TERMS OF LIGHT

Eon & Eze Stryker

www.sahaqielbooks.com

Terms of Light by Eon & Eze Stryker
Copyright © 2022

Beyond the Sea © 1947 by Bobby Darin
You Are My Sunshine © 1940 by Jimmie Davis and Charles Mitchell

Published by Sahaqiel Books
www.sahaqielbooks.com

For permissions contact: sahaqielbooks@gmail.com

ISBN: 9781958898123 (print)
ISBN: 9781958898246 (digital)

Printed in the United States, or whatever print partner finds its way to see it printed.

For those still looking for their way home

TERMS OF LIGHT

1

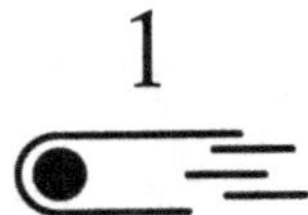

The door opens an hour before the sun, and I am pulled awake. Something in my brain itches in a way I have not felt since the war, but I have forgotten its name. I had forgotten it had a name.

The Shadows accompany a spark of light as it is shoved into my cage. The sound of dull, hollow laughter follows. For a moment, just a moment, I breathe in the unfamiliar smell.

It tastes like space dust and a warmth that tickles its way down my throat. My mind paints the world in stars, even as something new bobs around in my star sea. That spark...

The spark of light is red, and I understand the empty howls of the Shadows as they whisper to themselves about its fate.

"Stop here. This is it. Put it in there."

"How can you tell?"

"Doesn't matter. Daylight's in there, I can feel it. Bet you ten extra rations this one doesn't survive the night."

"That's only an hour from now," the new Shadow's voice is like fire to my ears. It has not yet become one of us and my fingers twitch with some unspoken, long-forgotten desire. The spark is motionless on the floor, a shock of red with white along its head, the rest of it in dull browns and grays that look so bright against the stone and ash.

I turn away.

I wait.

The spark stays silent. Perhaps it is dead?

My mind sighs in envy of the thought.

Daylight.

We used to have a name for this time, but now it was easier to think of time in terms of light: warmer that way, too. They would like it best if: when those iron bars closed around us, it also silenced us, but here in the darkness is where we have always worked best. I stand on one of the short horizontal bars and wait.

I tap the ring on my left hand — once silver, now a rusted core of copper and iron — gently against the bar. It rings, a dull, hollow sound in E flat, barely audible.

One. Two.

One. Two.

Further down the pit, I hear the ringing return to me. It amplifies, calls out; with it, a low, deep hum of voices rises. It is a whisper when it starts. The voices of my brothers and sisters at the bottom of the giant hollow spiral that is our prison. I keep tight to the edge of my cage even though it is where the heat is; even though it is where the light will be. If the comet is turned wrong, if there is a small variance in the prison's trajectory, that single bright beam could kill us all. There are days I want nothing more than to fall back into that eternal sleep.

One. Two.

One. Two.

The spark, no, the *he*. The new one sits in the corner,

unmoving. He's bundled in whatever he can find. He stares out from a different kind of darkness and it seems piled heavy on his bones. His eyes feel familiar and he notices me staring. The rest of us have turned to stone as the chill from the darkness freezes us where we lay.

Still, I recognize that look.

It's the same one the stars used to give me.

That was before the here, before this place, before this abyss that consumes all light. I move the thought away, back to the low hum of stone and voices rising up against the darkness. I know it is more likely New will freeze or starve before the terms become too short and the daylight disappears for a time, but I hope for him.

His spark, that damned red hair, may be enough to keep him alive.

Or maybe he will fall silent. Turn to stone. Disappear.

So will many of my brothers and sisters.

So might I.

One. Two.

One. Two.

"Daylight!" A scream is heard from across the hollow. The hum grows louder as a stream of light, blinding, falls over the center of the world from above us.

As the heat rises, the hum becomes something more than a sound; it is now like the beating in my chest. I can feel it rise around me, filling the darkness and stone and kicking at the darkness that fills my head.

I can feel a warm hand in mine that isn't there.

I can feel breath on my breath.

"Daylight!"

"Oh, in the shadows of death," I whisper into the hollow, "Oh, for the waking call of light."

"Hah. Hah. Ooo," the darkness chants back. A hundred voices, soft and dark as the stone we've become. "Hah. Hah. Ooo."

"Rising tides won't find us here," another cell whispers. "Waking light will hold us dear."

"Oh, for the shadows of death." I breathe the words into the darkness.

"Daylight!" The fading darkness screams again, this time in acceptance.

A streak of fire passes our cages. It falls past and tumbles endlessly down into the bottom. The pit's gravity core roars in response. Another brother gone.

3,228.

He belongs to the Whispers now.

"Hah…" There is one last breath from the room as the last of the light flickers and spreads across the expanse of our prison. I can see the color of my skin, now ashen brown against the gray of stone and wall.

We can see the ash and dirt that floats between the cells. I can see them all, lining the ramp that leads us to salvation. I can see a hundred cells, a thousand bars, and for a moment, I am fleetingly alive. The warmth on the skin from the light stings and makes me shiver, but it feels like I remember life should feel.

It feels Human.

In that moment, there is silence.

I count the last seconds of sun, sticking my arms outside of bars they used to not fit through, and revel in it, even through the ash and the heaviness of what comes next.

One.

Two.

Three.

Four.

Five.

The shutters above us close and darkness returns to remind us what we no longer are. To wear away the stone we have become. The hum recedes back into the depths of the pit, back down to the

Whispers, and for a moment, fresh air fills our lungs. We all take a breath while we can, all except New, but almost as soon as it is in our mouths, it is replaced with stale, recycled air.

Some refuse to let it go. I hear the quiet collapse of bodies all around me.

My lungs burn before I let it out. The new one chokes with the unfamiliar sensation of fresh air against the stale. Something in my mind still itches when I look at him.

I move away from the bars.

"In for a song?" one of the stones in my cell comes to life and asks New. "What did you sing?"

"Nothing," New mutters. "They got the wrong guy."

A shrill voice parrots his words, chirping the words as he says, a manic edge to his voice. "They got the wrong guy, you hear that? They got the wrong guy!"

New's eyes gleam from the darkness with a powerful emotion. He tries not to spit out the words.

"You all look like... they said you were... GEMs? You're all here because you're GEMs, right? The war? Your war on humanity? They couldn't stop you from killing innocence?"

"Rebellion," I correct. My throat burns like the light and air is still on my tongue.

"Hah. Hah. Ooo..." The stones in the walls chant in response.

"Whatever," he grunts. "All I know is they lock you up on sight. Villains. Demonized, hated, unwanted, just because of what you are... I get that."

"They got the wrong guy," Parrot echoes. "So, what did you do?"

"Didn't." He swings his words up like a shield. "They think I got someone pregnant."

"What?" A large stone, one that the itch in my mind calls Nash, moves forward. "How they lock you up for creating new

WIPs?"

"I didn't!" He swings the shield again. "I'm sterile. I slept with her, sure, but the baby isn't mine."

"They got the wrong guy!"

"How is that a crime?" Nash repeats the words like they are glue, his fists very near New's face, "How is making the natural born a crime?!"

"Apparently, being half isn't half enough." New confesses to a sin we do not understand. The room is still like ice.

The shadows whisper: "Hah. Hah. Ooo."

"I don't understand." Nash's fists lower to the floor. He sits next to New, but it is only a moment before he leans against the wall and becomes part of it.

"I don't know. They said I lied. Said I was…" His words sour in his mouth as he confesses more. "I guess not all of us are natural enough. If I would've known that I was going to be quizzed about it, I guess I would have kept the condom."

He folds himself into his arms like wings around his dark figure.

Half isn't half enough.

My mind itches with so many new feelings - and that red hair!

We let his words sit between us, and then that itch reminds me. It pulls at the strings of a world I've left behind and all at once, I understand.

He's one of *them*. The ones the Humans call Ritz, though we gave them the word first. Aliens that came from the hole in the sky. The ones that our keepers were happy to feed us to while they sat behind to watch with disinterest.

Now we sit in stone, waiting for…

The thought is as hard as it is dark.

New shivers.

"It's so dark here," he whispers into his elbows.

"Dark ain't come yet," the ceilings whisper. "Dark ain't come yet."

"You got a name?" The voice from the stone this time is chill and calm. It is a voice I miss. I can see the owner in my mind's eye, at least the way she was once. Snow hair, snow nails, the same stone burnt skin as mine. We are mirrors, her and I, except her eyes still seek the stars. Snow.

"I used to." New lets out a long breath, the walls echo it. "Here, I feel more like a number, though."

Nash laughs. There's a sharp pain in the breath behind it. "Ain't no numbers here, Red."

"Just the shadows, whispers and stones," Snow whispers from the other side.

"And the snow," I add to smooth the heavy that sets in, rubbing the ashen snow between my fingers.

"And death," my Snow White adds.

"Oh, for the sweet shadow of death," I call out to the room now, taking in the swell of sound as it rises from below. "Oh, for the waking call to arms! We rise again, we sing again, but those allowed a single breath of light, we fall again."

"Hah. Hah. Ooo…" The hum rises behind me, the walls hum with the very life of stone and flesh, and the air itself chants. "Hah. Hah. Ooo - Ahhh…"

"One thousand, one hundred and sixty-eight days," I say, moving back to the edge of my cage. New looks up sharply but says nothing. There's an edge to his eyes and weight to his stare. The number echoes five stories down, then again ten, then again until it is a whisper on the floor of the dark pit at the center of our world.

"One thousand… sixty eight?" New asks as the number breathes life into the stones.

"Since we rebelled," Nash hums.

"Since we were put here," Snow spits.

"They got the wrong guy!" Parrot squeals.

The world shakes.

The air is sucked from our stone prison as a heavy sound moves the world from above. We hear the gears of the doors churn above us as they open. The others pull themselves from the dust.

I move to the other end of the cell.

No one speaks, but they move forward in one giant wave. I do not move, and no one comes near me. I stand to the side and I wait.

We hope today we are lucky.

The metal gate raises, leaving the bars in our way to taunt us.

"What's going on?" New asks, terror rising as stones shift forward from the wall, once again made of flesh, eyes dark with hunger and thirst. "What's going on?"

"It's time," Snow whispers from the other cell. "Shh, wait and watch."

The artificial light from above sends streaks of white and yellow to cascade down the walls like invaders. I watch as others fill the ramp and climb it slowly, packed like stock animals against stone.

I trace my fingers along the bars of the window. The door bars do not move.

Our number is not today then.

We are not lucky.

My hands quake slightly with this knowledge before the cold comfort settles in. The rest of those in my cage understand it almost as soon as I do, and return to their place in the darkness.

"Hah. Hah. Ooo-ahh," I call out to the hole.

"Hah. Hah. Ooo..." it responds.

A call to those also stuck in their cages. We cannot see them anymore, but we know.

Reaching my hand out, I try to touch the very air as the vibrations of song rise. I watch in silence as more doors and bars slide open, releasing those lucky enough to be chosen today. I gently rub my ring against the string of bars in front of me and it aches with sound.

I close my eyes and feel everything around me until the artificial light fades. The cold deepens into a bitter frost and again we are stones, we are shadows, and many huddle together near the new one. They form a cocoon of warmth, as much for themselves as it is for each other, and the outside-layer seals what cracks they can with what little clothing they have on their bodies.

As they settle, the great steel slab blocks our view into the world, stealing the fleeting moment I have with my brothers and sisters outside our cage. The darkness consumes every corner now; the cold becomes a being all its own as it stands with us, chanting.

Yet the stones behind me are silent. I can hear every move from the cocoon as they settle into a painless sleep, hoping to wake when the sun returns. I can hear the fright from New in the center of the pile. He moves and wrestles with the idea of leaving, but as the darkness settles in, I think he knows that the warmth is all we have to offer.

2

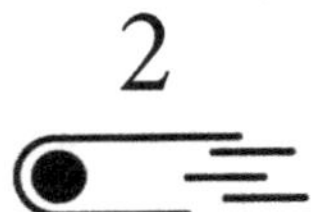

We are all awake before the next light, all except the New one.

As the room gets warmer, they all move closer and closer to the door.

All but me.

I remain where I am. They give me a berth of at least a meter; those at the edges of the cage move as far as the world will let them. Those that reach the door early touch and stroke steel bars that hold us fast. As the stone hums, the song does not rise.

The sun that rises today is not real. There is no chorus or whispers that join its rising. This is the light that the Shadows above us spread and we will not greet it.

A false hope.

Still, the artificial sun flashes brightly as it pours over us, lighting everything. The false sense of warmth fills the tiny room and in that moment we are imitations of beings again, individuals. As the slab slides away and shades of bright flow in through the bars, and prickles of light roll over my skin. I close my eyes.

You have to.

Even the false sun is blinding.

Memories of another sun, in another place, fill me, and my mind burns with a memory it is not willing to submerge me into.

I breathe out and let it pass.

Another day: we are not lucky, the doors do not move. We let the darkness take us, if it will, and return to stone. The New one paces. He whispers to himself in the quiet. My ears do not hear it, but I imagine him saying:

There's no place like home.

There's no place like home.

We wait.

We sleep.

The sun comes again.

There is a scream, a hiss of pain? It echoes through the halls in such a way that we cannot tell where it came from or even if it is real. Everyone is eager and the bars rattle with the pushing of thin fingers and bodies against it.

It starts gently.

Clack-clack, clack-clack: but soon it is a furious howl against the silence. Rampant, angry, rattling tears into the air from the top to the bottom as the howls of the hungry and thirsty soon join, in a symphony of sound that is like fire to those who had not yet felt it.

The howl creates a storm.

It reaches up for a fresh breath of air as cold fills our lungs and as quickly as it had started, it stops. The storm turns into a drizzle of rain as only the gentle caress of metal on flesh remains to echo against the stone.

Now, the quiet is too loud not to notice and New stands up. He takes his place as close to me as he dares to come, oblivious of the space the others give me, this perfect circle I have come to live in.

Then comes the sound, a gentle tap-tap-tap.

Footsteps, maybe, or chain, it is impossible to tell. The others press their fronts against the bars, against each other as New and I wait in silence behind them. Even though we are separate, even though he is apart from us, in that moment, we all breathe as one. We are all warmed by the same false hope as it seeps through the bars and litters the floor with light.

Gears turn.

Today, we are lucky.

Our door opens. Others are not; their doors stay closed.

No one dares to move too fast. The clicking comes again, tap-tap-tap, one-two, one-two, and you hear the stones sing again. The hum of those in cages, now open, follows it. E flat, A, C, all together in a harmonic, impatient stagger.

This is the rhythm of the sun.

I close my eyes and let the warmth of false hope roll over my skin as it scatters across my chest, my hands, my face.

"Walkers first," a voice bellows from on high. "Kneelers, then filth."

New glances around as everyone twitches eagerly in response. Even my fingers seem to itch, ready to follow orders, to die, *to kill* if needed.

We are ready to eat.

"What is it? What is it?!" Parrot gleefully shouts. "Walkers first!"

Nash shoves the new one with his shoulder and offers me a glare.

It takes me time to understand why. Perhaps he is upset that I have not reached out to New? I will never know, as the line forms quickly. Those who can walk go first, balancing themselves on the edge of the pit, waiting for the others in a silent act of defiance.

We let the worst of us go first. Hand in hand. As brothers.

Nash grabs Parrot and drags him in line.

I can almost tell them from the stone as they stand on the edge of oblivion.

Nash's skin is still ashen, but today it also carries the dark colors of clay and earth, with kinky hair and a thick beard to match his thick body. Even though he starves like the rest of us, his body shows none of it in his broad shoulders or narrow hips. His body is the idealized temple that Humans so wished it to be with none of the obedience they tried to program.

Perfection is always a true act of godlessness.

I can see the changes in him though, differences from the picture I keep in my mind. He is smaller, bent from years of engineering work that twist his body into shapes it does not hold well. The stones have made it more permanent, and he is missing two sections of finger on his right hand. He wears the scars of defiance like a badge and they stand out even against clothing that has gone so unwashed it carries the same ashen streaks that his skin and hair do.

Nash is almost more stone than man, except that he is thinning, weak, and angry. On a GEM as well designed as Nash, it is hard to see the wear of abuse and starvation if you do not know where to look. His legs are two small bamboo sticks in a sea of heavy green cloth. They shake as he clings to the barely there creature that is Parrot.

Parrot is mostly lip with a wide forehead: it speaks of his heritage. His space-pale sheen and narrow frame make him as alien as New is in our midst. He was colony born, not made, making him rare in that he had parents for a short time. Some think it drove him to madness sooner, knowing what a family was and having it all taken away.

His years show in every facet of his body.

Thin ribs poke out from a dangerously starved frame, eyes sparkle with a madness bordering on dangerous, but there is still something heavy there, something that keeps him willing to move.

It is hard to know what it is as he flails small, bone thin arms wildly near the edge. Nash will bruise him by the act of touching him.

The New one gives me a look before he steps past me, as if expecting more to happen. I'm not sure what to offer, but I watch as he moves closer to the edge of the pit. He knows not what darkness lies at the center, but I can see with the pressing of his eyebrows that he *wants* to know.

It is a dangerous thought to have as his dusty red shoes come to the edge of the stone pathway. I wonder if he can feel the beat of gravity as the core of the comet threatens? He leans towards the hole just a little, feeling that something we all ignore.

I can imagine his thoughts. What lies at the bottom? In the darkness? What song is there for us to hear?

Snow grabs his arm as before the gravity flux can pull him off of the edge. He steadies himself against her body, perhaps a little too close. He leans in, but she doesn't seem to care. Perhaps she enjoys the touch of someone else?

Hard to say. Hard to think about.

"Careful. That's a gravity well, and the light in this place, see the way it shimmers off this stone? It gives you vertigo. Almost impossible to tell what the real distance is, what the real depth is." She speaks to him, offering a hand on his back to guide him. "Keep your eyes on the ground - it's the only thing that's real here."

"Thanks, I'm ------" he says coyly. He says more, but it is all white noise to my ears as my senses are overwhelmed.

Too much noise.

Too much sun.

I focus on my breath as we pour out of our cage and begin the long march up the slopes. I focus on their footsteps, tap-tap-slide-tap, the dragging of bodies against stone, slide-slide-pull-stop, then finally, the wet slosh of movement that is almost not movement from those below.

The smell of red follows them.

Rusty, rosy, beautiful, and bothersome all at once.

The cages empty. Not all the cages, rarely all the cages. It is random: every day it is random and there is always a chance where you returned to will not open tomorrow or tomorrow, or tomorrow.

We have seen whole cages die, waste away as day after day we pass them on the way up. We have nothing to offer but song to them. A reminder they are alive, but the song can only fill so much before even that is taken.

When every body has moved, I exit. I lift the weakest one off the floor and carry her up to the top of the ramp. There we are met with the large, bright space where we sit and wait in silence.

I sit at the table with the fewest. The strongest looking.

One by one, the shadows grant us leave to lift our bodies, take our rations, and return. On each return, the next goes, all tables except mine. When the time for mine comes, they set down the rations in front of me, one full glass of water and a Pell.

We wait for a moment in silence. Only New stumbles, desperately sipping at his liquid. Once the moment passes, we consume.

When I finish, the rest at my table are allowed to move. To get their rations. They do their best not to look at me.

They will receive half of what I am given.

I wait for them all to finish in the silence.

3

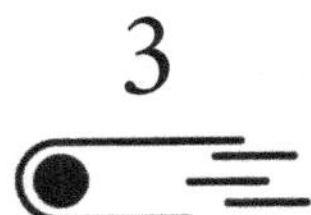

The work is not hard, but it lost meaning before we arrived here.

They put us in chains, weigh us down with gravity belts along our legs, and then attach the EGGs so we can move about the stone and look for bits that may have value. The alien life that is the EGG at my side is familiar. We do not know where they come from, but we know they grow to like certain entities, and the venom they inject into my blood makes the pain dull and takes the senses with it.

Some of us are left to mine the ancient tunnels that have long been sucked of value. Others are left to do menial tasks for the Shadows. I am left at the top to watch and be sent where I am needed most - to fill gaps where those that are weakest will die or fall over today. They set my gravity too high, and it makes it hard to walk.

They approach New, quietly muttering to themselves words I cannot hear. They attach the gravity belt and he begins to quietly scream, "Nonononono, NONO! Please! Please, wait. Don't turn it on yet - I have, that's - my bones -!"

They do not listen and turn it on, anyway. His entire body flinches as he waits for something terrible to happen, but it does not. Tears roll down his cheeks in something I imagine being relief as he is shoved past the guards and pointed to a pathway.

He gets in line behind the others, barely lifting his legs as he shuffles, not able to carry the same weight we can. He alone disappears as the group follows into the darkness. The rest light up like the gems they name us after in every shade of the rainbow. Some are colors Humans cannot see, and that is the only pleasure I have as I watch them leave.

Then I wait.

I do not move too far from where they post me, but I make my way as slow as I can to the great dome that covers the eating place. Behind that glass dome lives the water supply, and today it comes below my eyes as it sways with its murky movement. This is a sign that the sun's days are long, and if we were in another life, perhaps we would grace beaches and welcome its warmth.

I hold the information until they are ready to return us. They strip us down - EGG, gravity, chain - and move us like chattel back to our holes. As we shuffle back, I find Parrot in the lines.

"Below my eye, just about three centimeters." I whisper. He cackles madly in response as we move. I take a cage near the middle that is avoided by others and watch as the masses flow by.

I do not see the new one, and I wonder if he survived the day in the mines.

"Three days… three days," Parrot whispers from some distant cage. It fills me with something just short of a spark. As the door seals shut, no further sound escapes.

We exist only as vibration and shadow, because now we have something to look forward to.

Three days more.

Sleep comes easy.

"Hah. Hah. Ooo." Another rise of song.

Another rise of doors.

We are lucky again, but I notice there are many that are.

They are looking for something and I think I know what it is.

Pull-pull-side-stop. Pull-pull-side-pull.

I do not join them.

Slosh-slip-slosh-tap.

I wait in my cage, legs neatly folded on the floor, letting meditation hold my hunger away. If Parrot is correct, as he always is, I will have a visit today from a Shadow. So, I take in the light as a stone would. I let it sparkle and shimmer across my skin. Let them see me as they call me - a GEM.

I will sparkle for the Shadow that comes to me.

It does not take long.

The halls are silent for a long time until she appears. Tap-tap-click-tap of boots against smooth stone slopes. I can sense eyes on me, fiery and angry, as she offers up a long strip and a bowl. She pushes them towards me with the shine of her boots.

I do not meet her gaze; I look down. The strip has Pells on it, a few data crystals and a lighter. Sure, Pells are enough food for all of those in a cage for a month, but they act better as currency here for what little others have to offer. The rest is almost meaningless, but the lighter... some far gone part of me clings to.

The idea of it thrills me.

The strip fits easily into the lining of my jacket and connects to magnets there with a click. Satisfied, I stare at the bowl and I make no effort to reach for it. The way she taps her foot, the heaviness to her gaze tells me I should wait. This one still houses violence and killing her means this will go slowly for me.

"So you're it, huh?" she offers in annoyance.

I recognize the voice and know we often see new Shadows when new life comes down to the pit. She is too bright still; she has yet to learn she is as much part of the stone as we are. She will learn *or...* she will break. Goosebumps filter over my arms as a smile itches its way to my face.

I have been so itchy lately, and I kind of like it.

This will be fun.

I never let the Captain out of these requests without a proper fight, and for her to send fresh meat down here? An interesting play.

The Fresh meat continues to talk to me, even as I ignore the meaningless dust that pours from her teeth. Some dust I understand, but as separate things, not things that live together and hold meaning.

"They call you Daylight, huh? Big scary boogeyman? The one who makes them sing every night or some bullshit?"

"Hah. Hah. Ooo-ahh." I pump my fist in the air and tap my ring against the stone twice. It sings in a brassy whisper. Her face is clean and bright, but her light is anything but.

"Whatever. The Captain said we need a walk done in two days. Something you're being volunteered for, Tank." She smiles as if she has won something.

I give her no answer, but this is my game. I hold all the cards, because there is nothing she can take from me. They call me Daylight here, because I can shine a light on what kind of stone the shadows are made of.

Most are shale and pumice that crumble at the slightest pressure. She is... a brick, perhaps? Mud made hard only by another's will.

I know that if she returns with no answer; I receive a bigger reward.

She waits for only moments. I do not meet her eyes; I close them in gentle meditation.

Soon, she stops waiting, and impatient, and kicks the bowl closer to me.

"It's not poisoned, you know."

I catch it with the reflexes she will never have. The bowl is filled with a fine combination of egg, potato, Pell and something granular I've never been able to identify. Likely, something to keep me calm, to set the stage for this negotiation. As if we had not long passed the point I could say no, but the Captain likes pretense. She likes to assume some formal sense of reasonability, even though we have none here. It is something long extinct.

We are, after all, GEMs.

Monsters.

Killers.

Inhuman.

I run two fingers along the edge of the bowl and take small samples of its contents into my mouth. I can taste the sands of space, the dust of flesh and the cool soil of Terra in the mixture.

I must have made a sound because Fresh snorts.

"Disgusting."

"Oh, for the shadow of death," I say, gobs of mixture between my tongue and gums. "Oh, for the sweet call to death."

"Again with this chanting bullshit? Is this the fresh hell I have to get used to now?" She tosses a stone at the floor, missing me by accident, and she leans against the doorway. "Better than the shit show in Purgatory, I guess. Better docile cows than something actually scary."

"Purgatory?" My voice sounds strange against my skull as something else burns there.

"Oh, *great,* so you can speak.*"

"Purgatory. Is that not where you were?"

"I was a gate guard, GEM. I was happy to escort things in, but not out. Nothing ever comes out." She gives me a hand gesture I recall being quite fond of. "Now, because of pirates, I'm stuck *here* until my relief shows up."

The drops of smile on my face grow into a wide pool. Her expression turns into a frown of equal measure. The shadow - no - Fresh does not understand yet where she is.

That's good.

I contemplate the ways to play this game with her. My silence buys her impatience and likely me a beating, but I like the beatings. They remind me of a time when I was fighting for something.

However, this one seems... simple. I do not think she would appreciate being a pawn between the Captain's will and my own, even if it is the only entertainment I think that Captain Oswald has anymore.

Today, I will ruin her fun.

"I want the orb. Seve suits, sealed, I want the new one that you came with, Nash, Parrot, Snow and Perty - Oswald will have to talk to Naya about those arrangements - and you."

Her face is that of an animal that has run its head too many times into concrete.

"That is what the Captain wants to know, Fresh. I accept her offerings, but I want cards next time." I tap my head in the place where memory is best contained. She squints in irritation, and I gesture for her to leave. "Now go, before you forget."

She doesn't move.

Instead, she watches, twisting her face into various stages of disgust. I take a hearty bite of my offering, the protein and sugars filling my body with a long needed heat. The warmth sings over my flesh, burning small notes into each pore, reminding me I am human even if few see it that way. I take nothing else from her but looks and disgust and these roll off of me like the light.

Fresh eventually takes her leave, her steps echoing on the long path. Even those at the top can hear her coming. I know she will be praised for returning so easily with an answer.

When the others return from eating, they are as blind as they are quiet. Not the same ones, *rarely* the same ones, return to the same cages. There is always hope in the despair that tomorrow will be different, tomorrow will mean you eat twice, maybe you see the sun a moment longer. It is control and power, but I still wonder for whom? *They* are as much slaves to it as we are.

I only notice that New does not return, but I can hear his breathing in a cell that shares a window with mine. Snow likes that one, and maybe he likes her. She would never be into his body, no, but she is a good leader and a better sister.

She will guide him into the normal of… this.

I suppose life is what you could call it, but it is duller than that. Rounder.

How I miss being sharp.

No one enters my cell before the doors close. I am left to my solitary darkness. Heat rises in my body as calories flood my system. I am warm.

As the last hour of light fades, the hum begins. Slow, quiet, rising.

I imagine a sea of stars and the shores between them.

I tap my ring, but I make no call.

No one answers.

Two days more.

4

Today, all the doors are open and there is no work. We are told it is some glorious holiday. This holds no meaning for us, but in celebration, we are given full cups of water and rice. They see the gift to us as kindness.

We see it as a full glass of water and a cup of rice.

We take every inch we are given and gladly, without apology.

I watch New walk across the room with Snow near me, as if she does not see me. Maybe she doesn't, maybe she doesn't want him near me. I understand that. New is more dangerous than I ever believed.

I see that now.

That spark. That red. The itch that his existence seems to give me when he's near.

"So, what's with the blonde guy?" New asks Snow as he plays with the spoon in his bowl.

"Blonde guy? Oh, that's… the others call him Daylight." She

explains, "He's a dangerous prisoner, or haven't you figured that one out yet?"

She hesitates before she says my name, and even as it crosses her lips, it is foreign to my ears. It feels like space, and stars, and the sun. The entire room seems to swallow up the very thought before it can even become one.

Everyone near me backs away.

It is not the name I used to use. Not the name of a man free of artificial bonds, a man from back when we were star gone, and the sky called to us and we answered gladly. Now I begin to wonder when I became Daylight, and if that is now all I am?

"Dangerous," New repeats the word sarcastically, and I'm pulled back from the haze of my mind. "No one here seems particularly dangerous to me. A little off. Honestly, with as little as there is to do - and eat - and as dark as it is? I'm surprised you're not all a lot crazier."

"ONE DAY MORE!" Parrot says from his perch on a table. Someone scrambles after him when he dips his fingers in their bowl.

Snow smiles a little. It is something I haven't felt from her side of the room for a long time. I turn my gaze away now so the picture doesn't fade too fast.

"We're not crazy, we never were. We're tired." She lets out a sigh that is repeated by the room like a song. The word resonates in its own key.

Tired.

Then, the world gets a little louder, as if some knot of tension releases. New's words a massage on sore backs.

A moment to be reminded we are real. A holiday.

I want to thank him, to put my hand out to him and show him we are brothers, but my hands shake when I look at him. My fingertips get cold, my lips tight, and my skin itches. I can see the itch spread to others and I pick up my bowl and make my way to the hallway, away.

Away, away, away.

I lean against the wall and face away from the room, but my ears still tune in to Snow's words, to the mind's eye of her movements.

New asks questions, but they are never quite the right ones. Never, how is this, why is that, always who is this, when did that, why don't you then?

Snow almost laughs when he finally asks, "What is the whole two days more thing about?"

"ONE DAY MORE! ONE DAY MORE!" Parrot screams to anyone who comes near him as though they are the last words he'll ever say. He shakes wildly with anticipation and even in the chaos that is lunch, there's a chirping of excitement.

They can all feel it coming, the long sun, the turn of the comet's rotation.

Another year spent dead in here.

Others come to life as well, not just Snow and Parrot, but Nash. He threatens someone for touching his rations, but everyone treats them as sacred ornaments so no one would dare. Everyone knows, but they give him space.

Anger makes him feel alive.

"So, we're not all here to audition for Les Miserables?" New's anxiety spills from his teeth and Snow laughs, a sound that's so distant a memory it seems unreal, but it rings hollow against the walls.

Fresh watches over us, that disdainful smile so full of willful ignorance. Like a religious zealot now faced with the reality of a plague, she likes to think she knows better. That ignorance shows on her face as she goads one of the other Shadows and they wordlessly move away.

Even a few of the Whispers are up from the depths. Something rarely seen, and all give them a great berth as they move through us. I am surprised to see Perty is among them. My Perty Williams, but he makes no move for rations or Pells.

Instead, with the other Whispers they slam down their meal, proudly displaying their finest red meat upon the white slab that is the table. He washes his hands, his face, his mostly naked body before he sits. When he finally settles, he becomes part of the white slab, as though the marble itself was born from his pale flesh.

Most know of the Whispers, but they are easy to forget.

They live their strange lives in the gravity flux that is the base of this prison, far away from the rules of anything but the self. Most know to stay better and stay far away, but the seduction of *more* comes easy when there is nothing to lose. The Shadows are the only ones that stay far, far away. They have lost too many of their number to do anything but hide.

The smell of flesh, blood, the abundance of it as the Whispers move freely among us Stone. As Perty and Naya eat, some ask questions.

Where…

How…

What…

And in kind, like all whispers in the dark, they answer.

Their words are always true and never pulled back or softened. Even if it is a brutal truth, the act of speaking truths can turn any wrong into a right.

This is how many of the Whispers are born.

Naya is their keeper now, a tall, strong creature without fear. She wears white and rusty brown like a badge. We go back to long before we were here. She has led those I cannot, and she continues to steal those who have sunk into the darkest places from me.

I listen to lunch from my hallway with a smile. This may not be our celebration day, but for a moment, we are whole. We are brothers and sisters and I know tonight the song will be as grand and as defiant as it was when we started. The thought shivers me to the core and I enjoy the taste of it until I notice there's a presence next to me.

I take another spoon into my mouth to avoid unwanted speaking.

It is a hint that the presence does not take, and when I look, I see that bright spark of red that tells me it is New. New does not take the hint and… waits. I admire that he stands his ground better than Fresh did.

He is so close to me that I can smell him. It is foreign and brings to my mind memories long buried under ash. Notes of clean with a touch of romance make him almost smell delicious.

I tap my forehead against the thought, pushing it out of my skull and know that Perty is watching now through his mind's eye. It sits watching me now as I had watched Snow.

After a moment too long, New sits by my side. He watches me. It makes me shiver, and I cannot bring myself to look directly at him.

When I do it…

When I do…

The sky howls.

The world turns red with fear and blood as the smell of iron is all there is.

They are coming. The monsters from the tear in the sky. They look so Human, but they wear the scarves of red. When they smile, it feels as empty as the Humans always claim we are.

To fight them is to fight for our lives. To fight ourselves. To die as they smile empty smiles on our graves.

"Soren," he states definitely. "And before you start, I don't want any of your nickname crap. It's just Soren."

It makes a smile sketch its way onto my lips an old habits come far too easy. My mind suddenly blooms with a thousand other names for him. Most are fowl, but when I go to speak, my breath is ragged, short, and all I manage to get out is, "You...?"

"Look, I can see that there's an obvious dislike for you. I don't know what you did, or care I just wanted you to know that I don't care."

"Soren!" Snow's voice cuts the warning into the air, but it is too late.

It is the last thing I hear before I am back on the bloody shores of a colony whose name screams white light into me. Around me, fires burn, and the silence is so loud. My mind travels to another time, another place.

I feel the hollow bones crack under the pressure of my arm.
I love the sensation of life draining out of them before I let go. One. Two. Three. Four - the last bit of struggle as the light in their eyes lets go - Five.
It is what we were made for.
Might as well enjoy it.

The red scarves scream out as their forms twist together into giant monsters. Fire and lightning spew from the tips of their fingers, from alien wings and claws and beaks. They burn the world, and us, alive. I hear my brothers and sisters cry out and watch as they are turned to ash.

I reach for them, but they disintegrate and scatter to the winds.

My mind itches as, for a moment, I feel some missing part

of myself return. I am on fire. I grit my teeth and hold back these shadows lurking in my mind, but I feel New's thoughts on the outskirts of my own, even as I am pulled in again to the fire.

The ship sits in ruin above the ridge. We barely made it out of the escape pod. Oh God, all I can think of is his mother's face before she pushed us into it.

Peter, I'm so sorry.

This is all my fault, but the smell. That burning smell of gasoline, the fire that had to consume them on the ship, I can still see it pouring out of the back of the ship like a candle. Oh, God, what have I done? What have I DONE?!

...this is not my *memory...*

The red scarf in front of me screams.
Their screaming sets the world on fire.
I grab ahold of the one thing I know can make it stop. I grab the red scarf; I feel the gentle bending of bones in my hand. The cracking as a neck gives way to the honed strength of deadly hands.
Shuttles crash from the surrounding sky.
Bodies and ships burning into ash.

I need this all to stop.
He won't.
Stop.
SCREAMING.

"Hey! HEY! We're safe!!" Snow's voice is a dull drum against the fire of memory's bodies. "We're safe now, but I need you to let go now."

"He won't stop screaming." I mutter back.

I can hear the laughter all around me as the flock of Ritz tear into us. Knives, talons or jaws, it's hard to tell the difference. The creatures are the size of buildings. Wings and feathers fall between drops of blood. The cracking of their bones as they shift from something Human to something alien, the stretching of skin over bone and -

Pert's hands wrap around my wrists and pull them apart.

"Count with me. How many are there now? How many are there of us here?"

"How many…?" The world fades, the edges black and then too bright for my eyes. I squint, the dull hum of lights above us cutting through static noise anguish. The room smells of sweat and food.

Pells, ugh, barely food, but it doesn't matter to the dead tongue.

The edges of me are fuzzy and clear.

"3,228."

"Nine." There are fingers on my wrists as Perty and Snow hold them tight, fear screaming in the back of a mind that still reaches out to mine. "3,229 if you let go."

My hands release themselves without my command.

The vision of death, of fire and blood fades and I stare into the tangled mess of red hair and silver bangs that pulls itself up and moves as far away from me as it can. Tears run down pale flesh that turns ten shades paler. He gasps for air. His eyes blame me.

The actions replay in my mind.

Red hair, red scarves, hollow bones, alien bones, New

weeping under me, unable to speak as the dots finally connect. The reason my heart races, the sweat on my brow when I look at him.

"Half isn't half enough," I say the words, but he doesn't seem to understand what I'm trying to say.

I look to Snow to translate. I want her to let him know that I understand what happened, but she shakes her head.

There is nothing to be done.

I am hollow before him as my hands ache for killing and my mind for what could have been a friendship.

Friendship? Was that something you ever had a chance of?

No.

No.

I pull the lighter from the strip inside my jacket and I set it near his dirty red pair of shoes. They try to shuffle away from me as I draw near. I back away submissively and make my way to the ramp. I return to where I belong. I return to my place in the wall.

When the sun comes that day, it does nothing to warm me when it touches my skin. When it fades, I cannot find it in me to care. I melt into the stone, fade back into the darkness, and try to disappear.

The cells beside me are empty long before I am asleep and long after I awaken.

The stone does not hum and call us together that night. The slabs are left down so we may see the light as it passes over us as the comet makes its rotation.

Someone tries to reach out for it. There is always at least one who tries to touch the sun when it comes from a place we no longer belong.

The sun takes away the world.

Another body falls from above, burning as it falls down to the gravity heavy core of our prison. We all see the flash of fire before us.

3,228.

Farewell, brother.

"Hah. Hah. Ooo-ahh."

"You've got the wrong guy," calls back from the distance.

5

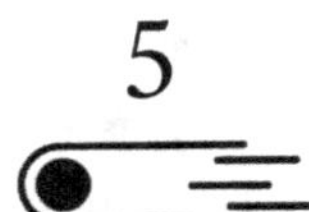

They bring me to the orb in chains.

It makes them feel better, but chains are not for me.

My mind itches as I near it, and it calls to me, floating there in the center of the large room. The Humans' feelings are distasteful to it, and its hunger is obvious as I draw closer.

The orb knows I'm here.

She is easily the size of a man, perfectly smooth and sings to me as I get closer. She is the moon, the sun, and the stars all wrapped up in one. She aches for her homeland, for the call of a Ritz mind, since she is a Ritz metal, but she settles for me.

My mind aches from so much time in the dark, and it is hard to hear her song. It activates something deep in the center of me that wiggles thick scales around in my mind. The itch returns. It is scratched as we touch, just lightly on the outermost shores of what is the orb and what is me.

I reach up to place my hand on it, but the chains hold me back. I flick my wrist, and by an unspoken agreement the orb removes the chains, consumes them. The Shadows take a step back as pools of silver moonlight gather around my feet before leaping up and wrapping itself around my body. For a moment, I am more metal than man, and then it vanishes. It is now part of me, at least, for now.

Fresh takes ten steps back, startled.

"What the hell was that?"

"Cession." Captain Oswald doesn't flinch. She stands watch over the process with dull dead eyes. "Fall in, soldier."

I stare at her for a moment; there is a fragment of her death that sits between us. It glimmers. She does not blink. I take my place by her side and catch Fresh's eye with a smile. My hands stay where they would be if I still had my shackles.

"Forsyte, get the others together," Captain commands.

"Sir?" Fresh questions. "Others?"

"Yes. The ones he requested. Get them out and suited up. They're going for a walk." The Captain glances at me and sighs. "Then suit yourself up, too. You're their escort."

Fresh balks. "Captain?"

My smile must have silenced her. It is inappropriate and I revel in it. I tilt my head to see her a little better, the expressions of frustration, anger, distrust now etched in memory.

These would be good to revisit in the quiet hours.

"Suit up." The Captain is not one for many words. "Stanten, since Forsyte seems to not understand her orders, please get the others from the pit."

"Even Naya's man?" The Shadow called Staten asks.

Captain grunts and looks at me, spitting at my feet. The orb pools and absorbs the organic material with glee. She turns her back to me, plucking at thick curls of hair before letting out a long breath. "No, I'll handle Naya."

"Aye." The Shadow Staten peels itself from the walls and slips out into the darkness.

I shiver with delight as the metal roils along my outsides,

exploring my flesh, consuming all the unnecessaries. The Captain doesn't make eye contact with me, but I can feel her heartbeat - no - her *hate* beat within her.

It is slow.

Triggers for hate are never from what you expect: it is always the small things, rarely the big. I can taste her hate in the way her eyes will not meet me. Perhaps it is that I remind her of what her life has become? Or is it the way I speak?

The way I smile?

The way I stare?

The way I chew, or don't chew? Breathe, laugh, talk, sing… or the silence that follows me?

Does it follow her the same way? Up here? The way the Shadows give her a wide berth, she must be very lonely. Good. Her privilege seeps out even in a place like this.

Captain already knows the lesson that Fresh will soon have to learn. Here we are forgotten, here we are all equal except in the eyes of those in denial. Ultimately, she believes her life is worth more than mine - that she would sacrifice me without a thought if it meant she would live.

The metal undulates on my skin with feelings I do not have names for anymore.

They bring in the others.

The new one is small and is ready to fight as they put him next to Snow. The others take a few more minutes. Parrot and Nash arrive together, and Parrot is a small sliver of a thing against him. We are tossed suits. Forsyte slips hers on over her uncomfortable looking uniform, but we strip down to nothing.

The suits fit poorly, our feet are dipped in the heavy pools that are boots as oxygen and glass are settled over our skin. They run a quick test for seals, but not a thorough one before they place gravity belts on us. New again flinches, but this time we are free to alter them ourselves.

When we are almost finished, Perty bends his thin frame through the door. The streak of blood across his chest tells me the Captain had to negotiate the hard way. When he sees us, there is a flash of a smile across his face before it disappears.

"You know what is at stake here. If you fuck this up, Pechard, you fuck everyone in here."

Captain folds her arms on her chest as she comes through the door. Her forehead is beaded with sweat and I wonder what transpired in the gravity wells. The backwards glare Captain gives me is enough to tell me it was a thing that was more effort than she wanted to give. This glare is supposed to be menacing but all it makes me want to do is take a bite out of her flesh.

Perty licks his lips as the orb mirrors his thoughts to mine. His pale skin is painted with ash from the stone and the soot down below and he gives all the Shadows a vicious, large smile before he slips his body into his suit. Nash barks at one of the Shadows and they scatter, unwilling to deal with conflict.

Fresh grumbles low, and another Shadow on the side is seal testing her suit. "This is ridiculous."

"This is needed. You will shut up and you will do your damn job," Captain Oswald orders. I wonder if she's upset because she didn't get to play more with me?

"I'm not a goddamn mechanic," Fresh barks, glaring at us, "They aren't either."

"I'll lead ya," I say through my glass. It was meant to be comforting, but she scoffs in reply.

"Know the way!" Parrot laughs over the internal mic. "WE KNOW THE WAY! Today! Today!"

New looks as nervous as Fresh. His eyes sparkle with confusion and determination all in one glimmer. Fresh shoves her weapon into my side and barks an order.

"Let's get moving then, trash!"

"Please," I mutter. I stare at Parrot, that spark that New

brings with him giving me a bit of sparkle that has been dull for a long time. "Please, please don't kill me."

"Kill me!" Parrot shakes his head, and screams through the intercom. "Please, don't kill me!"

Snow hides the smile that threatens its way onto her lips as the chanting from down the hall echoes Parrots' noise.

"Kill me"

"Please."

"Please don't."

The sound emerges in a grand shriek from outside the hallway. As the noise swells up and over the hole, the Shadows are quick to find their guns. They are cautious, scared, and huddle together in anticipation of something that won't come.

They remember in that moment, that we may be stone, but stones outnumber Shadows.

But enough of this show. Enough of this Human ceremony, there is important work to do.

With a great roar, I raise my arms, and the metal roils and rotates around me. I lift my arms as great metal wings surround me and wrap themselves around my body. Underneath, it eats away at the suit and replaces it with its own forms.

It becomes my second skin.

I stretch small pieces to form a single straight blade razor with a flip handle, and an empty necklace. The wings fall away, and what is left is a clear dome around my head and a well-fitting space suit, ready for a walk.

The room around us still sings with the echoes of our brothers and sisters.

"Kill me."

"Please."

"Please don't."

"Kill me! Please!" Parrot cackles, each time moving closer to Fresh.

"Forsyte!" Captain's voice is almost enough to cut through the chaos and Fresh's attention is pulled to her Captain. The Captain motions to a box where my EGG sits. "Get him dressed."

In her confusion, she spits words back at her commander, but they are lost in the surrounding noise. They fight, and we wait. Finally, the more obedient of the Shadows, Staten, places the EGG on my arm. The orb makes room for it, even adjusts to its alien legs as it settles in my skin.

It injects its proboscis, and the pain numbs and the mind eases.

I glance at Perty and give the faintest of nods as another shadow places an EGG on him as well. Then he stands at full height, and the glass of his helmet touches the ceiling. He spreads his shoulders wide, and it draws the attention of all. Parrot and Nash both fall in quietly behind him.

The rest of the room follows.

The echo from below quiets. All that I can hear is the chirping of the metal as it tries to tell me it is ready to connect with others. I run my finger along my ear to ease its screaming. It is not time for that, I tell it with my mind, and it seems sated with that option for now.

"Forsyte." The Captain motions to me, disgusted. "Follow his lead, but don't let them get out of hand."

"Uh, yeah, so I hate to interrupt this ceremony and all..." New interrupts, "But uh, what exactly are we doing?"

"Shut up RIP." Forsyte bites the words that are projected through her helmet's speakers. Her reflexes tell me she wants to slam a fist across his face but her gravity is too high for such a move.

I do not move.

I am surprised when it is New that jumps at her. He lunges with his words and chains and I hold him back easily.

"SCREW you, Forsyte! You sick, twisted bitch! You think you know somethin' about me?! You think you are something? I could kill you in six languages!" New shouts. Snow comes over and pulls him back, but it is Perty that now moves between them.

The room empties of Shadows.

"This is all your damn fault, RIP. We wouldn't be here if it weren't for you," she says in response, but turns towards the airlock.

New continues to scream insane threats that make no sense at Fresh as she enters her codes into the door. Snow and Perty let him, holding him a safe distance away before the doors open.

The air rushes out.

It catches everyone's attention, as the gears deeply frozen on the outermost layer churn and pull. The doors fully part, and all that stands between us and freedom is the vast everything of space. There is a light, distant, far away, but I can feel the burn on the outside of my body long before I see it.

It is the sun, even if it is only a faint echo.

I let the image imprint deep in my mind. Streams of light across stone, across the core of our flying prison, burning like a scar that has been remembered. With it come some memories of my own.

Some I thought long burnt away.

Ships falling from the sky. Lives taken as the sun takes away the world, but this time I am still here, and I understand the light in its entirety.

I embrace it.

Snow's voice is the backdrop to my sightless embrace.

"Alright everyone, we're going out."

"You can't be serious? We'll die out there." A long pause from New. "Won't we?"

I won't let that happen. I say nothing as the doors part enough to let the steps descend on a wretched wasteland ahead of us.

"No," Snow assures over the radio.

The voice in my ear feels too close, like it is closer than my mind, and my mouth repeats the words as they're spoken.

I touch my gravity belt, setting it low so we can accommodate the long path ahead of us.

"It's time!" Parrot shouts. "The time has come! NO DAY MORE!"

"Daylight!"

The voices behind us rise as the light reaches them. It spreads far behind us and we step out onto the vast, empty surface of our prison.

6

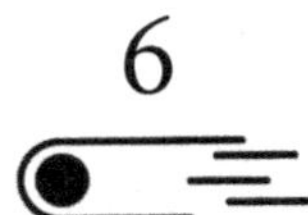

The comet is a desert beneath our feet as we take slow, agonizing steps to our destination. But the stars are more than enough payment for this. Everyone is a voice in my ear or in my head. It is hard to tell the difference against the darkness of the surface.

The glass in front of me displays icons, shows me distances, and tells me where everyone is, but I only have eyes for the stars.

New: "So, what the hell are we supposed to do out here?"

Nash: "You always ask too many damn questions. Why did we bring him, Daylight?"

Fresh: "Shut up! All of you! Fall in!"

Fresh's voice rings over our intercoms.

Fresh: "We're out here to make sure the water collector is running. Now shut up!"

Parrot: "Water. Water. Life, water. Where, where, oh where, oh where, oh where?"

His com becomes silent.

Fresh: "The faster we get this done, the faster we can go back."

It is unclear if she is telling us or herself.

For us there was little reason to want to return: out here on the surface, we had some semblance of freedom at least. Something new: beyond the hole, beyond the rhythm, beyond the dark.

My HUD beeps with a warning.

"New." I motion with my palm down. "C'mere."

Snow: "Hey…"

I hear the warning in her tone.

I do not hurry him; I let the empty expanse of space before us twinkle around my helmet. The EGG on my arm seems to ache with the homesickness brought by those stars. Energy surges through my whole body, filling my hair with light and lighting me up like one of the stars.

As New comes closer, I see that he's a small thing: frail, barely able to move in a suit made for a human. They should have let him touch the orb too: part of me wonders if that's a grounded idea, but my bones tell me the metal would have enjoyed it.

It moves on my skin excitedly as he nears.

"It's about to happen." I motion to the crest of the hill ahead of us.

The craters and meteors around us are dark and unfathomable. There are occasional flecks of dust and dirt around us to let us know it is not metal, but it is the only way we know. The heavy curve at the edge of the horizon reminds us where we stand.

A comet.

Our prison, a truly unreachable place from which escape is almost impossible. The edge of the horizon brightens, and our helmets darken to compensate. The new one, out of instinct, covers his face and hands, but I tug his arm away. He jerks away at the touch, but I still hold his wrist.

New: "Holy shit. We're on a COMET?!"

He looks down: seeing before the others do, the mist that creeps up, biting at the feet and legs of his suit until he is covered head to toe in a thick mist that hides everything below his belt. Our suits breathe for us, taking in the water, letting out CO_2.

New: "It's *beautiful*."

Then he runs. It is like he's trying to catch the horizon as he makes his way with surprising speed towards the light. Fresh does not see, so I let him run for a moment. When he has gone far enough, I extend the tendrils from my EGG and they attach to him. It jolts him back gently against the light gravity settings of his belt.

He is gently pulled back towards us.

New: "I! But! I want to - !"

Parrot: "BURN ALIVE! You got the wrong guy!"

Nash and Pert chuckled over the com, and Fresh finally seems to notice. She signs.

Fresh spits: "Let him burn, Daylight."

"That's not my name…" A long forgotten reflection in my mind screams the response even if I don't.

New: "I-want-to-see-the-tail!."

His words are barely a whisper with no breath between them. I tilt my head before Snow catches up to me.

"The edge is dangerous, New. Too hot. Too bright."

Snow: "S---n…"

She takes heavy breaths and grabs his shoulders as he floats by us.
Snow: "We have to be careful where we go out here. The comet isn't as predictable as a planet. If anything is off on the rotation, the sun gets closer. Then this turns into a very short trip."

New: "Can…can I see the tail?"

Nash scoffs: "One track mind."

I turn my gravity down and make a large leap forward. Perty follows suit as I set our destination in my HUD. As we move, the mist gets thinner. It means we move away from the side that sees the sun. It means we move in the darkness - what we are good at.

My body cools with every step I take away, but the conversation continues.

Snow sighs: "Maybe before we go back in, that's when it's the brightest."

Nash: "God… we really are stuck out here - this the first time I've seen the outside."

Fresh: "Shut up, all of you!"

Parrot: "Wrong guy! You got the wrong guy!"

It is a day's hike to the water collector. The HUD ahead of me flickers as the orb hungers for something to eat. Keeping up with the heat and cooling on the comet's surface is taxing, so I let it have one of my Pells.

Still, the signal is weak from the station, and I only hope we are going the right way.

On the other hand, even if we go the wrong way, maybe we'll get to see the tail.

7

Among the stars, I begin our song.

"Oh, for a glimpse of sunlight!"

Perty, Parrot, Nash: "Hah. Hah. Ooo-ahh."

This time instead of a low, droll hum that sounds like we are stone, there is something else in it. A breathy chant that echoes our military days.

Fresh: "You can't be serious. Don't you freaks get enough of this in the pit?"

A choking sound makes me pause. I turn to see Perty has Fresh lifted, so she is eye level with him, not an easy feat for most. She struggles against him as he grips her air hose.

I let her struggle.

I watch.

The metal on my skin churns with my unspoken delight. I try not to let the delight show on my face because I know it will make my Snow nervous. I see flickers at that moment. A body struggling for air as a red scarf wraps tightly around a neck — more mind shadows.

"Oh, for the sweet embrace of war." I turn and continue in the thinning mists.

Snow: "Give us hope - ahh - peace - ahh. Let us rest."

Parrot: "Oh for the sun… Oh for the embrace…"

Parrot mimics, but never quite gets the tempo right.

New: "Why… the song?"

There is hesitation in his words. It is Perty who laughs, setting down Fresh with a heavy crunch. She chokes as air rushes into her suit, but she will be fine. I can still hear her too-sweet breath over the com.

Perty: "Counting."

Perty brushes past New with the single word. He would not explain further, even if he were interested.

Nash sighs: "The rhythm of the song is in time with the cycles. This rock has 42 cycles, six seasons and years don't matter because there isn't a star to orbit around. We're on cycle 32, season of the longest sun. Today is a short glimpse of sun."

New: "Wait, you're… telling the time?"

There's an irritated sigh, which I know means Nash is quite happy to explain. It is one of his languages, knowledge.

Nash: "Scratching don't work. We can't keep our nails too long or they break in labor. Ain't enough light to see marks, anyway. What we got to write with ain't too visible on the dark stone. So..."

"Hah. Hah. Ooo-ahh." Me and Snow sing it together. It is the breathy rasp of the stone beneath us again.

New: "Right. So that's what it meant. Three days more? You knew we'd have to come up here to do whatever maintenance before...? It gets too cold?"

Nash: "Every 17 rotations or so, rock turns. Water runs low. It means the collector needs to be recalibrated. Crays don't bother doing it anymore: send out the slays to."

"Hah. Hah. Ooo." I raise my hand and wait to catch Fresh's retort.
It does not come.
The silence catches me in a steady haze of heartbeat and footstep, as New takes his place next to Fresh.

New: "Aren't they worried you'll escape?"

Fresh: "To where? We're as far from civilization as a gravity engine can go. Ritz cargo travels along the planetary ellipses and..."

New: "What about the pirates?"

Fresh: "Shut up."

Fresh's voice cracks.

Pirates? A word I haven't heard in a long time. If we were close enough to the solar system, pirates were a very real possibility. I missed being a pirate.

"They are as punished as we are," I add. "Is that part she ain't sayin', Sunshine."

Fresh: "What did you say, Daylight?"

New: "Sunshine?"

Snow laughs: "He means you really have to piss someone off to get this assignment. It's practically retirement. The only way to leave is if someone replaces you and few are gullible enough or unliked enough to take it."

Fresh: "We didn't come here intentionally. We were redirected mid-prisoner transfer because of pirates. My replacement will be here in 2 weeks."

"Ooo. Ooo. HAH!" We all sing it at once, even New joins in at the end.

New: "I think I'm starting to get it."
I can hear the smile on New's face.

Parrot: "You got the wrong guy! You got the wrong GUY!"

New: "So is there like… a whole song or is it just -?"

Snow: "Oh, there's a whole song."

Snow smiles and playfully pushes him.

Snow: "I'll share it with you sometime, but it takes a bit to get used to for newcomers, especially when you're not-"

New: "Not a GEM? Honestly, I do not get the propaganda. You guys have been nicer to me than any - what's the word you used? WIPs?."

"So imperfect, they had to make us perfect and punish us for it. Works in fucking progress," I chuckle.

Parrot laughs, jumping around in the lighter gravity.

Parrot: "You got the wrong guy! You got the wrong guy!"

New: "Oh shut up, bird man."

I feel New's flush on my own face. His mind touching mine. Something about him being Ritz made it easy. It felt like a glove on a hand, like it was...

My HUD lights up red and interrupts my thoughts.

"Target spotted."

The others go quiet. I do not need to speak for them to fall in line behind me. They let me go first, Perty and Snow covering my flank as I briskly move towards our goal. My suit makes it easier to move, but for the EGG to work properly, I have to turn my gravity up.

I dial the switch by my legs and the soft outer layer of the comet cracks beneath my boots.

I can feel New's intake of breath and the gentle caress of Snow's thoughts as I make my way to where the target should be. It is hard to see it in the mist and easy to miss entirely. It only takes a few yards closer before we can finally see it.

Giant turbines wrapped in layers of metal create the water processing station. It is easily the size of two or three of the cells we live in. The great beast before us is attached to a station that vibrates gently, roughly, stuttering and stopping with a lack of water to process.

It is easy to tell why it struggles. The turbines are covered in thick layers of ice. Dark, thick, immovable ice.

"Fresh?" She does not answer or make a move to come closer as I call, "What're the water levels at in the hole?"

Fresh: "Shut up and get it operational."

"It's important. I need to know if the water system is just recycling or if we've had new stock at all." The EGG, eager to work, places tendrils in strategic places around the ice. It plucks away with its strange tentacles, but makes little progress.

Fresh: "It's not my damn job to know that shit."

Snow: "You don't watch the water levels?"

Fresh: "Who cares? FIX IT!"

Snow: "Idiot. Nash? Parrot?"

Nash is stone still beside me, even as the EGG continues to tear away at ice.

Nash: "This is bad. Maybe damage. All black ice."
Nash's answers are a barrel of smoke as they come from his mouth.

The EGG tears away the thinnest barrier of ice. I approach and see we may be able to lift something off the turbine. The EGG gleefully complies. Launching the ice above us, it keeps one tendril up to suspend it. The others navigate their way into the machinery, dancing delicately around pieces that remain.

Perty's EGG joins mine after some time. His is difficult to see in the mist since his EGG is black and blends too well with the sound around us. The EGG's energy lights his skin in ultraviolets and blacks and his eyes are gaps between stars, focused and containing uncertain feelings within.

After tearing away at the station, we finally uncover two filters above the frozen turbine. One collection device is completely encapsulated in dark ice, but the other…

The other everyone begins to work on.

Snow's body sings of frustration and annoyance. New and Fresh send out a wave of hopelessness. Nash and Parrot eagerly get to work.

Parrot: "Get to work! Get to work!"

New: "How does this even operate?"

New snaps the best he can in too-thick gloves. His thoughts pour out like mist.

New: "Since the sun is normally on this side, this thing collects water from the mist, and when we're rotated like this, the ice gathers so it can melt - holy crap that's brilliant. But the ice is so thick. No way it could all melt before a rotation."

Snow: "Yeah. It's broken."

Parrot: "Get to work!"

"Hah. Hah. Ooo." I kneel and inspect what I can. We only have two more days before the rotation returns and we will be part of the mist that is collected.

My HUD beeps a few more times, calling to me, whispering to me even as my orb echoes the call. There's a vibration in the air that I cannot place, but it is… menacing.

Snow: "St----. Your EGG? Needs a break."

Snow touches the arm my EGG sits on. I follow the tendrils up to where it still holds most of the dark ice chunks into the air, waving them dangerously over Fresh's location. I ask it to drop the chunks some place in the mist behind us.

"What would I do without you?" I tease.

Snow: "I don't know S---n, but I missed this."

Fresh: "Don't get cozy."

Perty reads my body language wrong and takes a step towards me.

I hold out my non-EGG arm and signal him down as best I can in a spacesuit. It is easier for me since my suit is fitted, sleeker, more like biking leather, unlike what the others wear. I thank the orb for that.

Perty nods in understanding. He shifts his glance to Fresh.

We both watch her. The laser at her hand and note the safety is on, and we know. We know how fast, how far, and how easy it would be to acquire it. We briefly consider how to take the base, what to do with the prisoners once we've turned our guardians into refuse.

We contemplate a freedom we cannot have, but one that still itches at our very being. And before we can become invested, we stop.

We exchange glances, knowing better than to have such thoughts. Knowing they would murder our brothers and sisters for even having them.

Frustrated, Perty says, 'I will patrol, and I need space,' with a glance and I nod.

For now, I watch the show that is Parrot and New as they work on the filter.

8

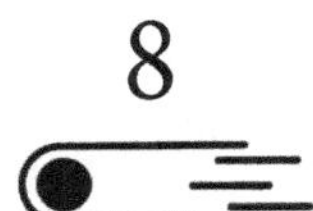

We work for hours. We work until we cannot.

This is work that has meaning. We do it gladly, and softly, some even sing. Not our song, no, disparate ones. Some about rings. Some about seas.

I watch the light move closer as some of the others dare to sleep. Not being part of the wall, not being part of the stone, it makes my mind feel looser.

I watch the stars: even though the sky is black from this side of the comet; I know what they would look like from here and revisit this in my mind's eye. Along with it, I replay Fresh's disgust and anger.

It soothes the soul.

New: "I think I can help."

He sits far away from me, knees tucked tight against his chest as he speaks.

New: "I'm no expert, but if I can get your help, I think I can repair it."

"There may be nothing to repair." I do not look away from the sky to talk to him. Maybe it will comfort him not to see my eyes? It is hard to say.

New: "That thing on your arm?"

He motions to my arm. I glance down, the alien and yet familiar visage of the EGG that sits there as it hums along with my body.

New: "And the orb? What is all this? I've never seen it before."

"Cession." I motion to my thin, beautiful air bubble, then to my arm. "EGG."

New: "The Cession egg then? It's more alien than I am."

I chuckle and start again. I motion to the alien thing in my arm. It, too, rests. The pain has dulled, but it is stronger now than before. I appreciate its efforts.

"This is an E.G.G. Exterior Gravity Gauntlet... maybe? Extraterrestrial Gravity Gear, sometimes. Either way. Found working the mines like us. Works best for unnaturals."

New: "Would it work for me?"

He hesitantly moves a little closer, likely to look closer at my EGG. My brief glance towards him makes his whole body shift backward.

"Bonded." I close my eyes, imagining a dock where GEMs used to load and unload with ease. A world where life was almost normal. "It would work, but not as well as its bonded patron. They bond us early, if they can. Usually, they are kept in cold storage, or in their natural atmosphere, like the comet."

New: "Freaking amazing."

I sit in the silence for a bit and wait for the next part. He doesn't disappoint.

New: "Sooo, Cession? What the heck is that? It was like… whoosh and then turned into your suit. So, can it form anything or just a suit?"

"Cession is from the same place you are. From the Rift. There are many breeds of it but this one is very rare. It is smart. Smart Cession forms what it wants, dumb Cession only forms what it is well accustomed too. It is connected to -"
The metal slithers across my skin, aching to be near a mind that it can touch with ease. "It hungers for you."

I hear him make a shadow of himself against the ground.
His breathing slows.
The music of the world grows heavy. The heartbeat of the stone throbs beneath me and I touch it, my eyes still cast to the sky. "Oh, for the sweet embrace of death… "

New: "Oh, for a call to arms - one, two, one, two."

He taps on the ground with a chunk of ice in his hand and turns his gaze upward. For just a moment, I remember him as a spark, an itch, and I feel something else in my mind. I feel connection.
I used to have a word for this.

A link? A join, a plug?
It matters little as we connect in the rhythm of the world.

Snow's voice is mostly white noise: "So--n. S--r--n."

New: "Over here, sorry. I was resting."

Snow: "It's better you not try to learn it."
She does not say why, but I think he knows. She stands near him, pulls him away from me. My brain sings of a long ago concept. A brain sickness. A dissolving of the self, a stirring of the self into another by the sun.
Then the thought fades. It is probably better that way.
He is too warm. Too HOT.
I'd burn away around him and never know.
In the distance, Perty's mind whispers a warning to me without words, without need.
I know. I know.
"Ooo. Ooo. Hah." I whisper.

Snow: "So you think there's hope to repair it?"

I'm not sure if Snow is asking me or New, but it doesn't matter. Hope has no place here.

New: "I mean… I was studying to be an engineer before I got caught up with the Breeders."

I can hear his awkward adjustments even in the silence.

New: "I can try."

Fresh: "Shut up already. No one cares if you die out here, Rip."

I imagine slitting her throat with the straight blade in my pocket, and it soothes my soul.

Snow's voice is soft over the intercom: "The first time they asked, St-... Daylight... volunteered to come out. The comet's rotation moves, but there are two gathering portals so it doesn't matter too much. That is until we got hit by a ship"

Parrot: "END OF TIMES! Please don't kill me!"

Fresh: "SHUT UP! Goddamn it!"

Snow: "It doesn't happen much, but when it does, it can throw us off. The days got longer, stranger. So we had to keep count as a whole instead of just a few of us."

Nash: "Hah. Hah. Ooo."

Snow: "Now, he goes every time. He knows the way."

I interrupt. "The sky is hungry."

Snow's heavy breath lets me know she is laying down now, staring up at the same black sky I am. She is tired and needs rest. We all do, but there is no shelter here, no comfort.

Snow: "If we get it working, we go back in. For a while, it will mean more rations and more water for everyone. The work never changes but -"

"The sky is hungry!" I am not sure how else to say it, as the HUD on my screen flashes with life.

It paints my world in shades of red.

Nash: "Hah. Hah. Ooo."

New: "Sky? Hungry?"

Snow: "It's what we used to say when an army of Ritz would attack."

There's a pause, and the voice becomes weary against my red flashes.

Snow: "Honestly, I only understand about half of what he says now. Things like that, I'm sure it all has some greater meaning in that fucked up head of his."

I turn the warning light off and settle in. Perhaps this is all a part of my fucked up mind.

New: "Did he? Did you all...? Why?"

Snow: "Why?"
She laughs.
Snow: "Is this your favorite word?"

I smile as she does, the whisper of her mind bringing me images of another time when we smiled much more.
"Why?" I repeat. "Why?"
"...got the wrong guy..." Parrot babbles from his sleep.

New: "I mean it. I don't understand why this is happening. What did we do to deserve this? This is beyond punishment. You guys are..."

He puts his hand up to the sky.

New: "Everything here is so black. It's like color doesn't even want to exist out here. I feel gray. Like I might become one of the walls one day. Doesn't that terrify any of the rest of you?"

"Hah. Hah. Ooo."

Only Fresh does not join the chant.

In that moment, I think New understands.

He can sense the rhythm of the stone, the terms of the light as the pulse beneath us - inside us, and I can hear the faint whispers of his mind against mine.

It feels… warm.

The sky screams. I tear myself out of space to make it stop. The stars, in their dying whisper, say: "The sky is hungry. The sun is coming."

I burn.

I fall.

I grab Perty's neck as I am awakened from the sensations that are hard to discern from reality. My skin is on fire. The metal beneath me aches with something it cannot describe with words, but my EGG knows, too.

The sky is screaming. No, my HUD is again. It paints the world in flashing reds and one word.

Warning.

WARNING.

"The sky is hungry!" I scream as Perty grabs my face.

His eyes burrow into the depths of my thoughts and pull out something that used to be. He puts it into solid words in my mouth and I say them as if reading from a script. "The trajectory and rotation are all off. We need to move. Now."

Nash: "What? We still have layers of ice to break and electrical to fix."

"THE SUN IS TOO CLOSE!" I do not mean to scream it, but I can feel the sun on every inch of my skin. My whole body burns with the unfamiliar heat. "Look at it. Our rotation is completely off. We're off. The whole damn comet is off."

New: "Well that was terrifyingly coherent."

Parrot: "Rotation too fast. Not three days, no, six hours and then - and then - and then...."

The horizon is thick with fog. It is high and distant, but I know my eyes play tricks. They are used to the darkness, but this is not the dark. The sky is a black hole against the rhythm of the stone.
No.
No, it is a few kilometers against a 10 kilometer circumference of darkness.
Think - damn it - think.
My mind floods all of theirs at once as I say words they don't need to hear.
"Measure the sky. Measure the distance between Perty and the ground, use it as a point of reference for the mist. Factor in the distance walked, where you know the collectors are in relation to the door. Do the math!"

New: "Parrot just said it. We're six hours behind."

New's eyes go wide as the sensation of his mind wraps around all of us.
Fear. Anxiety.

Parrot: "Hah. Hah. Ooo-ahh!"

Fresh: "What the hell does that mean?"
Fresh gasps the words as she stumbles to her feet from
sleep.

New: "It means we need to move. NOW!"

Snow carries anyone within reach as the wall of mist barrels
towards us.

68

TERMS OF LIGHT

9

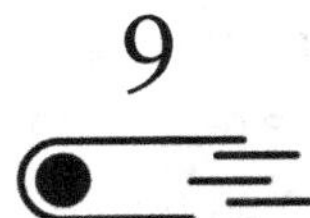

The world turns beneath my feet like a treadmill. Every ten steps is the same as ten steps before.

Nothing changes.

The crags and rocks are like passive eyes on us as we run. Heavy breath is shared between us as we all feel the panic that comes with the unchanging landscape.

Fresh: "The instruments would have calculated this."

Her words are for herself, not for us. Perhaps she hopes to reach the Shadows left behind?

One-two.

One-two.

"Oh, for the glory of the sun!"

Fresh: "NOT NOW!"

New: "We're thirty minutes ahead of the wall. He's counting. Keeping track of how long we have. You know - more than you're doing."

I remind myself, if we make it past this sun, to appreciate our new spark a little more.

Snow: "We need to... we need to slow down."
Snow's air is heavy as she talks.
Snow: "If we don't, we're going to run out of stamina. All we need to do is stay one minute ahead."

Nash: "One minute ahead? Not enough. We will be dead fast. We won't even feel the fire that burns us alive."

Snow: "Better that than a slow death?"
Snow stumbles, Perty is there to catch her and they are back to moving like nothing has slowed us down. Their breath is still heavy. The metal hungers along my skin, eager for one to fall so it can feed.
I keep it tame, but it is excited. Excited to fight, excited to run, excited to be what it is supposed to be.
My feet are lighter than feathers as the orb helps to push me a little faster, a little beyond what my gifts will do. It taps into what I am, into the genes they gave me to make me the perfect creature. Energy, long unburned, ignites in my legs and in my core.
My body wants to fight. Fight the sun?
My memory begins to static in and out again. If only it knew we had already tried.

Perty: "Shelter."

Fresh: "Great thinking. Where exactly are we going to find some?! The whole point of this place is there isn't a way OFF OF IT!"

Snow: "How long would we need?"

Parrot: "Too fast to build! TOO FAST TO FLY! 3 days in shelter! The sun will pass!"

"The sky is screaming," I mention again.

No one answers. This is all too familiar. Like a place we've been before, a time.

I can see an emerald sky singing in my mind's eye and in theirs.

A word comes to it. One that is entombed in fire and static. E----a.

New: "How big is the comet? If we can keep a decent pace ahead of it, we'll be right back to the entrance won't we? How far? How long?"

Parrot: "Other side. Water for the shadows, weeping, weeping from the sky. Not for us! No rest for us!"

New: "I liked it better when he spoke in riddles. I pretty much got the gist of that."

The energy in my legs, in my bones, weakens. Sleep I didn't complete nips at my eyes.

I call out, "Break."

The others are hesitant to agree. We have at least 20 minutes to rest, less if we're smart. We can see the wall of mist beside us rising like an ominous dragon against the pitch black of sky. My scanner flashes warnings at me again.

I sigh and swipe them away.

Snow touches my hand, but it takes my mind, my skin, too long to register, so she tugs at me. I see my face momentarily reflected in hers. Our hair is too long, our faces are covered in sweat that only serves to emphasize the hollow of our eyes.

Snow: "The Cession. That orb was huge, is there any way we can make it into a shelter? A… ship or a roof? Anything that could keep us from the heat? Or a…"

I know she hopes I will finish her thoughts for her. Perhaps another me would have, but I have nothing. The leader she craves was left in an empty circle for too long.

The orb eagerly reaches out and covers her hand, forming on it a small bracelet.

An offering.

As if to say 'hey, at least your beautiful head will survive.'

Snow: "S---n. St----. Captain! I need you. I need my leader back! We can't wait for a moment of clarity."

Her eyes are like two empty holes in the darkness pulling me towards them. Blue as a sky that I can now only remember in shades of gray and red. The thought alone makes me ache for war, for blood for -

"Hah. Hah. Ooo-hah."

My HUD again lights up, but this time it shares with me an old piece of data. There is something in the distance, something far, but near enough we could alter course. Calculations spin in distant whirls of color and Snow again tugs on my hand. Her fury flows through our link and a smile tugs on the edge of my corners.

The calculations say we need to move fast.

Need to move now.

"Left. 16 degrees. Two signals, one weak."

Snow turns her head instinctively in the direction, but I do not wait for her to see.

I run.

I let my body, worn, thin and aching for movement, melt into the alien metal that surrounds my body. I can hear, distantly, reactions over the com but they are static noise against my skull.

Fresh, lungs burning, tries her best to scream her lack of understanding. Perty, heart beating in sync with mine, runs at my side, Nash not far behind breaths heavy. New - New is the reaction I expect the least as he tries his best to keep up with us but the GEM in our blood far outweighs his Ritz.

Parrot stumbles authentically, rolling up and slipping the redhead over his back before continuing a sprint I was not sure he would make. He joins us as we try to push forward, our bodies weak. The world becomes a cloud.

The scent of ozone is so strong it makes it through the air filters on our suits and deep into our lungs.

It smells like hope.

New, bouncingly: "Do we know what the signals are?"

Fresh: "Stop! You have to stop! We're going to hit the wall. We're going to burn!"

New: "No, we've still got minutes between us and -"

We all fall silent as the clouds part. The fog breaks way to the forest of overgrown ice and metal. It is a foreign sight, a strange one, and my brain becomes blind from it.

It is Perty that grabs me and pulls me to the side, breaking our formation and dragging me behind a stone large enough to hide us. The others stumble out of the fog behind us. Perty summons them with a wave.

He does not have to motion for us to maintain silence, because we all have nothing to say.

That is, until Fresh appears.

She is the last to emerge from the thick fog as it gathers around this strange site. She stumbles into the mist from her own exhaustion. When she sees it, when she sees the foreign sight in front of her, she instinctively aims her weapon, but just as quickly drops it.

Unlike us, her reaction is that of the freed, of the Shadows who own the world we weep in. She stands taller, waving her arms, and we all wince as her communication echoes out into the barren field.

Fresh: "HEY! Hello! Calling to the vessel in front of us! Identify yourselves and prepare to be boarded!"

Nash takes a step away from where he is crouched beside Perty. He pounds a clenched fist into his palm, but before he can do what he wants, Pert puts a hand on his shoulder.

Fresh: "HEY!"

She tumbles past where we hide, her duty to serve and protect now solely dedicated to the self. As it always was.

Fresh: "Hey!! Calling out to the vessel in front of us!"

Each step she takes crunches loudly into the comet's ancient sands. It is like a hundred knives against our skin. Even New, now trembling beside me, blind and eager for this to end, makes his breathing stop with every shout she gives.

We all stare at the ship in front of us and wait.

10

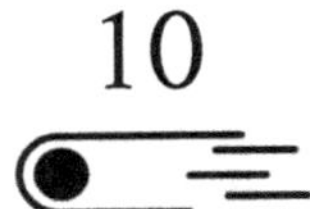

For every call that Fresh makes, the ship does not respond.

If there is life on board, they are far more preoccupied with something else. I glance at Parrot and I motion to the fog. It is too thick now to see the wall that will tell us how long we have until we may burn.

Parrot hops up, but Snow pulls him down again. I do not hear or see his answer if he gave one.

Fresh grunts, secures her gun and prowls closer to the ship. I can see every muscle of hers tense as her moves are stiff and clumsy. We all wait to see what comes next, even the darkness.

Snow looks to me from the small gap between our hiding spaces. Her eyes ask what the plan is. I put my finger over where my mouth would be. The plan is simple.

We wait.

Fresh will either set us free or die, and I am fine with either choice.

Fresh opens her external verbals and tries again.

Fresh: "Hail. I'm Lt. Cabera Forsyte. I'm a private security officer looking for transport off this damn rock."

New takes his chance while she talks. He's either brilliant or dumb as fuck.
New: "Is that a ship?"

Nash: "Yes."

New: "Think we can get in there before the sun line melts us alive?"

He tries to whisper his words, but hurry aches through his teeth. I feel an itch in my mind of... impatience?
It is not mine. Is this New's?
It is hard to describe. The words seem far away and I get lost in the thought.
What pulls me back is the musky smell of gravity as the air is pierced with a heavy sound. It is the sound of a ship as it thrums to life, her gravity engines engaging.
Perty, Snow, Nash and I exchange glances. We know this sound too well; we are pulled back to a place and a time with an emerald sky where ships like this fell like rain down on us.
The orb connects our minds and sings the song shared between us.

I hold up a hand and point in two directions. "Hah. Hah."
They respond, "Ooo-AH!"
One. Two.
One. Two.
Perty and Snow crawl through the heavy mist after Fresh.
One. Two.

One. Two.

Parrot pulls New away and tucks him into some secret place. He doesn't need to see this part of us. Not yet.

One. Two.

One. Two.

Nash and I crawl over the barriers at the same time. Our eyes, briefly blinded, see what Perty and Snow already know. Numerous shadows that dance in the ship's windows. Fresh engages those she cannot hope to negotiate with. Her voice, frustrated, still rings out.

Fresh: "You are in violation of the Purgatory Act. That's the system prisoner treaty act in case you're too stupid to understand where you are."

Fresh sounds a bit more like a goose as she waggles her arms uselessly at them.

Fresh: "This colony is -"

"Shutup."

What emerges from the ship sends me back to a time and place where I smiled more. They wear helmets and gear that remind me of leather and beatings. The one in the front wears a helmet that has sharp teeth and a pointed skull that make him look too much like a shark.

The other shadows behind him, that are visible, wear similar gear. Some are sharks, some are squids, others are unknown things with teeth eager to sink into fresh prey. I read the side of their ship and it says Calgary Haut. It bears the ancient symbol of a cracked skull on black paint.

Pirates.

I smile.

The crowd focuses on Fresh. Their maws wide, ready to cascade like sharks upon her frozen form. They pour from a mostly broken ramp around her, circling, sizing, investigating, intimidating.

My heart pumps gold into my veins as even my EGG trickles light into my hair and along my skin.

Their sharp leader calls out: "This is our ship, our rock - and now, you're ours too."

Fresh: "You have no idea where you are, do you?"

Sharp laughs: "And I don't care. Soon, we'll be off this rock and we're taking everything we can with us."

A vicious fanged creature steps into Fresh's shadow. She is oblivious as they wear her skin without touching.

Fresh: "Great. Then consider yourself under arrest. I'm taking you in to join the other scum."

Sharp: "Really?"
The sharp one glances around into the darkness and laughs, the weapon at its side glowing to life with foul scented light.
Sharp: "You and what army?"

The smirk tugs at the corner of my lips.
We all burn with urges we have not fulfilled in a long time. The swarm of pirates around Fresh do not know we are here. They cannot possibly expect what comes next.
We wait until each of us is in place, and then the orb helps conduct as we act as one.
I watch Perty's quiet movements as he pinches the air of one man. Then arms wrap around the thick fabric of their neck.

Snow is efficient, she pushes her weight against one so that his own helmet works against him, slamming his face into the front. The body lays heavy on her chest as she silently returns to her place in the mist.

Nash is brute force. He takes a large, flat rock to the back of one of the foul smelling weapons. It tumbles to the ground, and he is quick to grasp it. He knows he cannot fire it, so he uses it to beat them into the ground.

My orb knows what I want. I touch the back of one of the sharp creatures and the orb's tendrils slide under the metal, consuming it. It reaches his neck as he twitches a little, focused on Fresh and not me. Then, like a whisper, it slides across his neck and drowns him in red.

A howl fills the air.

Realization washes over the ones that remain like the fog.

Sharp screams: "What the HELL are you playing at?!"

Another yells as they fire: "YOU ARE OVER! You are OVER!"

Fresh backs away, aiming her gun but shaking too hard to use it. The Sharp one says something, but I do not hear it. Instead, my focus is on a familiar electronic howl as something ripples around us like water.

Gravity mine.

We fall back and Sharp screams at Fresh's retreating form.

Parrot whistles a song, sharp and harsh in our ears. It is five beats long.

The ripple of gravity hits just above the ground and turns into a whirlpool. The waves of force fluctuate around us, pulling, twisting and biting at our bodies. We lower the gravity levels on our belts, knowing better than to pull against the tide.

We wait.

We count.

One.

Fresh tries her best to move away, but the whirlpool pulls her towards Sharp.

Two.

Sharp fares better. His grav belt pulls against the waves that crash against him. This is his tactic, his mine, and with a smile hidden by metal teeth, he charges at Fresh with the ferocity of the predator.

Three.

The ripple compresses in the center before surging outward. It warps the air, the fog and pushes it all outward.

We engage our gravity belts.

The air warps around us as the tide reverses and pulls everything, even the stone at our feet, back towards the center. Sharp picks up the center, his skin and bones rippling and fighting against the reality they exist in as he lifts the mine's core. A morning star of gravity swells within the predator's hands, ready to tear Fresh's head from her body.

Four.

The force pulls against us. Sharp moves slowly towards Fresh. A blade forms at my hand as the orb reminds me it would like attention.

I am happy to comply.

Five.

I have learned in many years as a prisoner and as a rebel to never fight against the forces not meant to be fought. Gravity is the very force that taught me that. My EGG is unintimidated by this small flex of gravity in its presence.

White tendrils reach out and wrap around Sharp's wrist and the gravity mine's core. To the EGG, it is heavy, but little else. With a flick, Sharp is flung away from Fresh and onto the ground.

Six.

We breathe out as one.

All except Fresh. She cowers as the few other predators pull themselves out from distant hiding places. The gravity pulls at Sharp's body, his belt pushing against it, confusing his organs as parts of his body twist in unnatural ways.

We watch, but we do not wait.

Perty, Nash and Snow make quick work of those that remain. The need to stay quiet now gone, they make gleeful work of painting the comet's stone with red. There are screams. They are sweet music from another time but as they soothe me they find something new in my mind. I find myself petrified.

I cannot move.

Memories that are not mine again wash over me. I am hiding in the dark, waiting for the Shadows to find me. I am hearing the screams of those I love and my stomach twists in fear.

I think of New.

Of his Ritz mind that can connect to ours so easily, but it can project too. Even as the world turns a comfortable red, all I can feel is the sun.

My skin boils, my head becomes lighter than air.

I am staring at the sky.

I am now far from the center of the world and Snow touches my shoulder.

Snow: "Sir?"

It takes too long to look at her. She is… more colorful than I have ever seen her. Eyes are blue, hair is white, and her skin is the color of the soil, but that's not what I mean. Something else radiates from her center.

Something alive.

We are inside, my helmet removed. I have no memory of coming here. Is this the Calgary Haut?

"I think..." I touch my hair and twist it beneath gloved fingers. I glance behind me where rows of electronics and seating lay, welcoming, waiting.

I do not know how I got here or when we entered.

I touch the glass of the ship's display window. It is small, old, but functional. The computer's settings enhance the stars, but they are still distant and hard to see.

Snow settles near me.

My hands wrap around a steering column and the HUD in front of me lights up with a sequence of suggested destinations, even as the console below me scream with damage notifications.

"Where are we?"

Snow raises an eyebrow and takes a long breath before answering with, "Safe."

For the first time in an eternity, I can feel my heart beat.

11

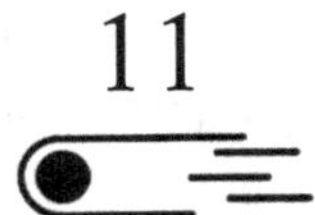

"This ship is shot to hell." the approaching wall of fog emphasizes Nash's words.

Parrot chimes behind him, "NO HOPE! YOU GOT THE WRONG GUY!"

"Shut up!" Forsyte demands from somewhere in the ship.

"I knew this was too much to hope for," Snow sighs, taking another swig of whatever it is she is drinking.

Everyone's minds are silent now as the metal is calm, satiated. It settles around me like a warm blanket. I run my fingers along the ancient steel and rusted together bolts that make up the wall beside me.

"It is nice though."

"It will barely cover us from the sun wash," Nash argues. "We need another solution."

"This was a miracle as it is." Snow takes another sip, aware of how precious whatever she holds is. She clings to it like if she doesn't, it will be lost.

"What about the other ship?" New's quiet form creeps out of the many tunnels of the ship. His head has changed. His hair is cut short, itching around his ears like it's looking for lost friends.

"Other ship?" I find myself asking a question I didn't have. My mind recalls running in the fog. Two signals. Two destinations. I lead us to the closest one.

I smile.

"Other ship."

It is Parrot's turn to roll into center stage. "Come see. Come see. These are pirates, yes, SHARP pirates, but they ruined their ship when they hunted."

"That was surprisingly coherent," New reiterates, staring at Parrot as if he had one head. "Yeah, no, he's right. This thing got screwed up when they hit the comet. I was trying to figure out how you HIT a comet, but then I saw the other ship. It's still on the foggy side. Further back. Looks like it might be safe if we can rig some kind of transport between the two. I mean… I wasn't sure if we needed equipment or to worry about the sun. Oxygen. Stuff like that?"

"Oxygen~ STUFF LIKE THAT!" Parrot cackles.

"Comet Chasers," Perty's gruff words break through the shadows he sits in even as they cling to his body like a mist. He is still in his suit, still ready to run at a moment's notice.

Most of them are.

"Comet Chasers? No way!" New is suddenly at Perty's side like a butterfly finding its first flower. "Really? I've never seen a Comet Chaser ship. Why would they be hunting this comet? I thought they only hunted class R and lower stones. Who would they be collecting for? How? Why?"

I smile.

Maybe I should have named him Why.

I feel something, but it is hard to tell the source. The warmth that came from the room or maybe from myself is too much to ignore. I tap the metal band on my hand against the door frame.

One-two.

One-two.

I whisper, "Oh, for the sweet embrace of home."

"Hah. Hah. Ooo."

"Oh, for the way to the stars once more."

"Hah. Hah. Ooo-ahh."

Yes. That's it. My fingers tingle with anticipation.

"What are we going to do with Forsyte?" Nash motions to Fresh, who's tied up to a chair. She struggles against it as I enter the room and tilt my head. I study her for a moment.

Finally, she spits. She is still in her helmet, so it hits glass.

"We're going back!" she screams, "As soon as you fix the water collectors."

"Nah." I wave at her with a smile.

"Hah. Hah!" Nash says, punching my shoulder. "So, we leave her here? She'll bake or starve."

"Mmm," I shrug. "The sun is still ten minutes out. Let us walk if we want to walk."

"We won't be able to come back." Snow warns. "We need to really think about this. This ship isn't completely sealed, but we can make it that way."

Nash scoffs, "We can improvise sealing, but we don't know nothin' about the other ship."

"It's an hour outside of the sun's danger zone, I think." New chimes in like he's been part of the crew all along. "We need to get to it and wait until the sun passes."

"All wrong! Trajectory all wrong! The sun is all wrong." Parrot warns, grasping at me, half out of his suit. He clutches at my arm and whispers, "Don't leave me."

I stroke what little there is left of his thinning hair and smile. "We're going. Taking everyone, even Fresh."

"Fresh?" New asks.

"That's what he calls Forsyte," Snow explains with an itch to her fingers. "Also, I think there's something with shielding we can use in the bay. It can't take all of us. Some of us have to walk, the others can get it together and meet up at the other ship."

Nash is now the one to tilt his head.

"I looked in the bay, ain't nothin' there."

"They're pirates." Snow's eyes roll so loudly I can hear them. "It's hidden, dumbass."

There is a buoyancy to their barbs that makes me smile as their words fade out. They argue. Nash insists he's right, Snow *knows* she is. They disappear.

"Then we walk." I look at the others. Perty is the only one that participates with a nod.

"So, we're really doing this?" New asks hesitantly.

"You can walk with them, if you like." I put my hands on New's shoulders and he flinches, ready for violence, but trying not to show it. I kiss his forehead. "We go. You stay. Parrot. Perty. Fresh is with us."

Even New did not need an invitation to understand. He will be more help to those two than to us. And then...?

Perty reluctantly lifts Fresh by her bindings and slides her over his shoulder like a fresh kill. I wonder if he took his share of the kill outside, but I pass the thought off for another time.

We all reseal ourselves and take a step out into the thick mist. We can all feel the heat, the warning of something we all fear.

But we will move fast.

We have new motivation now - and the stars. The stars are closer than ever before.

As we step back out into the frozen dust, we sing.

One. Two.

One. Two.

All in sync with one another, all except Fresh.

"Oh, for the sweet embrace of home."

"Hah. Hah. Ooo."
"Oh, for the way to the stars once more."
"Hah. Hah. Ooo-ahh."

Parrot: "What is the place that we call home?"

We answer: "The stars. The sea. The sky. Beyond. Hah. Hah. Ooo."

"Oh, for the shadow of death. Oh, for the call to arms." I echo, "To walk as One among the Others. To wake to Daylight's call."

Parrot: "Daylight!"

His is a scream. A call to the sky.

Perty: "Daylight."

Perty's whisper is a wish to the earth.
We chant.
We walk.
A song not complete since the sun was stolen. I feel the rhythm through the stones beneath and the electricity above. It tethers us as we walk through ice, frost, and the threat of heat death at our edges.

Then, from the mist, it emerges. The faint outline of something barely recognizable as a ship. It is a compact sphere of a ship. We approach and find that New was right. This place is outside the threat of the sun, as the mist is thin and easy to see through.

We enter the ship without a challenge, like it was waiting for us.

We find bodies where they died. Most bracing for impact, still tightly tied in seats.

We push them out and make the first round of diagnostics. Fresh struggles. Perty assists and Parrot… waits.

It is not long before the others join us. I do not know what they find or how they get here; only that the airlock opens and I am met with New's bright spark.

"Holy shit." New's breath is at my back. "It's beautiful."

"And probably shit." Nash balks, pulling off his thick gloves. "At least she look intact."

"You're here. Good." I nod to myself and let the diagnostics run. This was never my game, so it is all gibberish to me.

While we wait, Captain Oswald's words ring in my head.

If you fuck this up, Pechard, you fuck everyone in here.

I glance at Perty and Snow and sigh.

"We will water the stone - you." I press my finger into New's shoulder and push him to Nash and Parrot. "Sing me a song of home."

"… This is all starting to make sense. I think that's the part that bothers me the most," New mutters as he picks up tools and is dragged to the small space that is the engine.

Snow shakes her head and touches my shoulder. "Nice to see you back in action, Captain."

The words light my mind up with white noise. If she says more, I don't hear it. I squeeze her hand and get ready.

There is still so much work to do.

12

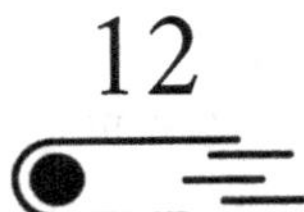

We are on and off Sharp's ship with little effort.

The amount of weapons they have in their care will make easy work of what we need. Melt the ice, get the turbines running and… the thought beyond that is like black ice on the blades of my brain's filter.

We could die.

We lost our lives long before now, but I cannot leave the others to die this way.

We can - no, we WILL sustain the lives of those below if we free the filter from the ice. It will only last a few terms. A few… a few cycles of…

I rub my head, furiously trying not to track every sound I hear as we drive the little car the others have rescued from Sharp's ship.

My mind replays the last few hours over and over. The detail is vibrant, my orb roils and wiggles with anticipation of another fight.

My breath is heavy. I finally verbalize.

"What if it works?"

"It will."

"What if we -"

"Shh." Perty looks even paler than the stars. "It will."

We get to work.

The work has meaning. The damage to the water flow system is substantial. We have likely been drinking in from only one side for more terms that most of us remember how to count. That explains the more frequent intervals and why I still have gifts from the Captain from the last walk.

Perty sits with me. We say little. There's not much to say that our eyes do not tell.

With some effort we get to the water, and the sun does damage to the thick sheets of ice, but it does little to that which is shadowed. The collector itself is mostly in the crater, making it easy for the ice to stay, and hard for maintenance.

Perty and I take turns using sonic and heat weapons on the outside of our little sun shielded dune buggy to break away at the ice. We take turns using our EGGs to help it along. I pull some of the ice inside and we make water for ourselves.

It is too cold and tastes of dust.

It tastes better than any water I have ever had.

My hair, the EGG, is all the light we really use inside our little car. I study Perty; I see his pale flesh is rust colored and grimy and a little piece of memory that cuts into the now. I pull some of the ice into a bowl and warm it with my hands until it is water.

I sit next to Perty with it. He stares at me, then at the water, and for a moment I see his body shake.

He strips quickly, taking a piece of cloth he tears from a seat and dips it into the water. He washes his skin, his face, his hair. I leave him to do this on his own. This is for him, a sacred thing, a missing piece perhaps he also has recalled.

I turn my attention to the ice.

I line the filters with another round of sonic and heat. My EGG tears at it, and then something deep and bassy shakes the cart. I can hear the cracking deep down in the hole. I watch as the ice gives in.

Explodes.

Dances in the air like diamond knives.

I find myself laughing and give Perty a wink as he comes to see. His smile is a ghost of what it should be. We hear the turbines churn, and the lights on the pump station come to life as mist rises and dissipates. The fans hum.

The water flows, channeled down to those below.

We make our way back to Sharp's ship, but say little. The small success is enough, but now we face something much harder.

I have an itch on my mind as we gather what supplies the others have staged and prepare. We load oxygen, food, and I stare for a moment at some gravity bombs and the engines.

The rotation is off.

Even though we have fixed the water supply, for now, it may not be enough. My heart is heavy, but I have a thought.

Fortunately, I know how to sabotage a ship as if it is second nature.

It comes easy.

It comes fast.

"Hey baby," I whisper to the black screen as I finish my tasks, "You're going to give us one last run, okay, but then I promise we'll let you sleep."

"Calgary Haut," Perty mutters.

"Cally," I smile. "One last job, okay?"

We return to the Comet Chaser without speaking. Seeing her reminds me of home, and my heart races.

"This could work."

"It will."

"... This could work."

My thoughts weigh heavy and blank.

Snow touches my hair, tugging on it gently when I do not respond at first. I give her a look of acknowledgement before sinking back into thought. We - I - am on the Comet Chaser ship again.

I have no memory of how.

"Parrot says we're ready." Snow adds, "We should be ready to get off of this rock any time, but we're going to need to drop-jump her."

"I should help."

"You should stay" She sits across from me in a chair too small for her broad GEM frame.

GEM.

GEM.

I repeat the word in my mind. It is strange, alien, but shinier than *stone*.

"Pert said you got most of the ice cleared up and then started to lose yourself again." She rubs the inside of the Comet Chaser's hull. "I'm... glad you got the water fixed."

"This is stupid."

"This is... scary." I can imagine the pit in her stomach growing. Mine did, too.

"What's her name?" I touch the ship's wall, mirroring Snow's motions.

"It's been scratched off. The parts from the Calgary Haut will cover the holes from their crash soon, and she'll be someone new." Snow affirms. "And then... ?"

"This could work." I whisper.

"This could... work," she says with me.

"Oxygen~!" Parrot chimes from the back of the ship. "SOMETHING LIKE THAT."

13

The way the artificial light touches my skin after so many years in darkness feels like fire.

Even if it is a little. I pull away, but no matter what I do, it lingers. It is everywhere as I sit under it, unprotected by my orb.

In the darkness above us, there's a song. In the light, somewhere, there's another.

The sun's song tells me the darkness will go away, that worlds will go away if I sing with it. For a moment, I listen - just a moment - then I am pulled back to the place where the world ended.

The sky turns emerald; it sparkles with alien light.

The sun is gone. We stand on ------ alone.

The desert that the sun has left behind is hot.

Those few survivors that I can bring from the rain of ships have little of themselves. They are different, changed, like I am.

I pull them to safety, into the shade of broken buildings and ruined homes. There are few others that help - that *can* help.

The sun takes away all of my feelings.

I have nothing left except rage and fire.

I pull my hand away from the dashboard as I wake up.

The thin crack in the window's tint is enough to have the sun pour through it. My entire body wakes up before my mind, grabs the controls of the ship, and starts it up.

"DAYLIGHT!" I call out.

The rest react before they can understand what it means.

"Daylight!"

"Daylight!"

"Daylight!"

I am left breathless. A firm hand lands on my shoulder; it is Perty's. He is a vibrant, brilliant white, and I am reminded how much he *hates* to be called Perty. I smirk.

"Hey, Pert."

He nods. Hoarsely he says, "We are ready when you are, Captain."

I swallow.

Jump-dropping isn't something I've done before, and no one else on the ship has piloting experience. I've done more dangerous things, *probably*. So, that means it is up to me to get us up in the air, drop us off the comet's side, and hope we pull out of her gravity as her velocity pushes her past us.

Also, I have to make sure we do not freeze or melt in the tail.

Easy peasy.

I grab the controls.

"Countdown Parrot, please."

"ONE! ONE! ONE! ONE! GO!"

I flick a switch. The universe rumbles to life.

Nash cries something I can not hear over the vibrato of metal being pulled against the gravity engine. Mist fills the air as we fully compress and seal, and the ship slides violently back against the stone.

Parrot pops his head by my shoulder and whispers in my ear.

"Might not make it. No tests worked. Could die."

"Not a first."

The small burn engine lifts us up off the stone.

I pull us higher.

The thrusters smash into the ground, pouring fuel, fire and death into the comet's surface and us into the air. The heavy scent of atmosphere seeps through - at least, I think it does. No one says anything as we crawl our way into the sky.

Higher.

Higher.

The sun peers at me through the hole in the shading, daring - *daring* - daring me to fail. Come at me.

Come to me.

Come get me.

I cycle the engines on full and turn thrusters off as we pull far enough off the ground.

I kill the engines.

I can see that there is fuel left. It is not enough for us to try again, but it may be enough to burn us all alive if we need it. We float. For just a moment, we do not know if I've gone up far enough and we have to let gravity do the rest.

It is less dramatic than it sounds, as we fall into orbit around the comet. We go around her once; the sun makes half the surface a blinding bright mass. We pass over the wreckage, the water collectors, the door to our hole in the ground, a docking station, and we watch breathlessly.

We are grateful that the thin lining of the comet chaser does not crack or break against the strain, but as we float it cradles us. There is a comfortable silence that wraps itself around us, even as it threatens to strangle us.

Parrot is still beside me as we fall further and further away. His eyes are too wide, too bright and full of stars as he glances at me and smiles with an almost toothless grin. "All's well, all's quiet, all's well."

"Hah. Hah. Ooo-ah," I whisper into the console. "Thank you."

No one speaks another word as our orbit becomes wider. The comet chaser's screens display our trajectory failure as the gravity engine roars to life under our feet. Slowly, gently, we fall back towards her natural gravity.

"We're falling!" Nash yells.

"We don't have the fuel to pull away. Gravity engine won't work unless we can get away from her full pull." New says panicked. "Shit. Shit. SHIT. Please, not now. We're so… close."

"So close. Oxygen and things." Parrot whispers.

It was a little selfish of me, but I wait until we pass the Calgary Haut. I salute her and with a smile I can no longer suppress; I pull something from my pocket. It is an old school device, made of parts of a com device and a radio signal that spreads further than anyone ever expects.

"Boom," I say as I press the button and cackle.

The others come to my window, waiting for something to happen and, as we pass it on the horizon, just before it is out of view, Cally implodes. The way she compacts makes the entire comet shudder under us.

Then, it pulls away, and so do we.

I laugh.

I'm not sure at what anymore, but the madness in my stomach rolls out onto my tongue as I slap the console and laugh. No one joins me as another signal beeps behind me.

"We're… clear," Nash says.

"What. The. FUCK was that?" New asks.

"I unfucked us," I smile.

"Unfucked us," Parrot mimics in something that sounds like disbelief.

"You ass," Snow says, punching my arm. "Neptune's colonies, you ass!"

"What's happening?" Fresh asks from behind. "What the hell is happening?"

No one answers.

Instead, we watch. There is a pit deep in my stomach that takes the place of my laughter as I watch our comet grow to a size that fits in my window. We are showered in ice with the comet's tail as small chunks of debris hit our screen and sides. With every cycle towards the sun, the ice melts away in thin layers.

Our prison is little more than a dot as we pull further and further away from it. The calculations put us as staying still as it moves on without us. She is little more than a faded corporate logo and a door.

Our home.

Our prison.

Our stone.

Ourselves.

All of these things fall away.

What takes their place is a thousand bright bits of light, and the daunting echo of a burning star. I let the silence settle in before I stand. The alien orb of metal that surrounds my body now crawls into compact pieces around me.

They are familiar things that no longer exist except in memory: a necklace, dog tags, a razor still in my pocket, and a shackle against my wrist.

Where I go, a thousand eyes follow. No, less now. I ignore how small the world is now and how crushed it makes me feel, and I stop in front of one set.

Fresh.

She is tied to a new chair, and she is terrified.

"Forsyte." Saying the name is like diagnosing cancer. "You... have a choice."

"You got the wrong guy!" Parrot chimes, cackling madly afterward.

"Captain?" Snow is the one to raise the question the others dare not answer. "Is now the time?"

"We can leave you here." I motion to the door. "Or you can come. I promise no fate after you leave our care."

"Your care?" she growls. "If that damn pirate hadn't attacked - if you-!"

"They SAVED you!" New wields his shield at her.

"You have a choice." I press my boot against her knee. The dull sound underneath it shuts her up as her face twists. "We can leave you here or you can stay with us."

"What the hell chance do you bunch have in a real fight?" she spits at me. "Look at you! You can barely STAND! Let me go and I'll show you what a real fighter is, you relic."

She surprises us all by standing; the ropes falling at her feet. We overestimate how fast she can move, and how tired we are after so much work. She fumbles her way to New first, and she slams his head against the hull.

He falls. My metal boils, ready for action.

Before I can move, Pert lifts her by her throat in the air and she touches the ceiling with her head. His eyes are wide, his skin the shining white it is in my memory as he stares at her with a stony expression.

She struggles against him, pulling, kicking, but he is stone. Something her people taught us, and all of us relax. He releases her before she passes out, much to my personal sadness, and it is Nash who moves first to help New off the floor.

His eyes are wide with panic for a moment before he sees that things have returned to the status quo. New makes a sound like the ticking of a clock that makes me smile a bit. He must have noticed the attention because he unconsciously steps closer to Pert when I glance his way.

I look at Pert, and we understand each other.

He accepts the mission I give him. Fresh is his now. She has made the challenge, and he has accepted.

"Well, now that the air has returned to the room. Next order of business." I grip the razor in my pocket tightly. If it were open, it would cut into my flesh, a thought that comforts enough to keep me calm. "What comes next?"

No one answers.

After a moment of choking, with ice in her throat, Fresh wheezes. "You've got nowhere to go, tank born. No friends. No money. No payment to offer. No-one will accept you. You are alone. Extinct. Forgotten."

Her words are venomous only to herself.

It is Nash that steps up. I expect a punch to silence her, but he puts a roll in her mouth instead. Even Shadow cannot deny the urges of the body when given a choice.

After a moment, she chews.

"What... choices do we have? Where are we?" Snow asks the obvious, such a good right hand.

"Projections put us near the gravity drift between most of the Jupiter Alliance Colonies," I offer. "If we do some research, I'm sure there are still many colonies we can land safely. Supply and plan from there."

"But what about — ?" New covers his mouth as soon as everyone looks his way.

"It's okay, S--en. Ask." Snow motions to the center of the room.

"What about everyone else? What about those still on the... comet?" He asks without looking for our reactions.

It is for the best. There is silence heavier than the ship's core.

The words bubble up from beneath me; the words taste lava red and sting my eyes. "We can't take them alone. We do not know the worlds anymore and even if we escape, the Shadows are many. They have strings beyond our rock and we would be giving them what they've always wanted."

"A reason," Snow answers for me.

"A reason." I look at each of them.

Fresh is defiant.

Nash looks conflicted but relieved.

Pert, stone and blood, disappointed and frustrated - but accepting of the idea.

New, thoughtful, angry, frustrated.

Parrot, eager to be back in a place that resembles home, more lost than most of us.

Snow... her face is a mirror of mine. Her expression is sad, lost, but accepting. She knows we will return to this place, be it by will or by bondage.

"We have to lose this battle to win the war," I whisper. "We will be back."

It is a promise we make in blood, in space, in sunlight. They hate it as much as I, but we both know there never really was a choice.

This was never our battle to win.

"I don't want to die here," Snow says what others dare not say aloud. "Let's find a place to land."

14

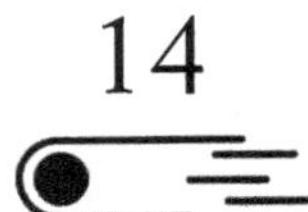

"They don't teach the GEM rebellion on Earth." New stares out the window next to me. It is the first time he has spoken in many hours. As the prison fades from our view, only a few distant stones make themselves known in an otherwise endless sea of twinkling darkness.

I grunt in response. He winces at the noise.

"I mean… not that they should, I just… my foster father told me about it. He wasn't in the war, but he knew many people that were." He was attempting something I didn't have a word for anymore. It was like swallowing something sweet, but it was stuck in the throat. "He said the GEMs fought instead of human soldiers until they turned against us. They stopped fighting, and that's when more people died. More Earthers."

"GEMs." I touch the air like I'm grasping at the word. "Genetically Engineered Miners, then Military when the war came. We stopped calling ourselves that a few years in."

I try to wave away the buzzing sound that the concept of time makes in my head. I tap my metal ring against the seat beneath me to calm it.

One. Two.

One. Two.

It helps my mind feel less hazy.

"Then… what should I call you?" he hesitates to ask, but his foot taps along. A slightly different rhythm with the same beat.

One, two. Three, four.

A memory sings to me.

We look up at the stars together, his small hand against mine. I let him have my coat because the cold and heat stopped bothering me earlier this year. He knows all about GEMs, even though they taught him the twisted version of history in his classes. Perfect soldiers, faster, stronger, smarter, but wrong. Broken.

Soulless.

That's the way it's read.

Property.

Best handled by those who made them.

I wonder if he sees me as property?

"You're going to explore the stars, aren't you?" His small voice asks with certainty. The way he speaks, I know it is not a question. It's a fact, a belief. He believes it until he cannot anymore.

Worse, I think I believe it too.

"Maybe," I tease. "You'll come with me, yeah? You can be my number two, little brother."

"Yeah, right. Number one, you can be my number two mister star gone man." He laughs. It's a phrase they use for people like me, the ones that come out here and stare too much at the stars.

Wanderlust. Adventurer. Spacers. We've had lots of names in the past, but the latest is that: star gone, so far gone for the stars, you need to be in them.

The name sticks.

My lips twitch at the edges as I catch a piece of myself.

I wonder if he got to see the comet's tail as we fell away from the gravity well? I wonder if he got to enjoy that?

"We went through quite a few names after GEM. Haoriri, Armik, Fazqui... our focus was always on the idea that we were the enemy. We were what the others needed us to be. We were made by them and destroyed by them. It was a long time before we decided: maybe we didn't want others to tell us who we were. So we became-" I touch my chest. "Self."

There is a long silence, but it is contemplative. It is lit by the stars around us. "I get it."

"Half ain't half enough, huh?" I twist my fingers through my hair. "Sad. WIPs are always so eager to find a hate they can forge and wield. Makes sense the Rips were next."

"Please, don't call me that." It was mumbled. "I don't even... get it."

"Rip. Tear. Sky terrors. Night fury - that was a good one - nephilim. When the Ritz came, they tore open the sky and changed the world. Rips, that was the name we gave to the enemy, sympathizers were Tears. The humans took the word and twisted it up, called them Ritz, like the crackers. All jargon, something among soldiers to keep hate a warm blade. I always called them Reds." I make the mark of twin triangles with a circle between them at my chest. "Not sure why anymore, really. They were them and you're not them. So, what do I call you?"

"Soren." He takes a breath and I hear it clearly. "Just Soren."

"That's going to take a bit." I rub the name around in my head and between thoughts. It is hard to really hold on to.

New feels more real, New feels less… human. Sometimes it was nice to forget the part of my mind that was human. "New… I like New better."

"New?" He contemplates it, then continues, annoyed. "Is that what you call me?"

I take the time to look at him now, red hair still brighter than the sun, eyes green like the color of broken skies. His nose is too sharp and his hair has those damn feathers that sit poorly in his scalp. Not quite Ritz, not quite human. A beautiful mix. A forgiving mix. "What do you call me?"

"Big guy, spacer, scary," he hesitates. "Daylight."

I stop the tapping.

I pull my hand up to my face and stare at my ring. I twist it in my hands and try to remember where it came from, and why it is warm when I look at it.

It feels very heavy, very hard to lift, to hold.

My body shudders as it throws me another memory.

"They took the food." It is a distant ringing of memory that comes on like a star, but shines brighter as I turn it in my mind.

"When we first said no, they took the food and refused to let us sleep. Our hands, our minds, began to break. They thought we would break completely. They were used to the other kind of GEM. The kind they taught only what was needed to work, but I was different.

When things began to fall apart, I kept us together. I taught them song, I taught them laughter. I taught them pride.

Instead of folding us into pieces they could pick up, we got angry. They had all found their pride, their determination. They thought it would break us, but all they showed us is they had nothing left to offer.

So they shipped us out to die at the hands of their enemies.

The Ritz came.

The Ritz died.

We took their ships. Ritz ships were stronger, faster than WIP ships. We learned to speak to their metal. Then we took HUDO cargo ships. We never had to break civilians, because they never did their own work. The GEMs: we were always there - on the docks, loading ships, in the gutters, anywhere a WIP didn't want to work. So, we took what they had.

Then it became easy.

They took our food. We took our truth back.

We said no.

We rebelled.

We lost.

We died.

Now, we are stones that live by terms of light cast at another's hand.

Nothing but dust."

He stares at me as the ringing light dies away from my mind.

It has been so long since these thoughts have burned in my blood, but it feels branded on my bones. Still, I feel like I should know more about... us.

What happened to us?

I shake my head and shrug.

"The disadvantage of those who oppress is often the resourcefulness of the oppressed. They rely on the status quo and we worked around it. The world grows with or without those willing to change. You take away the food, we eat your hands instead."

"Yeah. Well, I don't really want to be called New anymore, okay?" he offers it up without an ultimatum, without a threat. "Soren. Think you can get that?"

"Your father. Foster." I nod in acknowledgement, repeating the name again and again to myself. "Soren's dad, maybe he knew stones like us?"

Soren offers meekly: "As far as I know, I never saw any on Earth, but my dad knew a few before the camps, before the deportation."

"Deportation?" I trace lines along the seat between us. "To where? Earth? Mars? Saturn?"

"I don't know. I just know that the solar system went a little crazy after the Ritz war. Jupiter and Io were the first to open up trade again a few years ago and the rest are following. ------ is still locked down, I think, but I'm not really sure, honestly. They lie to us about, well - they lie to us about a lot of things. The deportation was pretty early on.

Doesn't this sound familiar at all?

I mean, how... long did they have you guys locked up?"

Snow offers New a cup of something and he takes it. I can see a bit of steam rise from it and his eyes light up.

"Three years, two months, four days and 2 hours. Those last two may be wrong. I have lost a lot of time since we left the hole," I offer with a shrug.

"That's a long time. Still, the war ended almost 5 years ago." Soren sips at his drink. "It makes me wonder if you have, like, GEM celebrities down there. The Y kids, or whatever."

Snow laughs, "Those are a rumor, kid."

"Alleged." I add.

"No, a legend, but impossible to find if they do exist," Snow says with a bitter laugh. "We crawled a lot of colonies looking for them to support us. Immortal GEMs that could exist in space without help. That would have been nice to have around."

I nod. "Instead, they were stuck with me."

"Daylight."

Snow raises her hand and shakes her head. "No. That's…"

"The rebellion came from a womb born set. Younger than the ones born for mining, older than those bred for war. They were raised Human, experimented on to see if we could graft their DNA onto WIPs." I roll my fingers around my thumb. "Their minds were like those of the WIPs. So they could teach the others how to fight and what to fight for."

"Oh, so by 'like you,' you mean you were born outside of the GEM vats? Were there others?"

"Three, I think? Never met over three." I shrug.

"You're looking at the original." Snow's hair is white. It is so white it makes my eyes burn when I look at her. Her smile is brighter, her teeth are too. "This is him, the original, badass. Rebellion leader and most of his right hands. We started all this shit, organized, unified, and led most of the rebellion."

I cannot see his eyebrow quirk at the comment, but I can imagine it.

I smile.

"This guy? You all? GEM rebellion leaders?"

"Then along came the sun and swallowed us whole." I cover my eyes as even the memory is too bright. The sensations all boil together, I can feel every breath, every frown, every blink around me. It makes my skin crawl. I want to keep it inside. I cover everything I can to get away from it.

From the sun.

From the sky.

"…Right." New stands and disappears into the ship as I remain paralyzed by the stars.

15

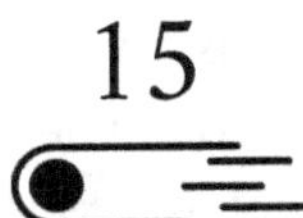

Somewhere beyond the sea.

Somewhere, waiting for me…

This song is the song the dark sings to me. It is not like the one the sun will sing to me in my sleep. It does not threaten to take away the world, and yet…

"Much better. Now, I'll ask one more time, are you going to cut it? You always felt like a short hair kind of girl to me," Soren says as he looks Snow over.

"If the conditions are right, I'll cut it." She shrugs. She smells good.

Fresh.

Clean.

I look down at my too long nails and put my teeth to the task of fixing them.

"Alright, so let's do this." Snow takes in a deep, refreshing breath and looks at all of us. We sit in a circle - well, most of a circle if you count Parrot's inability to sit still, and wait.

Nash starts: "Best I can tell, we've been out of the hole for about 72 hours. They likely know we aren't coming back. We don't have a lot of supplies. I don't understand how the water recycler on this thing works and a lot of the pods are sealed shut. Don't know what's in'm. I give us 5 days to figure things out before we'll be stuck in whatever Drift we land in."

"So, we have to make some choices." Snow nods and looks to Pert and Parrot. "I imagine Forsyte has a lot to say on the subject."

Pert nods grimly, there is no need to touch his mind to know he dreams of hands still tight around her neck. I do not disagree, but it is a topic we will take up when we can turn the lights on in the ship for more than fleeting moments.

"Shower is limited, so is a lot of the water," Soren adds with a sigh.

"Hah. Hah. Ooo," we respond.

"Right. So, I want you guys to get showers in as soon as we know more, but right now?" He motioned to Snow. "That one felt necessary. Next up: food."

My stomach churns in envy, but I recall something important. I pull a lighter out of my pocket and hand it to Soren with a smile. He takes it with a raised eyebrow and shakes his head.

I think perhaps I am more like Parrot than I want to admit. Recovery will be slow; at least, Snow implies it will be. Not just the ship, and learning her ways, but us. It is a frustrating thought.

It has been difficult for everyone.

I pull Pells out of my jacket and I pass them around.

Everyone but Soren perks as they break them into parts and hold them in front of them. We all pause, Pert handing a piece of Pell to Soren as we wait, then eat. He watches us without taking part with a sigh.

"What... is this stuff, exactly?"

"Pell," Pert explains.

Nash groans. "Nutrient food from the Rips-er, it's a Ritz nutrient pill. They don't cook, but they eat this. WIPs figured out the formula during the war. Full week of food for a growing human body. Lightweight, easy to store, lasts for a long time. For GEMs... a day of food. Higher metabolism makes us faster, sleep less, but hungry."

"Good to know." Soren takes a step closer to Snow.

"This gives us at least 5 days of food if we ration. It's a start," Snow adds.

"No offense, guys, but where are we going to land?" New - no, no, Soren, my mind corrects - asks. "To land somewhere, we're going to need docking codes. Docking codes are port specific and... expensive. I very much doubt that someone's going to let freed prisoners without real names land without too many questions."

"You were saying the JAC was a GEM friendly place," Snow offered.

Immediately defensive, Soren raises both hands.

"Now look, I said a lot of things, but after the Ritz war there was a big civil war between all the colonies and Earth. Something about treaties and the Jupiter Alliance Colonies not being real colonies? Everything in the solar system is a mess and I've been hopping through it as a stowaway until I hit that breeder ship. Most of what I know is that the other worlds don't like to share, and what they do share is weird. Apparently, Mars even renamed her moons, and I couldn't even tell you that until a year ago."

"So, we have no known allies, no knowable place to land, no hope, no chance," Pert summarizes. He looks at me and every fiber in my being itches. I clutch at the blade in my pocket, fiddling with the latch, touching the smooth edges as a little devil at my shoulder whispers in mute and wordless glee.

Sometimes I wish I could still hear those devils. Perhaps it is better that I cannot.

"We've had worse odds." I mimic Snow's words with my mouth.

"Had it WORSE!" Parrot repeats firmly. "HAD IT WORSE."

Soren winces at Parrot's repeating banter. "Well, the ship probably has codes - and - no promises here, but I might be able to dig them out."

"You kiddin' right?" Nash takes a step forward and Soren a step back. "You gonna pull codes out a ship you've never seen before? What, you can't be older than 16?"

"I am-" his lips barely believe the words. "21! Probably! God, what month is it?"

Snow glances at me and pulls Soren a little closer.

I must be staring.

I stand up and make my way towards the end of the room, but Snow tries to stop me. I raise my hand.

"Ports... ports... ports," I chant.

"Ports! PORTS! PORTS!" Parrot joins in with a smile and a little dance.

"Safe Ports."

"Yes, but where are we going to find one?" Snow glares daggers into the back of my head.

I run my hands along the silky metal wall that separates us from space and wonder how easy it would be to slip through it. The orb that has condensed itself into my bracelet reaches out to touch it along with me.

We can feel the insides of the ship together, but I do not let it off of its chain. I know it would let me pull out codes, pull out information that would let us dock, but it's more important to keep dragons tamed, lest they think it okay to eat their masters.

"Somewhere beyond the sea," I say matter-of-factly.

Parrot twists behind me, and I hear Soren groan a little into his cup. "Great. I'll just put that in the nav computer now."

I open a small panel, most ignore me as I do.

I press buttons in a pattern, a rhythm, a song.

"You used to be JAC." Nash bites his words. "Maybe you still know someone, Snow."

"Right." I can hear the cock in her voice. "I'll call up a few old friends, who are probably dead, and whoever answers won't get us sent back to the hell we just escaped from."

"FROM HELL!" Parrot argues back at Nash.

It makes me smile, and the ring on my hand is heavy again. *Somewhere, waiting for me…*

"It was just a thought." Nash moves too close to Parrot and Pert takes a single step to grow between them like an anaconda from high branches and they move apart.

He stares both down until they are both at corners.

"Somewhere…" I twist at a few frequencies on the device, listening to the voidless static that greets me. The song takes shape around my throat. "Somewhere… beyond the sea."

"Captain, any ideas here would be helpful." Nash and Snow seem to say it at the same time, or perhaps I hear it wrong. It is hard to tell. I let out a long sigh and turn to them.

"We should chase a comet." I motion to Soren. "He wants to see the tail."

"I don't really see how… comet!" Nash chokes on his own words as his brain catches up with them.

"Yeah… great… let's do that - why?" Soren's spunk makes even my metal smile.

I pull out a small transistor and attach it to my bracelet. The orb is eager to assimilate it. I press it to my bracelet and it comes to life with a few numbers on it. It displays something I haven't seen in a very long time. It tells me the time, and shows the faint outlines of planets, drifts, and where we are in the system.

"Don't rip that up… sir. Please?" Nash sighs.

We are beyond the reaches of the belt, way past the Saturn Stretch, but nowhere near the Rift.

"Comets," I mutter into the inside of the ship's panel as I push it all back together haphazardly. "Water. Food. Fuel."

Parrot is the first to hop and glance at my arm. With a chirp and a cheer he nods. "COMET!"

"Ten days to get anywhere." I hold up the configuration so it displays. I highlight a few things. "We have to follow the drift; the drift will take us to this, this or this one."

"Wait. You're serious." Soren is chewing on something small. He's always doing that now, snacking, and my stomach becomes a desert as I watch him. Before he can put another bite into his mouth, I take it from him. Whatever it is, it is chewy - a texture my tongue barely remembers and instantly rejects. "Oh - and you spit it out. Thaaat's lovely."

"Better than waiting to die," Nash barks, a little too close to Snow as he makes his way towards the ship's engines. She winces. He continues, "I can figure out the technicals, but I can't fly. Daylight can, unless anyone else wants to volunteer? It's only the deadliest profession in the solar system."

Snow studies me as I pull tiny seeds off my tongue between the chewy leftovers. "Well..."

16

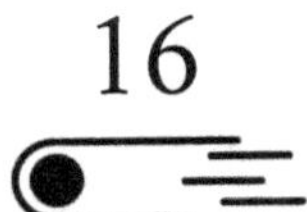

The deeper we fall into space, the more pieces of us come loose.

We do not mean to be difficult, but the cracks begin to show.

"Okay, yeah, I know, but give it a try. Please?" Soren coaxes us all towards the small bowls next to our Pells. He lifts some of the whitish soup and puts it to his lips. "Rice pudding, I promise, it's okay."

We do not *mean* to be difficult, but…

"Pudding?" Pert surprises us all with the question. "Where is it from?"

"The supplies we took from the Calgary Haut? There are supplies on the ship too, but it looks like they unlock as we gain something called, I dunno, comet points? It's all in Ikean." Soren waves his hand somewhere behind him, where I imagine the supplies live. "As soon as we get done chasing a comet or whatever, we'll have more food, but guys, there aren't that many Pells left. Those are emergency rations, and you guys need to learn to eat."

Pert sneers.

In another life, when he was still himself, anything not caught by his own hand entering his body was a taboo. I guess it is a part of him that's coming back.

My fingers are cold; when I look down, they are full of pudding. Unlike Pert, I am anything but picky, and I spin the substance around a few times before I put it in my mouth. The texture is smooth, the taste dull. It reminds me of the Shadows.

And it... whispers things to me.

Pieces of a past me itch in the back of my mind, pleading to be released.

"Pudding?" I ask.

"RICE pudding!" Parrot corrects, putting the bowl to his mouth. It dribbles down the side of his chin and back onto the table.

"Oh - look at that - you got a little... Yeah. Great." New - *Soren* - hands Parrot a napkin that he nibbles on. A long sigh escapes Soren, and I do my best not to laugh at his expense.

The others exchange looks with each other, some having tested it, others unwilling to. Then, as if one, we take our fragmented Pells and lift them up for a moment, taking a single sip of water.

And we wait.

"It was that or potatoes, but we don't have any potatoes." New rambles, "I really think you should -"

"Shh." It is Nash that quiets him. "A moment, please."

"Moment?"

"Shh."

We let the silence settle over the table. There's a feeling between us, a familiar one, but today it is heavier. Dark blue, I would call it, as it hangs on our shoulders.

It is in this silence that we remember our fallen.

Water.

Silence.

Pell.

Drink. Remember. Eat.

"To absent friends," I pull from my throat.

"To absent friends," they mutter behind me.

Then, in turn, we all take our pudding and study it. Parrot studies it with his nose, mostly decorating his face with the color. I - well - I think I finished mine before I recall eating it.

A low noise emits from my body. "Mmmm…"

"Pudding," Parrot appreciates as his long tongue dabbles it off of his face. "Yes. Very much."

"To the cook," Snow teases, passing her pudding bowl my way.

I gladly down that one too.

"Potatoes?" Nash contemplates the words. "I can't even remember the taste."

Soren perks, his ears red with excitement.

"So, you guys like it?"

"We…" Pert pauses, his spoon between his lips and his bowl. He makes a sound in his throat, like something is caught, and glances at me. "We hunger. This is food."

"Pudding," Parrot corrects.

"Fuckin' delicious." I nod and hold my spoon up to Soren.

"Oh, good, cause I've got like ten bowls of the stuff. Couldn't really find the recipe for less." It is hard to tell if he's joking or not.

"Oh. Good." Snow's pursed lips speak more for her than any words.

We all chuckle.

We all enjoy.

We all… feel.

It feels foreign. It feels strange.

It feels free.

17

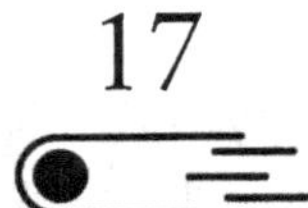

Sleep.

We take shifts, even though there is little to do as the Drift takes control of the ship. We have aimed it towards a comet, a thing with only numbers and symbols as a name. I have named her Bonnie, and hope this lady comet treats me better than a car that sits in some distant photo in my head.

Baby pink with rims too tall. She used that archaic substance to run on.

Rubber wheels.

Wind in my hair and the smell of Terra at my back. We ride as the stars twinkle above.

Bonnie.

There are two rooms and six bunks. The two rooms, we agree, go to the two who care. Pert and Soren. The rest of us pile onto one of the shelves and keep ourselves there quietly for the few hours our bodies insist on, but it is hard.

We do not speak of it to each other, but I think the others find it difficult as well.

Our bodies are rested, rejuvenated and not starved for... everything. It feels wrong.

I lose track of the numbers, even as the device on my watch keeps them for me. It's disorienting, and the darkness is heavier without my song. I find, after a few attempts, that if I am alone in my bunk, I do not sleep.

I wait for someone to come and when their breathing is all I can hear, my heart will slow, my body will return to stone, and I can rest, but sleep doesn't come. I still watch, sometimes, hoping to see the flash of light filter in from a door that no longer exists above me.

Instead, I have the stars.

They consume my mind for hours on end outside of the fiction I chase called sleep.

The dark has a different kind of meaning here. I try to convey that in a way that makes sense, but Pert is the only one that gets it.

In confinement, the mind resigns itself to a certain degree of silence; freed, a mind goes mad without something to make it spin. I try a lot of things, but most of them put me where I am now. I have found something that helps me pass the time.

Staring in the darkness, I am perched, waiting.

Like a dozen times before, the slow, steady breathing of the living is comforting in its own way. I let it count the beats between terms and try to let go of counting. It is hard. There is shuffling as I shift a little and the bed creaks with my weight.

"What the hell?" A pillow soars over my head, and I catch it instinctively. I toss it back at Soren, who glares at me through the dim light of his makeshift lamp. "Man, are you just staring at me again?!"

I raise an eyebrow and shrug in response.

"Did the others all kick you out or something?"

I smile and roll off the end of his bed.

"Alright, go away without saying anything then, you damn creeper."

His breathing resumes soon after. I sit outside this time and listen.

Sleep doesn't come.

Terms of Light

18

The Drift is kind to us and we come upon the comet earlier than expected. Still, it brings an air of nervousness to everyone but me.

I pull Soren up to the console. Nash is on the other side, but I'm not sure why. In a normal ship, I would expect this to be uncomfortable, but it is not. This cockpit is meant for cooperative effort and it is easy to tell. There is space, there is ease and placement to compensate for others. It is unusual for human construction.

Must not be from Earth.

Spacer-tech usually is meant for cooperation, I remind myself. This must be a colony made ship. I smile and stroke her again, understanding now her thin walls and sturdy construction. She was born out here, like we were.

She still doesn't have a name, and I hate that.

"We're going to have to name her before we do this chase," I say, and Soren seems annoyed at my distraction.

"So, the only thing I've ever driven is a tractor and, well, one car. That I stole," Soren spouts nervously. "I'm not really sure you should let me chase a comet with this thing."

Nash grinds his teeth as he talks.

"I agree, but we need backup in case one of us has to go fix something on the fly - or he goes blank again. You want to tangle outside with a bulkhead instead?"

"Nope!" Soren sighs. "Okay, so this side is the comet engagement controls, and this is the piloting?"

"They're the same," Nash grumbles, irritated.

"They got the wrong guy," I chuckle to myself.

Soren frowns and nudges me, and Nash makes a sound he's made more lately. It is half irritation and yet he is blushing.

"They are the same, like Nash says." I put my hands on the controls and summon up the piloting interface. "This button is engagement. This one is for piloting controls."

"Piloting. Engagement," Soren repeats, switching between the two consoles on his side. "Got it."

"What did Snow teach you?" I ask.

He stares at me blankly.

"Rotational orbits should match the path configuration along with your Drift calibration, so make sure you keep your dingaling in the singsong samba. Or something. Honestly, no idea what she taught me, except that line going over there is bad."

I laugh and for a moment; I think the itch returns to my mind. My mind summons up an image of Snow as she once was, working docks, guiding in great behemoths from space. She controlled so much of the world then, and no one even knew her power.

"Snow pulled ships into docks, not flew them," I explain, and I hope he understands. "She is correct, yes, do not let that line go over there. It means we've lost the drift and have to pray that some gravitational pull picks us up again. Not good for Comet Chasers."

"Got it. That's the 'we're fucked' line."

I nod.

"This is the male, and this is the female. They do not look that way, but trust me." I motion to the controls. "Male instruments require some roughness with a gentle touch in sensitive places. Pull this, guide that, stroke this, you'll get what you want. This is the female. You listen to what it says and you will have what you need. More pressure, less power, ease the knobs, never rush. She can go all night."

"I'm not sure I'm really comfortable with that description but, okay, I think I get that better than 'rotate the proforma.'" He places his hands on the control set and strokes, pulls, listens. The ship purrs and roars in response, and Nash gives me a look that is both a threat and appreciation.

I shrug.

"I hope you don't have sex like that." Nash motions to the controls Soren grabs. Soren lets go, his face turning a bright shade of red as he tucks his arms under his armpits.

"I also sincerely hope I don't," he retorts. "But I think I get it. I think if I had to, I could figure this out."

I tap my head where memory is best stored and I tap his too.

"I think he's syncing with me," he says quietly. "That's a terrifying thought."

"More than you know," Nash mutters, pushing me out of the seat and sitting next to Soren. "You have no idea what he's like."

Syncing.

Syncing. Syncing. Syncing.

A dozen images come to mind, but they are spread across years. I see myself in a facility. It is white and blue and labeled Humanity United Defense Organization - Humanity's Last Hope, across the side of it.

I am training, feeling the minds of others, taking in their skills, laying mine over their own. We become something better than we are, something stranger.

I sit in a room of pure white, with no shadows, and I stare at myself.

I fill in row after row of code, madly obsessing over every detail, every reaction, every thought.

I am sitting on a car hood in a place I have never been — no, no, this one is not mine.

"Syncing," I say out loud.

"Yeah." Soren breathes out heavily. "That's syncing alright. Intense."

"What'd you see?" Nash glares at me as he asks.

"Nothing that... matters. So, how do we do this comet collection materials thing? I get we chase it down, align with it, but then what? Do we just stay in its tail long enough to collect materials and then hope our gravity is strong enough to get away?"

"Well, that's the basics. Yep. We chase, we latch on, and we fall away. The hooks do most of the work; they can wrestle Jupiter whales if needed, so a comet should be nothing."

Nash motions to the side of the screens outside of the ship. There are large, thick slabs of metal that look almost like crab hands stuck into our cute little orb ship's face.

"See those parts of the ship? Those are big, old energy hooks. They latch in with little propulsors, act like a second thing we're steering. Those are the engagement controls. We turn on all the collection gear, they sort through all the materials like water or minerals, collect it, ionize it, or whatever it needs to do. Then, when we are done, we drop off.

Worse comes to worse, you pick comets that are going by larger bodies and use the gravity drift differential to pull away from both."

"Wow," Soren smiles at him with the same wonder he did when he knew he could see the tail of a comet. "Did you do this in another life?"

"No!" Nash scoffs, and I know he's had the brain itch, too. "I don't know how I know it."

"Learned it from the sun," I note.

Soren groans with a pained look.

"So, I only see one hook out there. How are *we* going to latch on?"

Nash grumbles.

"Well, one is still better than none, so we're going to hope that's enough. Should get a good enough haul that maybe we can trade our way into a port, or, like you said, earn 'Comet Points' for food, or whatever."

I think about pudding as he speaks. Trading for more varieties, more colors, my mouth waters.

"Oh, I like that idea."

Soren looks at me. I know how the sync goes both ways as he can hear my thoughts, my hunger.

"You really liked my pudding that much, huh?"

I give him my best smile and he pushes me out of the way. I lay down between the seats and stare up at the stars through the window.

"You really think if we get the right resources, we can land somewhere?" Soren's voice shakes as he speaks.

Nash lets out a long breath.

"One thing at a time. I guess we should name the damn ship."

19

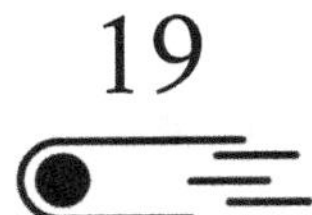

I settle myself as the others prepare.

I do not sit in the pilot's chair like Snow wants because Nash has discovered what I have tried to explain over and over to him. The sun took more than our lives, but it gave something back, too.

As I stare out at space, I play a piano in my mind. Something I have never done before, and yet, my fingers are so very good at it. It gave me this. It gave *him* comet chasing.

And he is very good.

Nash brings us into range, and the comet shines before us.

Snow: "We have the target in sight, estimating contact in five minutes."

Nash: "You guys hear that? I hope you're ready. This is going to be rocky. I'm no goddamn pilot."

Parrot: "ROCK! ROCK! ROCK!"

Soren: "Are you sure I can't help with anything?"

Nash: "Buckle up in case this gets rough. If we crash on that comet, at least you'd survive. Pert, are you sure that Forsyte's secured?"

Pert grunts in response.

Nash: "Did you at least torment her ass, like I ask?"

Soren: "Yep. Ate a granola bar in front of her and everything."

Snow: "Soren…"

Nash: "Good man."

Snow: "Nash. You should have told him to eat one of those little pies that Parrot made. She loves pie."

They laugh. It makes my soul sing to hear that sound.
We draw closer to our second target.
Bonnie's hunt didn't go so well. I told them it was because we didn't name our ship. I also know that our hooks were not fast, my piloting was not as delicate, even if my daring was at the right level. No one enjoyed being so close to the comet that we almost crashed.
I reminded them we did not crash.
Nash volunteered shortly after to pilot and we named her by committee. The committee being Parrot screaming 'V'ger V'ger V'ger' until we all agreed.
That's okay.
This new comet is a better fit for us; she is small, young, and beautiful. She also contains high levels of a few elements we know

nothing about except that they are rated high in Comet Points, so they are worth a lot to us.

Now to do what we do best.

Snow: "Contact in four minutes. Let's try not to screw this one up, *boys.*"

Nash: "Soren. You know that lower cubby that Parrot always nests in?"

Soren: "Hard to forget it."

Nash: "There's one on the upper part of the ship, near the dining hub. It's mostly storage, but in two minutes, I want you to get up there."

Soren: "Seriously? Now?"

Nash: "Trust me."

Pert: "Dampeners."

The ship rolls and stumbles, but she does it with grace. We enter the comet's tail, just the trailing ends of it. The ship's dampeners shimmer like the aurora borealis as ice, dust and debris evaporate on contact. The ship shakes, but finds a rhythm in her wake.

The light is beautiful and fills me up with a sensation I have been missing. Light and heat prickle on my skin.

"Daylight."

Parrot: "DAYLIGHT!"

"Oh, for the sweet embrace of darkness."

All: "Hah. Hah. Oooh."

Snow: "Three minutes."

Parrot: "Daylight! THRUSTERS! Daylight! TARGET!"

Nash: "We're taking too much heat on the rear. Parrot!"

Pert: "I'll take it."

Nash: "Then who's going to run engagement?"
Scrambling. Noise. A shuffling as the ship rocks with motion.

Snow: "Engaging hook in Three. Two."

"Hook affixed," I call.

Soren: "Alright, I've found this hatch you were talking about. What am I looking for?"

Nash: "Heat levels are returning to normal."

Soren: "I'm not seeing anything."

Parrot: "Don't see the LEVELS!"

Nash: "Ugh, shut up! Soren, move the damn tools."

Soren: "Got it."

Snow: "One minute. You're about to miss a show, Soren."

Soren: "I think… oh, I see it!! Holy crap… oh my god is that really the tail? Is that the comet? It's like a rainbow. Holy shit. I've never seen that color before! WHAT IS THAT?!"

Parrot: "IS THAT?! Is that! A rainbow! Colors!"

Snow: "Engaging in 45."

Soren: "Uh… guys."

Pert: "Collector's on. Engaging drag in 30."

Nash: "We're getting some heavy drag, but I think we might just make this work."

Soren: "Guys. GUYS. GUYS!"

Snow: "What is it?"

Soren: "Is the-fucking-Daylight-is-on-the-OUTSIDE-OF-THE-SHIP!!"

A few seconds of silence follow, and I stand up. I thought I would be out of the way of the window. Oh well. He is right, though. It is beautiful. I move from my perch, arms spread, and let the metal do with me what it will.

The orb expands wings around me, lifting me into the air as I attach myself to the ship with an alien metal cord. I breathe in, and I smell space and atmosphere and death all around me.

I fly.

I am joined by small bots, little more than giant filter buckets with gaping mouths attached to the ship. They shimmer and wiggle as they adjust their gravity to match the ship's pull.

These must be the collectors.

Snow: "Comet engaged. Initiating Collection - Goddamn it, Captain. I'm going out."

Pert: "Let him fly."

Soren: "SHIT GUYS IS HE - How... what the FUCK?!"

Nash: "Fucking asshole."

Snow: "Soren, come back down. We need you monitoring our 'Points.'"

"No, wait. You'll miss the view," I call over the com.

Cold waves of ice and stone flow around me as they envelope our ship, twisting and turning, embracing me like some beautiful lover. I lift higher off the ship, but I turn the gravity up a bit to compensate. My EGG is anxious on my arm, desperate to cling to something, disliking the idea of flying away, but the Cession - the orb - wants to fly more.

It wants to turn into a ship and take us to a place so clearly painted in my head, beyond the red and blue lights of the Rift's opening.

I want to fly there too.

I howl with excitement and roll to the side of the ship.

Snow: "Captain - damn it! STARGON!"

That name sends tingles down my spine. It lifts me up; it fills me in.

Around.

Up.

Down.

To the side. Everything pours over my senses in shades of dullness. I can taste the space around me. I can hear the darkness sing to me.

"Somewhere beyond the sea.
Somewhere waiting for me."

Soren: "I can get a suit or -?"

Pert: "Just let him fly."

Nash: "We've got bigger problems. Hooks are not disengaging, engines are running too hot. Too much longer like this and she'll steal our Drift."

My EGG pleads with me like the song in my head. I let out a happy sigh and nod to myself.

"On it, Nash," I call.

Parrot: "Let him fly. Let him fly!"

Soren: "How did he even get out there? We don't exactly have a HATCH."

Nash: "That dick always finds a hole."

Snow: "Nash."

Nash: "What?"

I summon a HUD in front of me. The computer does its best to calculate how I disengage our giant hook and not implode the ship from the gravity shock as I do it. I can see on the sides more collectors and analyzers working overtime to catch what it can around the ship. Three giant panels are open and taking in everything my little flying friends miss.

That's when I finally see the front of our ship. Our little *V'ger*. She is round and stubby-nosed, but behind the comet she spreads her great maw like some sort of alien queen moth. She takes in everything she can as we ride wild and free, trying to pick up the scraps.

My HUD locates the best angle for us to grab the hook, and I lock myself down to the ship with my gravity belt. My EGG injects more painkillers before we begin as it eagerly gets to the task. It wiggles its legs under my skin.

With the orb's help, I brace and guide my EGG to our designated target. It takes longer than I want it to as the tendrils test their ability to withstand the fluxes around them. Finally, it grabs the hook, testing the girth, strength, and gravity. It tries to tell me what it finds by speaking to the orb through the make-shift interface on my arm.

The HUD tells me that the connection between chain and ship is the weakest point on the ship. It would be easier to repair the ship if we tore off the grappling hook. That would mean easier repairs, but we would also be without the ability to hunt.

I ask it to evaluate ripping the hook off of the comet. It returns unfavorable odds.

We try anyway.

It is heavy as the EGG attaches.

One-two.

One-two.

It pulls hard against me and the alien tendrils of the EGG, pushing with micro gravity engines of its own. It pushes at my EGG's tendrils in unwelcome ways as I share the pain in my fingers and arm.

My enhanced strength can only help so much in this case, so I jump to the other side of the ship, holding my EGG as steady as I can to see if I can get us more leverage.

Snow: "I don't mean to rush, but we can only do this for another five minutes and then we will be the comet's new tail."

Soren: "Shit. Shit. Shit. Not again. Not again."

"Soren," I call over the com with gritted teeth. My arm feels like it's about to explode from the inside. "Soren, are you still in that window?"

Soren: "Yeah."

"Is there an emergency release for the hooks in there?" My arm aches, alien chemicals pouring into it to increase my adrenaline. My heart beats faster.
The world slows down.
Over the com there is unintelligible whispering.
Shuffling.
Loud noises, heavy breathing.

Soren: "No. I mean, it's not here. I don't see anything where they attach!"

Pert: "This is not a new enough ship."

"Just our luck. A'ight. Here we go." The EGG injects me one more time. I turn my gravity up more than I should and my knees ache deep in the tendons down to my foot. I pull again, bracing against the ship, and make small dents on either side of the hull.

Nash: "That's it!! That's it! Hook is disengaging. Disengaging and dropping in thirty, twenty-nine, twenty-eight..."

The line floats free above me, whipping for a moment wildly between all the gravities, and I release myself from my belt and float. My EGG manages the rest, the chains retract into V'ger's ports and my entire body aches.

Nash: "Nine. Eight."

Now to survive the fall.

I adjust the gravity as quickly as I can, pulling in my wings, even as the orb protests. The EGG retracts its limbs in time so as not to lose a tendril. The rope floats in front of me, and for a moment, I swear I can see time stop.

It is engulfed in ice and dust and the world is painted in shades of blue and white I haven't seen since -----.

My mind burns with fire.

No, not now.

Not now. I need to stay with it.

The white noise returns. It fills every hole it can find with ice and pain.

Nash: "Four. Th---. T--. ---."

Then the ship drops away from me.

Things move too fast and too slow all at once. V'ger falls one way, I move another, the comet another. I feel sick. It has been so long since there has been something in my stomach that I do not recognize the feeling right away.

All I can hear is screaming.

It is me. It is my screaming.

Then we are torn violently back. I am yanked down by arms that I cannot see.

Snow: "Captain!"

I slam into the ship.

Pert stands over me, an ancient space suit tucked around him. His frown is deep and takes up most of his face. His EGG, that deep, rich black, turns his eyes into lightless pools. The EGG takes a moment before it releases my body to settle it against the ship's pull.

He grunts and points at me and then gives me a thumbs down.

All I can do is laugh.

20

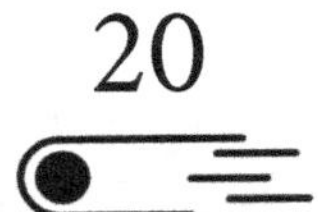

"So, was he always an asshole, or is this a new trend?" Soren's words try to sting, but only make my smile widen. Snow and Pert gather to lecture me, but the ship purrs with new life, satisfied she got to do what she was meant for.

Stardust and ice fall away from windows as we pull further and further from the comet's gravity.

"Hard to say."

Pert pulls his suit off with disdain. He hates pants almost as much as he hates chains. I jingle the one I've made on my wrist at him and laugh breathlessly.

"Oh," Soren whispers.

"What was that?" Snow's tone is less forgiving. She isn't angry so much as - "Are you even listening?"

"Sorry," I shrug. I motion to Soren with the elegant silver edges of my suit. "Ever seen one of these before?"

"Pardon?" Soren blinks a few times, trying to ignore the view out of the window. "Yeah, when we were on the comet like 2 days ago?"

Snow throws up her hands in surrender.

Parrot quickly hops over with his arms full of potatoes. "Eggies!"

"Snow!" Nash growls. "Pert! Help me, he broke into the food that opened up!"

"EGGIES!"

The two look at each other. Pert tosses aside his suit and puts his hand on Soren's shoulder. They exchange barely heard words as I stare up at the sky. If they're going to ignore me, I might as well enjoy the scenery.

"No." Soren stands a little closer, arms crossed cautiously. "I haven't seen anything like that. The orb. The suit. The wings?"

"Angel Suit." I hold back a snicker I cannot help or explain. "For your flying half its standard gear. Built in propulsion, ATMO-shield, auto-generating oxygen, water, even lets you pee."

"That's... gross. So, this is made of what? Cession?" He's hesitant to touch it. I can only imagine what he's been told about the metal in a world that still hates the Ritz. It doesn't respond to him as he nears, but it wants to. It *enjoys* feeling his mind, feeling his sync through me. I wonder how much of this transformation was me, how much was the will the metal has.

"Yeah. Cession. Not sure how it is now, but when the Ritz first lost bits of it, the Human scientists became obsessed. Unfortunately it requires a," I tap my head.

"Sync."

"Yeah. Sync. Humans are not so good, but the GEMs, well, we were much better." I hold out my hand and the orb happily changes shapes, showing off. It changes into a square, a knife, then a lighter.

Wait, did it eat my lighter?

I search my pockets, frustrated.

"... Did you pee in it?"

I smirk, but do not answer.

"Did you get those docking codes yet?"

"I! Hey! You flying around on the top of the ship with the damn comet doesn't exactly help me focus." He pushes away all responsibility. "What the hell were you thinking?"

"I was thinking..." I stare up as the last dregs of the comet fade into sparkles of ice along the window. "I was thinking it sure would be beautiful."

We both stare up at the small window. Our minds touch again, this time without the itch. We exchange a look; he is embarrassed. I pull him closer and shove him into my chest. He tries to push away, and I let him.

"Sorry." I try to explain why I did it. It's so much easier to say things when you don't have to be restricted to verbal language. "I still smell like the comet."

Soren looks me over at first in awe, but then skeptically. Moving a little closer, he takes a deep breath. Then another.

He can smell it.

"Wow."

"Wow," I repeat with a smile.

"So, this is Cession. You said there were types. It can turn into an... Angel Suit? Why would they give it to you then? I mean, it's clearly powerful." He touches my chest absently. The orb tries to touch him back.

"This is Mech grade Cession. Third highest grade," I shrug, having wondered that myself. Then I am reminded and I try to let my mind numb around the memories. "At first, Oswald did not let us use it, but we lost guards, and GEMs when we had to walk. The cycles got shorter, so she gave in. At the end of the day, we came back. She stopped thinking about it after that. Because we were objects. Part of the stone. Where would we go?"

"Okay, so I get that you have this EGG thing, but why do your hair and eyes glow, then?" He asks. "You said you were bonded? It makes you glow?"

I touch my hair.

The EGG makes it glow like a strand of thin LEDs through my hair, and my eyes sing along. I share with him in my head an old promotional poster for genetically engineered miners. The image is clear to me; it is human forms painted in black silhouettes with bright colors to accentuate parts of them. People used to show us off in the dark like that, so they could see how fancy we were. We'd glow like gemstones in purple, blue, green, white, red - all colors of the rainbow, but otherwise covered in soot and mining grease.

They used to have devices in all the ports, Shimmers, we called them, that would light us right up. That way people could tell. That way you couldn't pass as Human and get something you weren't allowed.

I do not know if the fact he doesn't know that brings me hope or...

"Cause it's in my blood. I control it like it controls me. WIPs have a hard time with it, not sure about the Ritz. They like us. Kin almost. Not of this world, not of another." I shrug. "Like the halfers."

"You think of halfers as kin to GEMs?" He asks.

"When the world abandons you, who else we got but each other?"

21

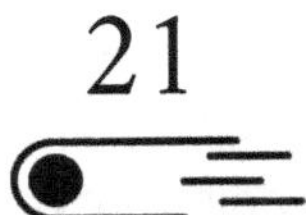

"Potatoes, rice, beans, and toast." Soren stands proudly over the table he's pulled from the basement storage room. We all stare at it absently. He looks disappointed when we don't clap. "I liked you guys a little better when you were more musical."

I lower my head.

I motion dramatically over the food.

"Oh, for the sweet embrace of potato,

Oh, for the call to rice."

"Hah. Hah. Ooo-ahh," they respond with the deadest of faces.

We take our sip of water.

We wait a moment in silence. Even Soren waits this time.

Then with a deep breath, we all dig in. Food. Warm food with flavor - not a lot yet, but that's because the curry that Nash made was a regrettable choice. The silence sits with us while we eat, but it is not the same heavy silence. It is the confident companion that all of us missed.

Soren pokes at his food a few times before he sits up. We have all come to learn this means it is question time.

"So -?"

"So, Soren." Snow catches the ball, fast as ever. "Tell us about being a half-Ritz."

"Pardon?" His eyebrows speak more for him than his body. He was surprised and hates the subject. Welcome to the party. "I, well, what do you mean?"

"We know nothing about you other than -"

"You got the wrong guy!"

"You were put in the hole with us for poor aim." Snow spreads her potatoes on the toast and makes a taco out of it, staring intently as she waits.

We all match the intensity of her stare.

"I mean…" he takes a moment to compose himself. "I don't know what it means. I've never met anyone like me. So far, it means I can't take pain medication - hell, any kind of medication, and I have," he hesitates. "Powers?"

We all shift a little when he says that.

He winces.

"Snow told me you guys fought a lot of Ritz with powers. That the red reminded you of them? That's why I cut my hair."

Nash shakes his head as he cuts each toast into four same sized pieces. "Your accent is Earth based. The math is bad. How does a half-breed your age exist on Earth?"

"I don't know? I'm from Michigan, United States, at least I was, for a while. I was raised there until my brother went to war. Taken away from mom. Foster care." Soren takes a moment to study his food, and an ache runs along the table. "Then space."

"Hah. Hah. Ooo," Pert joins me.

"It sucks. Honestly, it sucks." Soren sits up, now defensive. "My bones are hollow in some places, my appetite is unquenchable

146

and frankly, I can't do anything with these damn silver feathers. I can hide them if I need to, but that's it. Happy?"

Snow shakes her head.

"There was a lot of information there. Thank you."

"What about you?" Soren sits up, now eager to throw the ball back.

"Me?" her lips perked up a bit.

"No, him." Soren points at Pert. "You shaved your head when we got on this boat. You've got that water thing you Daylight does with you, now you have swirlies drawn on your skin. I wanted to know, is there something I should know? Like, is it a religious thing or...?"

He left the question open, and Parrot chirped madly at the opportunity.

"TELL HIM ABOUT THE EGGIES!"

"The potatoes are good," is Pert's only answer.

"I just don't want to do something *wrong*," Soren offers meekly as Pert chews the bite of potato with an aching slowness.

"Have you ever met one?" Snow asks.

"One what? A Ritz?" Soren stops using his food as a distraction and studies us instead. He watches our expressions, careful what might come out of us. "One, but it was brief. I don't know much about them other than what Spacers have told me. Hell, I didn't even really know I was one until the one I met told me."

Snow lifts her eyebrow now, sipping at the warm liquid she has started making herself for these meals.

"I'm surprised we can interbreed, if I'm honest."

"Well," Soren laughs bitterly. "At least Humans and Ritz can. Not sure if I'm special or it's all of us that are sterile."

"I'm sorry, Soren," she adds somberly. "I know you wanted a family."

"Not like that, I didn't." His venom is bitter in the air. "I mean... I'm happy to adopt. Biology doesn't matter to me."

We all sit in quietness for a moment, taking in something that is just to the left of family. It makes me feel warm, even warmer than Snow's beans and some of Nash's potato in my stomach.

"I do not like meat that I do not catch and kill myself," Pert's low tone offers up as payment for the penny of knowledge. "I prefer fresh fruit."

"Oh. Well, that's easy enough to figure out." Soren seems to relax.

"We don't like questions," Nash states in his obvious fashion. "Sometimes it helps keep us in the present, but there are a lot of things that are better to forget."

"The sun is coming~" Parrot echoes in a whisper, "Time to hide!"

"Hah. Hah. Ooo-ahh."

"Yeah… you guys are a little obsessed with the sun," Soren teases. "Then again, I guess it's been a while since you've seen it?"

I slide my spoon into some of Nash's rice before putting more of it onto my plate. "Not long enough."

Soren throws his pillow at me as he wakes. His eyes are heavy stones in the pockets of his drowning body as he tries to pull himself out of sleep.

"You have got to stop doing this. There are better ways to get my attention," he mutters.

"Rest, not attention," I explain and I take his hand; he briefly tugs it away, but stops just short of removing it. Reluctantly, he lets me lead him across the hall to the room that is Pert's.

It is little more than a bed, a small sink and a table that folds out, but it is more than he has ever had. Pert sits cross-legged in the center waiting for us. Today he drapes a cloth over his genitalia in hopes of easing Soren's inevitable - "Oh GOD, you're naked. Okay."

I strip as well and Soren raises his hands, half covering his own view, half trying to push us away.

"Okay, hey, hey, what are we doing, guys?"

"Sit," Pert points to a seat next to them.

"You wanted to know." I offer my best smile, but Soren looks at me skeptically. He lowers himself in a way that only comes from a heavy weight of poor sleep and hides his head in his hands as I finish stripping.

Pert places a bowl of water in the center of all of us and hums lowly. He dips a clean bit of cloth in it and washes his hands first. Soren watches, silent.

He rubs his face after a moment, as Pert gets to his arms and shoulders, and a dawning happens in his mind.

"You want to show me your ritual?"

I tap his head lightly where the memory is best kept, and he stops before batting my hand away. He watches as I watch. Pert runs the cloth over his body, his head, his face, his chest, his legs, before pausing. I slide behind him and slowly wash his back.

"Cleansing," Pert explains in the way that Pert does.

"So, is this for germs, or is this for some other reason?" Soren asks.

Pert taps his head knowingly. I laugh when the tiredness seeping through Soren's pores spills out onto his face in frustration.

"Meditative. Clean the mind, clean the soul," I say, and hesitate only for a moment to add, "He started it after his family died."

Pert hisses when I say it, but it is not because I share, but because it brings tears to the corners of his eyes. I finish his back and he takes the cloth and begins again. This is not a normal part of his ritual, but I have reminded his mind it needs more cleansing.

We have so much further to go.

This time, I take my cloth, and dip it in the water. I start on my hands and clean my nails. They are much cleaner here, but still,

I crave tools I don't have anymore, even as the Cession offers them to me.

"Ritz," I say it aloud, and Soren's tired gaze turns towards me. "What do you want to know?"

"Know?" Soren sits up a little more. "Oh, I wasn't aware this was a sharing thing."

"Pert meditates in silence, I do not," I tease. "We fought them. A lot of them. Powers and all."

"The red," he asks, unconsciously pulling his too short hair back from his ears. "What is it about red?"

I laugh for a moment and trim the edges of my nails until they're rounded. I think deeply for a moment, past the images that knock on the corners of my brain. It is getting easier to pause it, but not stop it.

"Scarves of Red, those were the leaders. The powerful ones. I told you there were many grades of Cession? The most intelligent is the Planet grade, then Ship grade, then Mech grade. It goes down from there. The Reds carried ships on them like accessories. Belts, boots, bracelets. Shiny and fancy. When they walked, they rang like summer wind."

I can see the damn divas in my mind. They look so human when they pull down their hoods and their smiles are bright and wide with a few too many teeth.

"Do your teeth grow back?" I ask absently.

Soren unconsciously runs his tongue along his teeth and nods quietly. "Yeah. Never had to worry about a dentist, at least."

I mimic his action and touch my eye teeth, sucking on one I cannot feel anymore. "They love teeth. Did not get that our teeth do not do what theirs do. Ours do not grow back. They pull them raw, love to hear the screams, but when there were no more to pull, they would have to find something else to pluck."

I hiss and Pert splashes me with water.

I take a deep breath.

"Sorry, this isn't about the bad."

Soren squirms a little and looks at Pert with a soft expression.

"So, you fought them. Did you ever *meet* any?"

"Many," Pert says.

"Many," I echo. "They're lunatics. Happy people, lovely people. Boys are beautiful and the women want to beat you up. They love music and do not have a single language because they can sync with each other and BOOM - their minds all understand the language."

"Music?" his mind drifts off a little before he hesitates and grabs a cloth that sits in front of him. He dabs it in the water, taking only a little, and starts cleaning his hands. "I always wondered if I heard it differently than others."

"Possible," I offer. "You smell different than others."

He raises his eyebrow and frowns. "Look, the shower will happen when we do another run."

"No, no." I point to his nose and he pulls away, irritated. "Nose smell."

"Oh?"

Pert nods, shaking his head. "I cannot smell the blood in here."

"Really? This place reeks of - oh. Oh, I see." Soren cleans his other hand. "Guess I never really thought about it."

"If you ever have questions…" I offer.

"We spent a lot of time with them." Pert hands out more words than he has in a long time. "We can try to educate. Connect you. It is good to have a culture, a connection, even if you are an orphan from it."

"Thanks guys," he says with a sad smile.

Terms of Light

22

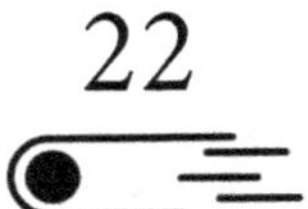

"This would all be a lot easier if you --!" Soren physically steps back from Fresh's chair. Pert had been her keeper and had cleared out a space in the smaller, lower storage area for her to *mostly* stand in. The lower part of the ship was poorly lit, but it was easy enough to see how disgruntled she was. How full of pride.

I imagine this is how this interaction always went.

"I'm not giving docking codes to a fuck like you," she growls the words like the animal she is. "As soon as I am free, I am making sure that every single one of you never sees the light of day again."

I laugh. It is not a funny thing, but there is irony in her thinking we ever want to see the sun again.

The stars are enough for us.

Always have been.

She growls another phrase, and I throw a look at Pert. It is a question to him as he sits quietly in the corner. He keeps his eyes on Soren. I gather Soren comes down here to feed her and ask for codes.

Admirable.

"Good to see you're doing well, Fresh," I tease.

"Oh, you taught it to talk too?" She rolls her eyes. "Next you'll have them working in a circus on E--r--a."

Her words set my mind ablaze, but only for a moment. There's a grunt of warning from Pert's side of the room, but I hold up my hand. Soren seemed oblivious of the whole interaction and turns to me, arms folded, body tilted in frustration.

"Sorry, I've been trying."

"No luck with the computers?" I run my fingers along the low ceiling, hoping V'ger might hear me.

"Nothing yet. Snow and Nash are working on it, and Parrot when he remembers where he is." There's a glance back towards Fresh as he moves closer to me. "It would just be easier for all of us if she'd cooperate."

"I could make her," I say it loud enough I know she hears. "But I think she'd enjoy it too much."

Now it is Fresh's turn to laugh, but it is an angry, bitter one. Not the one of someone who feels broken, but of someone who thinks they deserve what they had.

"You don't know anything about these monsters, do you, boy?" she growls back like iron wool on porcelain. "They probably haven't told you about the hundreds of innocents they've killed, or the reason they're out in the middle of the black."

I push past Soren and sit down across from her, legs folded. Pert looms behind me as I do. I imagine, for a moment, we look like a strange totem pole, until Pert's pale frame sinks back into the shadows.

"Why don't you tell him?" I prompt. "Tell him what you think you know, and maybe we'll even get you some warm food."

"The crazy one that repeats itself? Albatrossi? He built the weapon that obliterated E-----." I ignore the flashes of fire in my mind as she continues. "The pale one lost his mind in the war and came home to kill his wife and kids. They still haven't found the bodies. He ate them."

I watch her eyes scan us all, searching, begging for some kind of give. I don't look back at Soren's face, but I don't need to. He doesn't matter to her, but I think I see the thing that does.

"The other white-haired one? The girl? Actively poisoned civilians. Thousands of men, women, *children,* DEAD, so they could take ships and supplies from ailing colonies."

She puts her desperation on display for all to see.

She looks for an ally in someone that she had doomed to a life of stone and starvation. An interesting turn, but common in Human desperation.

"How did you get to the comet again, Soren?" I ask.

"She was transporting me to another place. We were being tailed by pirates, probably the ones on the Calgary Haut, and we made an emergency landing." He says it like it is practiced. I wonder if he knows how much she panics when he does.

"This one?! This one tortures. He revels in his sadism, killing innocents for information he could have easily gotten anywhere. During his time, he was responsible for the death of children, women, grandmas - an entire colony of people! Even his own!"

She's desperate for Soren to hear the words, but he gives nothing.

"She doesn't have the codes." I stand up slowly, her fingers dig into her restraints.

Soren's eyebrows flicker for a moment in consideration of this, and he glances back to Pert. I put my hand on Soren's shoulder as I pass.

I give Pert the order he's been waiting for with a nod.

We go back upstairs.

Soren follows quickly behind me. There's a tension in his shoulders that I am not used to seeing.

"How do you know she doesn't have codes?" Soren asks.

The tension of the room stays behind with Fresh and I feel a smile bounce on my lips.

"She has nothing to gain. She's stalling and hoping we make a mistake." My mind wanders to another time, another place, a colony, perhaps? That word she said, the one that's like fire in my mind. I can't remember it.

I cannot hear it. I wonder if the others can or if it is fire to them too?

I stroke the ring on my finger. It is rough and cuts into the flesh as I do.

"She would have taunted us by now, told us information even in subtle bites, but she screams and squawks like an infant."

"That doesn't mean she can't help us." His frustration shows as he twists his foot in small circles. "There's got to be some way to get her to help. We're in this together, right? She's just as stuck as we are?"

"Soren." I lift his silver feather bangs out of his face and his eyes go wide. "Help Snow and Parrot, they'll pull the codes out of the computer, I'm sure of it. We've had stronger foes."

"Is that - what - an order?" He takes a step back. In his place, I can imagine someone younger, with different hair and eyes that mirror my own.

Defiant.

Angry.

Unwilling.

"It was a joke. Captain?"

He puts his hands up to his neck, defensively and I pull myself back from wherever it is my mind takes me. It's getting easier and easier.

"It must be the light." I mutter.

"Right." He takes a few steps back before heading down the hallway.

I don't see him again until dinner. He makes pudding, candied corn, noodles and some bland sauce with a hint of butter. It tastes like the world feels: far away.

Most make conversation over dinner, but I only hear it in broken bits and distant thoughts.

Pert eats his meat in a somber silence.

23

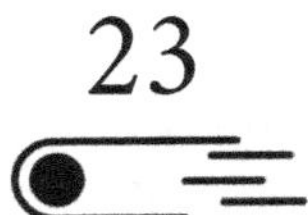

Time loses meaning, but we fall into a pattern of success and failure.

We learn what comets to take on and, by our fourth one, we are better. We know what to expect. Soren, on the other hand, finds something new to complain about every other hour. I think it is how he settles his anxiety.

Now that I have made him aware his sense of smell is better than all of ours, he focuses on getting us into showers. He learns that the water we collect during a Chase is water that's easy to replenish. So, he orders someone new into the showers during.

Real water, he insists, will do us some good.

We argued little. We don't know how.

Snow gets hers first, happily.

Then Pert - who was grateful - and this time it is mine.

The water feels... I don't really have a word for it. Silky? I feel like a canvas freshly painted for a gallery opening. It is something that is hard to grasp, like I feel new. No, not new, but... words are slippery.

The water is cold, but my body doesn't care. I can feel every millimeter of blood pumping through my body.

My fingers tingle.

My lungs burn.

My heart sings.

The sweet sound of music pours out of every cell in the universe and into my mouth. The ship shakes as we latch on.

I don't notice.

Somewhere beyond the sea.

Somewhere waiting for me?

Somewhere, somewhere… somewhere…

I go sailing

The ship turns round and round. She almost flips upside down as panic fills the crew. I can feel it in the air. I can feel as we struggle to release.

I don't care.

Time washes itself down the drain in circular motions.

I wipe my hand across the stream covered mirror.

My eyes are older than I remember. GEMs only live 40 years, and I have to be in my 30s now. I was never meant to look this way, something says in my mind, but my eyes are the least of my worries.

I tug at the carpet on my face and see the frown that goes with it. My hair drapes around my shoulders and neck in wet, tangled strands. I feel like a bushel of eyebrows tangled together and tug again at my chin.

Ugh.

The heavy moisture is unforgiving as I find my clothes on the misty floor. My fingers brush along my straight blade razor. I lift it to my eyes and tease along the edges of my hairs until it is shorter.

Millimeter by millimeter, I let my hands do something that feels like visiting an old friend.

They seem to know the way.

They trim, slice, cut but not flay, as easily as if I had practiced my whole life. On the counter sits… a cloud.

No, no. Cream? Milk?

I rub it in my hands, contemplating what rain from such a cloud might smell like.

Blue, maybe? Sand, maybe. I pull it off my cheeks with metal. Maybe it would smell like toast.

My stomach enjoys that thought. A toasty rain. One that smelled half like the street and half like the trash that laid on it. Echos of mildew as a city bubbles half beneath an ocean.

No.

Not there.

My mind wanders to an image of a city that didn't sleep. I see people too stubborn to move to clean transport, drive their rubber vehicles along the street and poison the urban farms as they drift by. Cats, human and otherwise, howl out the windows, begging for attention or destruction.

My memories lie in the sunken city. Where the scent of mold and mildew hangs even when you are long dry. Where you tapdance on the heads of skyscrapers as they bubble into the sea, taking with them dreams and forgotten crimes.

I tug at my chin.

Just skin now. I feel more… complete.

I slip on something fresh to wear. The shirt hangs too tightly on my shoulders and too loose around my gut, but they always did. It wears quite like a uniform for rebels. The jeans are torn and ragged, but I like them that way. Broken and bent, a little rough, but always reliable - that's a familiar tune.

They fit more like socks.

I brush hands through my hair; they stop too short of the familiar, but it feels good. My head is almost too light to wear on my shoulders. I take a step outside into the place we've called our room. The air smells different, like a toasty rain, as Soren is the first to glance my way. He's carrying a heavy container, no doubt from the latest round of supplies, but his eyes linger for a moment.

Recognition is slow, so I offer my hand. "Hey, how's it goin'? I'm Jason Pechard, but you can call me Stargon."

"Oh, shit." He fumbles with his cargo to shake my hand, but his eyes don't leave my face and his hand forgets to leave. "Wait, what? Not Daylight?"

Nash is the first to roll back into frame from his busy workings. He looks me over with a scoff.

"Hey Cap, welcome back."

"Lt. Nash," I nod. I set Soren's hand back on his heavy cargo and make my way up to the cockpit. I pull Snow's chair back and put my forehead on hers, letting my bangs brush along her eyebrows. She pulls up immediately, not giving in to any taunts or jeers offered, and wrapping her arms around me.

"Jay?"

"Hey, Minnie." My hand settles at her back. It's not romantic, but it's the best feeling in the world. She rubs her face against mine, cheek to cheek, and the edges of her lips creep up into a smile.

"Don't call me that, asshole."

Her grin mirrors my own, and we embrace again.

"How goes the search?" I motion to the equipment.

"Still no luck on codes. The comet hunts are going well. I think Parrot is -" she clears her throat, "Albatrossi still isn't quite making sense but his diagrams do."

"As always," I shrug. "How far out are we?"

"Not quite Neptune Outlay, not quite Jupiter Alliance Colony territory."

"Are you avoiding saying we're near Uranus?" I tease.

She frowns and glances at the darkness in front of us as the comet falls away. The ice still falls over us like snow and the entire ship smells like space, as even the atomizer shields can't keep out what space wants in.

"We only have about five days of supplies left, ten if we extend it, but Soren doesn't like those odds."

"So melancholy," I nudge her. "I think you need a haircut."

"Me?" she snorts and looks me over. "What, you don't like the mirror image look?"

"It's not my mirror anymore." I grab her arm and spin her towards the back. She catches herself in an elegant twist and makes a spar-like bow. "I'm not sure if I'm ready to… come all the way back yet. I'm not sure if I'm ready to be…"

"Minerva," I say it so she doesn't have to. "She's still out there, on E… E…" I cough as the word burns down my throat. "Don't worry, I'm not asking you to snap back into place, Snow. I'm just saying your hair looks like crap and it'd make me feel better to slice something up that doesn't scream for a change."

She laughs and shakes her head.

"How do you know I won't scream?"

"I would hope we would find you someone with a softer chest before we got to screaming."

I hold out a hand. She takes it reluctantly.

We make our way back towards the sleeping quarters and my fingers itch to slice up her hair. It's probably not the best idea to give into this feeling, but it is on the edge of joy, and I need that right now.

Soren returns from whatever he was doing and looks at both of us before we start.

"What the fuck?"

Snow smiles. "You'll have to be more specific."

"He needs a haircut, too." I sit her in a chair to avoid any more questions.

"I really… really don't want you to put a blade to my…" He touches the place on his throat where I can still see my hands around it. I swallow hard to push back the image, push at the itch in my back, my fingers, my throat, my brain.

"S'ok, Pert can do it too," I shrug. "But I think we could all use a little trim."

Nash barks from the back.

"Fuck you, sir."

"Except Nash," I shrug, "who hates bladed edges."

"Thank you, dickbag."

Pert nods to Soren warmly from his shadowy perch as I pull Snow's hair out in long strands and get to work.

24

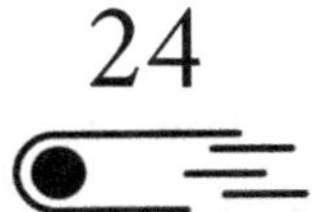

"I'm surprised you understand most of that." I look over the mess of papers, string and scribbles that make up Parrot's cubby. We gave him the topmost bunk but he wouldn't stay there, so Soren must have converted some nearby closet into Parrot's 'nest'. Albatrossi was always an excellent scientist, but always a terrible housekeeper.

"It makes a sort of sense." Soren tries to explain but just ends up holding his hands out, "At least all together?"

We mutually stare at the scattered papers that float on and around the numerous beds. Most don't mind because they are used to dust and stone, but Soren tries to gather the papers up. To make sense of them.

He frowns.

I laugh.

"Really ruins the idea that all GEMs get the cleaning compulsion, don't it?"

"Sorta." Soren moves to touch something, but Parrot bats his hands away.

"NOT that. Not that." He chirps and mutters as he continues to draw.

"So explain it to me." I tap the wall in a 4/4 rhythm as the engine goes quiet and the gravity drift drags us along. We must near a plant's orbital pull. Soren seems to instinctively match the beat with his foot, welcoming an end to the dead silence that consumes the ship.

One-two, three-four.

One-two, three-four.

"Well, you see, here - there is a little bit of a different spin of our current location." Soren takes steps in time, touching his freshly cut hair. I can't help but enjoy it. "Here we are, here are our comets we've chased, our general trajectory and an approximation of - I have no idea what these are."

"NESTS!" Parrot removes something from Soren's hand and puts it back where it was.

"He calls this the sea." Soren nods. "He calls this the Somewhere, and everywhere else is the beyond."

"Beyond." The answer is reflexive.

"Right." Soren gives me a suspicious look.

A song hits my mind again. I tap at my wrist and the device I mounted there. It's a reminder of time more than anything else, but it brings something to my mind, but my memories can't quite reach through the fog.

Something important... something...

Something...

Something...

Someone?

My mind aches with a memory.

We leave in a shuttle. We know this may be the last time we see home, but that is no different from every other time.

We are not sent off with fanfare; we leave when few would notice.
We are coming back, but I always look back.
Don't worry, we'll be back soon.
We just need one more push.
One more push and we can turn this into something so much bigger.
Still, that pang of regret as I leave her alone in the dark still lingers.
This place.
This city in the middle of nowhere.
Our home.

"The calculations he has are pretty decent. There are a few asteroids we could land on easy, but that doesn't exactly help us on the supply front. It almost feels like a treasure map." Soren touches one of the art pieces. "I feel like I could have learned some serious science from this guy."

"He was our navigator, physicist, and tactician. He knew all locations at all times." I motion to Parrot's head. The scars are in the place where memory is best kept. They are faded but still prominent on his skull. "It was his compulsion. They tortured him more than others to get locations. Unfortunately, his codes only ever made sense to him."

"Jesus," he whispers.

"Somewhere... beyond the sea..." The words escape me when I can't keep them in anymore. My mind is filled with a dozen images painted in blurry watercolor. "Someone waiting for we."

"You really like that song, don't you?" A thought pulls me into another room. Soren follows, "Um, okay, I thought we were getting over the crazy. Also, can we talk about your name? What am I supposed to call you?"

"The sea." I grab Snow's hand. She pulls back.

"What? I'm sort of busy, Star."

"So, it's Star now?" Soren questions.

"Somewhere beyond the sea," I sing.

Snow smiles and takes my hand. The annoyance in her eyebrows is evident now that I can see them through mirror cut bangs.

"Somewhere, waiting for me."

I pull her up and we dance. She glances at Soren. "Dancing, it always calmed his nerves - and it's Stargon. The other names don't matter, they are just pieces of the whole."

The grin on my face must have looked manic by the shades of pale Snow turns. "You're not listening."

"I... I am, sir." She whispers.

"We're trying, Dayl - er - Stargon, but you're not saying anything. You're just singing some old song you always do." Soren explains.

We spin for a moment more before I let Snow go. "One-Two. Two. Two. One-Two."

She stands by Soren and they both fold their arms, like a mirror. Then Parrot breaks between them. "Someone waits there. Yes. THE SEA! BEYOND!"

I snap and point at Parrot.

"Yes."

"Okay," Soren throws up his hands. "I'm lost. I was starting to understand this, but I'm lost."

"It's a base location." I motion to my com, which spins with a dozen local artifacts and names. "It's a signal. They look like debris, so they should be playing old radio tunes. That one should play every hour. Just an old song, on an old station."

"One that can reach out into space but doesn't have relevance to most people this far out." Snow's eyes light up. "A beacon for those who seek her out, an angel in the sky."

"Wait. Wait, wait, wait, wait - you mean all this nonsense is leading to a fucking base we can land at?" Soren looks between us.

"Somewhere beyond the sea." I grab Snow's hand again and we dance. "Someone is waiting for me."

"THE SEA! FOR ME!" Parrot adds with a clap.

Soren rubs his face in anger, but it quickly fades. He glances back at the closet and taps his chin in thought.

"Actually… looking at this as more of an astral projection map, the drawings make much more sense. Especially if you account for gravity drifts for something that wouldn't *move*."

"You got the wrong guy!" Parrot chirps proudly in response.

TERMS OF LIGHT

25

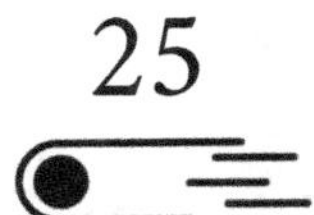

"Holy shit." Soren covers his mouth as he peers from another window. His excitement is easy to read in the bouncing of his shoulders. "You were not making it up. It's a freakin' space station. How does no one know about this? Where the hell even are we?!"

From a distance it's a shell - 'nest' - I can hear Parrot correct me before my thought finishes. From a distance, it's just a husk, a place for dead memories to be dug up, something forgotten and unused.

From a distance, it is us.

I touch the small pane of glass; it's chill to the touch, colder than I remember. My mind struggles to hold on to the present as I stare at that corpse of a space station.

I breathe in the stale air through a respirator. This place has been abandoned too long. There's no way it's going to be functional again.Walking through the dark halls, nothing could surprise me at that moment.

The station moans. She creaks as once tightly fit panels now move under the stress of weight. This place was meant to house millions, a bastion far from the ties of Earth's gravity somewhere between the Rift and Terra. A failed project, abandoned to the ages.

The angel of the sky: Sahaqiel.

"The military is pretty good at keeping things quiet when there's no one to tell a story."

Snow's bitterness is not missed. I want to send her a comforting glance, but all I can feel is the pull of a time that's gone. A time that barely makes itself known to me even as I can see it play out before me.

A place and time buried long past the reach of the sun.

"We can make it run," Nash perks from the bowels of the under-street workings. He's covered in grease, but smiling. "She's designed to take care of herself with little in terms of input. She's got it all, stealth, quiet, sustainability, repairability."

Albatrossi raises an eyebrow and looks over a screen at me.

"Initial estimates tell me we could house most of the GEM population here for a hundred years without planet side intervention. More if we have allies."

"That's what I like to hear." I give Nash a friendly punch on the shoulder and palm him some extra rations. "I just want to make sure everyone else believes it. That crack in the citydome is a bit… unsettling."

"Hell, an ATMO-shield is much stronger than glass. Makes air. Earth doesn't have a glass dome and everyone trusts that," Nash argues.

"Some things take more time to build trust with." I touch the station, but ice runs through my veins instead of comfort. "We'll get to know each other, won't we?"

"Or we'll suffocate slowly," Albatrossi mutters quietly, pushing up his glasses. "Either way, it's a preferable death."

"Think anyone's still alive in there?" Nash's voice cracks as he asks.

I try to hide a smile as I reply.

"If not, at least they're fat corpses."

"I'm serious." His tone cuts through the jest, but I don't feel the edge.

"So was I. If there are people there, Raven has taken them and we'll die to some Tidings tonight, or they're in there, scared to death because they've been discovered."

"Shit." He holds his breath. "Shit, we can't really relay the return signal, can we? They won't know it's us."

"They won't know it's us." I repeat the words and stand up. "I could always go out in my Angel Suit."

"No," Pert pushes me back down in my seat. "Stay where you are, rough one."

"Hah. Hah. Ooo," I purr as I stare blankly at the window. "When's the last time we were here?"

"That's- " Nash is annoyed by the question. "Soren?"

Silver bangs perk at his name, and he comes over, goosebumps running along his arm. It's hard to tell if it's from something he doesn't know he's feeling, or the chill the space near the window brings. I hope it is the latter.

Nash tells him without asking.

"We told you we've been trapped for 1168 days. We've been flying in this thing for, what, 12?"

"Eighteen," I correct.

Nash scoffs, but continues. "We tell you we been gone that long, but how long does that station look like it's been there?"

"Y… years?" Soren stares back out the window with even bigger eyes. "I mean - really, I have no idea. It's space. Decay works differently. Ten steps back, what's a Tidings? What's Ravyn?"

I roll my head back and look at him through my HUD, so I don't have to turn.

"Death God, death god's minions that eat abandoned space ships."

Soren's bangs floof more.

"That is not the comforting thing I was hoping you were going to say."

"They're superstitions," Snow says, annoyed.

I stare at the Sahaqiel as we slowly drift closer. The docking sequence is automated: she's code-free and trader friendly. We probably did that before we left.

Better to have unwelcome guests than none. A thought occurs to me: one I don't love. One that makes me doubt my own mind; the things that have kept me sane in the dark.

So, I ask, "When did the planetary civil war end?"

"I don't really know," Soren shrugged. "All I know is when the Ritz war ended."

"How long ago was that?" Nash's tone grew impatient. "Three years? Four?"

"Five," I say with Soren.

"Yeah, my brother was in the war. He was killed when I was 12. I was in foster care for 4 years after that - and that was, God, four-ish years ago?"

"He has no idea," Nash points to Snow as if winning some bet. "I told you."

"Give him a break," she folds her arms. "He has been through just as much shit as we have - not that you would know that. It would require you to *talk* to him to know that."

"I know plenty - like what his taste in music is and ------------
--"

"We can't stay here forever." Snow's voice is as cool as her namesake. I barely spare a glance. She says what I already know. The glowing lights of passing ship traffic tell me the time on the station was always limited.
"The longer we stay, the more chance they'll find it."
"I don't care if the military finds us," Snow scoffs. "You know as well as I do there's something out here that's much scarier than HUDO."
"That's a freakin' rumor." I dismiss the idea.
Snow balks.
"We've been over this."
"And yet…"
I hesitate to turn on the audio, but it's a reminder. All of us are tired of hearing it, but it echoes in our dreams. They started appearing a few weeks ago; eerie voices in the static.

"We bring tidings of joy,
tidings of death,
tidings of war,
tidings of love."

Snow hasn't slept since it started. She monitors it like our lives depend on it.

Over and over, but then they stop for no reason. A forgotten groan always follows. One long, continuous note that seems endless over the signal. Like a frog caught in a black hole.
"They haven't hit us yet, but we hear them whenever there's a shootout with HUDO and the Rift." I roll in my chair and look at her.

"But we haven't seen them. It's got to be some Ritz scare tactic."

She puts her hand over mine. Perfectly manicured nails, pale hair, calloused hands - in another life, in another gender, maybe a sister, maybe a lover. "We have to solve actual problems. Get back to the front. They need us. The GEMs, our sisters, they need us."

"Tidings... of... " I run my fingers over the com at my wrist and scan for signals. The calm, jazzing middle of the muted Beyond the Sea starts up again. Everything in between is static.

"Stargon?" Snow touches my shoulder. "Something wrong?"

"Worried about how we're going to dock. About what we'll find," I mutter.

"Like you care," Nash scoffs. "Leave it to us. You always trusted us implicitly before. Why ask questions now?"

I wonder if Nash is having memories, too. I wonder what his say about me? Who I was. Who I... am.

"Did I step on your ducks before they hatched this morning, Nash?"

His brow furrows in confusion at my statement.

"You seem utterly against the only plan we seem to have other than living in a Comet Chaser ship that needs an air refueling."

"We should have sought out a colony," Nash muttered. "We don't have a lot of burns left. There's no getting away from here if it's a bust."

"I'm confused." I feel years of commanding soldiers flow through my fingers as I step too close to him. "What part of 'we are wanted criminals on the brink of escaping forever' do you not understand? You think we can just waltz into a major port and we won't disappear into the black box of history instantly? Because that sounds like what you want right now."

"Maybe it would be better," Nash pushes at my shoulders, but it does not move me. "Maybe we should have stayed with the others. At least then we knew… at least we knew…"

"I know it's hard to understand this, but what Soren just said? He's telling me that while I have been counting hours, minutes, seconds, for almost three years, I'm off by almost two years and that doesn't bother you? We were still fighting the *Ritz* when we got put in the hole, Nash." I grab his collar. "We have no idea what is waiting for us out there. We have to at least try the station. Even if it means scavenging supplies, this is the only option where we live."

Snow touches my shoulder, but says nothing. Pert sits quietly, uninterested in anything but what is outside the window.

"I just don't think we have any options at all here, Pechard," he spits the words. "We all only have half a mind right now. All I can see are shadows of myself when I look at the insides of this ship and you want us to go do what? Crawl around in that corpse ONE MORE TIME?! Why?!"

"Why not?" I spin the ring on my finger, the rusted edges cut into my skin as I look towards Pert and Snow, then back to Nash. "Because it's an order, soldier."

The statement burns us both on the inside. Nash doesn't bite anymore, but huffs back to the front where Parrot supervises the docking procedure.

One we don't know will work.

"You know."

I can't find the face of this person. The sun swallowed it whole. Maybe it's not my memory anymore, maybe it's someone that doesn't exist.

"I'm going to miss you."

"We'll be back. We're just going to --r--a. The docks are calling."

"I know, I know, 'It's where we get our best intel. Always trust a dock worker to know what's what', yeah, yeah." A hand slides over mine. The rings match. Maybe. It's too bright to see clearly. All I know is it feels warm. We kiss. I can feel the passion behind it. I can feel overwhelming pain course through me as I twist the ring on my finger.

"Who are you?"

"Um. Soren. I'm Soren," New introduces himself again, calmly, like we've had this conversation a hundred times. "You're Stargon, remember?"

"Yeah. Sorry, just... memory shadows."

I am now standing near the docking rings as I feel the Sahaqiel connect to us with a rough shake. My Cession forms an Angel Suit around me, mostly. The helmet stays off.

"You guys don't really do anything undramatic, do you? It's either all in or *alllll* the way out." He laughs at something I don't understand the reference to. There's a sad sigh that follows. "So like, this is going to be creepy, is it?"

"It..." I'm not sure how to answer, so I don't.

26

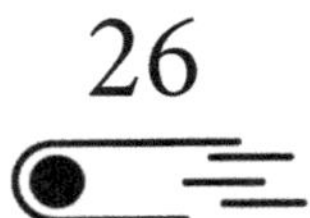

We move through the dock in silence. We wear suits because we don't know what to expect and the large crack in the atmospheric dome draws my eyes and the others' fears.

Worse, part of me itches for this, craves this, and I think this is the part of me that decided to touch the tail of a comet in person. This is a part of me I don't know how to do anything but embrace.

As we enter the docking area, we are met with silence. It is desolate, white, barren, but beautiful. Standing on solid ground, my body sways naturally. Too long at sea, too long at sea, I tell myself, but I'm not sure if I listen. My whole body feels lighter, tighter, somehow stranger in this place where I can still see reflections of something like… home.

Home once masqueraded as an apartment in Sunken Brooklyn where the smells of the mildew and booze below sifted through floorboards and the jazz music sang me to sleep. It pretended to be friends who shy away when people called me Tank and Owned like they were words that meant anything to me.

Home sometimes wore a uniform. That was the clearest reflection I could still hear. It was white with blue stripes and gold pips and came with few rights and long hours. There was always a sister or brother there to take my hand and lead me forward if I got lost. I knew that if I screamed, there would be a witness to the actions. I also knew that if I screamed too loud or pushed too hard, it wouldn't be me that suffered. That uniform taught me to see the cracks underneath the surface of home.

I run my fingers along my worn ring and wonder what other homes I've forgotten.

The lava seas of Io?

Perhaps the chilled docks of E------'s breeze, or maybe something warmer: something closer with a heartbeat and dark eyes. I glance back at Soren as he clings to the too-big suit he swims in. Nash says something to him on a private com. I wonder if they aren't getting along; I wonder if there is more, but the groan of the last door opening cuts my thoughts short.

This should lead us from the docking sanitation area into what would normally be greeting and registration. When all is said and done, darkness is all that greets us. Not the eerie darkness of a hallway, but the wide open, silent calm of space.

The glass and ATMO-dome overhead give way to the emptiness of the Neptune Outlay. We see several of Neptune's moons frozen in time and a few asteroid colonies that are frozen in place, staggered as they lead up to the wide-open eye of the Rift. From here you can see her inner layer, frothing edges of red with a deep, pulsating inner life of blues, whites, and purples. At her center, a crack in the dimension where all the Ritz nest.

I feel a shaky breath behind me. It mimics my own, and after a long moment, Snow takes a step closer to me.

"There's a lot of memories here."

"They're too far away for me to reach."

"Me too."

"This place." Soren takes in a sharp breath. "This is… so BIG. How the heck do we find anyone in here?"

I turn and look at him with a smile and point up at the top of the dome. He squints for a few minutes before he just gives me what I'm officially calling his huffy face. He does it all the time: when he's hungry, when he's angry, when he doesn't understand, when he can't see anything - which is often, I think he needs glasses - and my personal favorite, anytime I talk.

"You think they'd just build a giant dome and not have any surveillance?" I turn and skip forward down the open corridor, through the entry gates. "This was all state-of-the-art once unused, too. The rations are still here, the security. It's one giant dead city out in the middle of nowhere."

"Yeah, that's not actually helpful," Soren scolds. "How do we *find* anything with surveillance that's in the *sky*?"

"I guess we learn how to fly." I run my fingers along the metal wall and it lights up. "Or hope they don't see us first, if anyone's here."

I press my makeshift device to the wall where a panel lay, and let my orb do the work. After a few moments, I pull up a map of the ship. There are several display options and I swipe through a few until I get to the security display. I pluck one of the camera nodes out of the map and turn it until I can tickle the computer enough to let me turn it on. My orb works deep inside the walls to make things work for me.

After a few tries, it succeeds, and the pathway in front of us lights up with faint yellow guides.

"You could have just said 'there are access ports on this floor,' Soren," Soren mocks my accent as he talks. Snow gives him a bit of a bump to the shoulder and shakes her head. "What? I just don't understand why we went into the giant empty space station when we could have found a perfectly good colony to land on."

"We're fugitives." Snow points out what's obvious to the rest of us.

"We're criminals," Nash adds reluctantly.

"We're genetically engineered superhumans everyone is afraid of, are owned by a government that wanted us dead when we fought for freedom - oh and you failed at finding the docking codes for our little ship." I turn down a hall the lights guide me to.

Soren scoffs, but I can hear the humor in it. He's learning.

"Oh sure. Blame the new guy for everything."

"You got the wrong guy~" I sing.

"Yeah, uh, why did we leave Parrot on the ship again?" Soren tries his best to keep up with Snow, but lags. His speed tells me he's much lower on energy than he wants to admit.

"Just in case," Nash barks.

"Just in case?"

"We need a getaway driver," Nash confirms.

"We die and want someone else to finish our mission," Snow adds.

"He tries to nest on something that will kill him," I correct. "But the other two are why we left Pert there, too."

"He wouldn't try to nest on…" Soren pauses. "Fair enough."

We walk the rest of the way without words.

What is there to say?

The yellow lights end and what looks like an empty wall, and I run my fingers over it again. The Cession wrapped around my body churns and wiggles with anticipation. I wonder what it hears, what it sees that I can't. It's hard to tell if it is calling out to its siblings, the other mech-grade Cession orbs on this ship, or if it's trying to tell me something else.

I tap the panel three times and it clicks open. A few dozen screens appear around me and I toss them to the three beside me. They run footage from around the station.

"Start checking," I order. "Start from today and go back from there. See if you can find anyone, any*thing*."

"You've got to be kidding?" I expected that to come from Soren, but it comes from Snow. "We haven't been here in *years, Stargon. We* can't just go through *years* of recorded material and hope we find something."

"You got a better idea?"

She always does.

She takes away the security console and starts working her magic. She rarely volunteers for this kind of thing. She'd much rather be in the middle of the action than stuck behind doing tactical work - but she's so damn good at it. I feel the edges of a sword hilt form in my hand and finally think I know what my orb is telling me.

I don't *see* an enemy, but there's a very good chance that they see us.

"Hoo-ahh." I breathe.

The others perk for just a moment before the alarms go off.

The dead air fills with the sound of sirens blaring from the entire section of the station. Red and yellow lights bombard my senses.

My heart beats faster, my blood feels like fire, but I can't tell if it's panic or glee. I'm itching for a fight. At least part of me is, and I try to focus, but all I can feel is every inch of red along my skin.

They're going to find me!

I pull myself out of Soren's mind and do my best to stay alert and ready to fight.

I move Soren behind me, so he sits squarely between Nash and Snow.

Swords form from the hilts in my hands.

My blood pounds in my ears as I wait.

I wait.

I wait.

I wait.

"Sorry." The lights fade. The noise is now gone and part of my mind begs for its return.

I swear I see Shadows in the corners of the room, but they are gone before they are there.

No more silence. Not again. Not again.

My shaking hands touch my helmet and I try to focus as I can feel the reality slipping. I can feel the static of words I don't know anymore as the sun comes to take away the world.

Think of something else.

Something else.

Come on. Come on.

One-two.

One-no.

No. There's no rhythm in this place, no engines, no hum, no heartbeat - nothing. Nothing. Nothing. NOTHING.

"Hah. Hah. Ooo." It's whispered in my ear.

Soren's voice is shaky. "Oh for the shadow of death, Oh for the waking call to arms."

Nash echos, "Rising tides won't find us here, Waking times will hold us dear,"

"Here, forgotten in the dark

We will rise. We will rise. We will rise.

To Daylight," I finish.

"Hah. Hah. Ooo." Three voices in unison.

The blanket of silence lifts. I can feel - hear - the blood in my body with the steady beat.

One-two-three.

One-two-three.

"Ooo. Ah."

My helmet lowers as if I requested it. I run fingers through hair I don't remember being short. I touch my face, devoid of hair that seems like it should be there, and I roll my neck. I meet three sets of eyes.

Panicked, annoyed, worried.

"Anything?" I ask.

There's a moment as we wait to see if the ship reacts to our false alarm.

Nothing.

We are neither relieved nor comforted by the response.

"Yeah, can we not do that again?" Soren fills the void with noise. He would have been good to have in the first few years in the hole.

I can't help but smile.

"I'll do my best. I also see there's been a security breach alert." Snow motions to the console, her eyes still wide, "But that wasn't from me. Silent alarm."

Before I can speak, my body reacts too slowly and too fast. Blades, fully extended in front of me, as they touch the edge of a pistol as it's raised to my face. I meet masks that hide faces, sizes, races.

They are not airtight masks, just disguises.

In the darkness we see a few more move. The others stiffen and try to blend in without moving.

"Who are you?" The voice is female.

Unfamiliar.

I take in every detail I can. I can count five masked shadows behind her that are visible, likely at least two out of sight with some range coverage. The ship is their home; they have every advantage, but they likely don't know that Pert and Parrot are not that far off.

I see the front two have gravity belts, one has a laser net, three have guns, two knives and likely something else hidden under one of the back shadow's body. Hard to tell, hard to gauge.

I'm out of practice.

The soldier I was would have them dead already.

The chaos I am, smiles.

One sword edge slips a little and slices into the barrel. The orb jerks at the weapon and the owner steps back as the gun is consumed before it can hit the floor. I extend Cession wings from my suit's tightly packed frame to cover those behind me.

"I suggest you *run,*" I growl.

It's a feral thing in my throat that feels hot and hard and so good against me.

The Cession falls in front of my face, pulling from another source. It makes me shaped sharp, like a predator as the Cession seems to delight in the promise of what comes next.

A feast.

Destruction.

My fingertips sharpen into something not claw or blade. It will only take me ten seconds to eliminate the two targets in front of me. Enough time for Snow and Nash to run or take aim and try to save what we can. Soren may get hurt, and that is the only reason I do not move.

The net is an unknown — but nets are slow.

I am slow. I swallow.

They raise their arms; I hear the foul smelling light of sonic and heat as they activate their weapons. They aim for my brothers who do not have the advantage of Cession, even if my metal can protect them.

No options are good here.

All I know is we are NOT going back.

No more silence.

"You're not taking us alive."

"You invaded US!" the enemy screams as she pulls out her own knife and crouches.

"WAIT!" The sound comes over the intercom and we are all rattled.

The woman in front of us hesitates. She looks at us, then to the one at her side and they share the unsurest of shrugs.

I can't wait. I'm too anxious, too eager, too ready for blood and I grab her by the throat. The other one readies his net as Nash fumbles for his own weapon.

One of the distant shadows fires anyway. The shot grazes my shoulder and the Cession armor covers it before it can bleed.

"No! No no no no no! WAIT!" The voice is from behind the group now.

It gives us all pause even as the metal calls for flesh.

"Wait. Wait. Wait!" We see movement part the few soldiers that face us. The voice finally makes it to the front of our assailants.

He is not in armor or wearing a weapon. He is out of breath, with messy hair and a leather jacket that is older than I am. An aged smile crawls up his face when he gets to us.

"Oh… my god… it is you. It's you. Stargon - Snow? Garth?… oh… oh man."

I'm wrapped in an embrace, and I lower my captive. She scrambles away as my heart stops beating for a moment in my chest.

My finger burns.

The wings fall as weapons are lowered and Nash and Snow exchange the same confused look between us. Soren, still shaking, approaches the stranger.

"Uh, hi," He pushes his way forward from beneath my falling wing. "Soren. Hi, sorry I don't think we've met - who exactly are you?"

"Hi! Soren?" The voice takes Soren's hand without hesitation. "It's so nice to meet you. I'm Josh, and I'm Stargon's husband."

Terms of Light

27

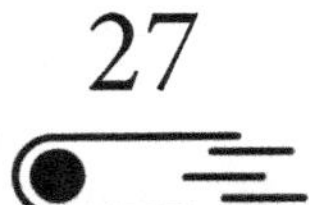

"We met on a cold day in November."

My memory paints the world in trees that are bare except for gowns of ice that twinkle against dim starlight.

Josh pauses.

"Wait, or was it, April?"

I look at him with a blank expression. The trees don't change, but the starlight does. The scene does. I am walking next to him on a bridge, his hand held in mine, the warm sun on my face, his smile confirming our future plans in the bedroom.

I sit in that warmth for a moment as I cup the mug in my hand and stare at the others. Well, more like past them. A date connects to my mind.

"It was January," I correct.

"Now he remembers?" Soren is red with anger. Or embarrassment? It's hard to tell, but he stands near Nash as he paces and listens to Josh talk.

"It's photographic." Josh motions like he's taking a picture, and taps my head. "But the sound isn't always there. Ever since you were caught in that bunker on Calibre - er, Station JX something, something. I don't remember the station number. You were always better at that, but you lost most of your hearing. Comes and goes. As for the rest, well, it looks like some of the film just needs some re-exposure."

The sensation when he touches my hand is like light is pouring over my body and filling it up with its brightness. Firelight. Smoke. Starlight.

I feel like my skin will fall away with that touch, but I don't want it to stop.

"It was during a riot." Josh's tone is calm as he speaks, the dissonance of violence and pleasure strong in my memory.

The pictures in my mind paint themselves without sound. A hundred people in a crowd, some with arms raised in protest, others with weapons. There's so much smoke. Then there's violence.

My head is against the pavement, a boot to my temple. I can feel the metal cuff holding back my arms as I smile. It hurts. I love it.

I hate it.

It is everything. All at once.

Josh continues.

"It was the first time that the GEMs had been openly protesting outside of a military facility. It was chaos."

Now there is screaming as they open fire on us like we're at a practice range. They throw smoke and it burns my eyes, but little else. The WIPs around me collapse.

I watch from an angle that hurts my neck.

They slam boots into my ribs, my head, my legs.

While they are busy with that, I slide the restraints off my wrists. There's a noise behind me that catches me off guard. It's a shout but I can't distinguish the words.

There's a crack, like a baseball being hit out of the park, and the boot falls away. A bat lands near me. I grab it and notice a trickle of blood near the edge.

That's the first time I see him. Sweaty. Angry. Tears of rage flowing down his face.

I fell in love even before I knew his name.

My Josh.

"They opened fire on us, but we stopped it before there were too many deaths. We overwhelmed them, but they used unfair weapons. Smoke bombs. Sonic grenades, you name it. Even as the injured were dragged away, the GEMs marched forward.

It wasn't peaceful anymore. The GEMs always mirrored what force was used. That was always their way, tit for tat. EGGs lit up like a thousand colored stones against the artificial backdrop of winter white; it was the most beautiful and terrifying thing I think those people had ever seen."

"So, what, you met in jail after the protest, then?" Soren asks.

Josh smiles at Soren like he's just caught him lying.

"Not quite. They didn't exactly put us in cells."

I laugh out loud as the memory catches up. It catches us all by surprise.

"We met when I decked you for touching me."

"Yeah," Josh rubs his jaw absently. "He punched me in the face after I tried to help him up. They had him on the ground and were screaming orders, but he either didn't hear them or didn't care.

Either way, I went down, but held onto his wrist, and he dragged me off into an alley. I think he only stopped because I apologized. I earned a whole wink before he disappeared back into the crowd."

"That's…" Soren shrugs. "That's nowhere near as romantic as I expected."

"Somewhere beyond the sea," I sing. Josh squeezes my hand and stands up, offering his arms out as I sing. "Somewhere, waiting for me."

Our hands intertwine, we move around each other like we're orbiting stars who have done this dance all our lives. It feels as natural as breathing. His voice matches mine, but it's smoother, deeper.

"My lover stands on golden sands and watches the ships that go sailing."

"Okay, that's more what I expected. So, what, love at first punch?" Soren's eyes are alight with interest and excitement, even as he pretends he doesn't care. Snow and Nash won't confess their curiosity, but I feel like this is new to them as well.

They are painted in vibrant colors against the white-gray of the station walls, and for the first time I feel like I see how much the stone took from us.

I stiffen and stop dancing. Josh doesn't seem to mind, as he just holds my hand.

"Sort of." Josh shrugs his shoulders and pulls me closer. "The next time we met was at a club, though, he didn't admit it at the time, he had been watching me for weeks. I had made myself a powerful ally in the fight for GEM rights - my wife was one before she was killed - and I wasn't going to let it happen again."

I close my eyes as I take in his scent. He smells like laundry soap and tobacco, with just a hint of coffee on his lips. The lights make it hard to pass anything but a subtle expression, but we talk, we introduce ourselves; we leave together wrapped in music and sweat and lust.

"The sex was good."

Josh scoffs.

"The sex was GREAT."

"Then we start talking about plans." I look at him with awe, with respect, as it plays out in front of me. "Organizing more than protests. Food lines, transports, safe houses. A way home for those that don't have it."

"Right. I quickly went from that really good ally to like number three in a large GEM rights organization. I didn't mind, it just went fast." Josh fans himself and we both sit, knowing too well what our bodies are eager to do next. "Then *it* happened."

There is a heavy silence that asks a question we can't.

"... Europa?" The word burns as Snow asks, defiant against the quiet.

"No," Josh squints at her, concerned, but then looks at me. "NaReau's assassination."

I see a pale man with pale hair and a cane as he stands at a podium. He raises his fist as we cheer. He shows us documents that say we're free. We are not owned, even as the solar system rejects his papers.

"He was the leader on the political side, the one trying to change the legal status of GEMs as property. His death left a tyrannical corporation in charge and they abducted and imprisoned their 'property' as fast as they could. That's when things got violent."

I see a body on a couch. There is spilled wine as his wife screams and panics. His little girl is sobbing in another GEM's arms. The GEM looks at me for guidance, for what he is supposed to do, but I have no answers.

All I have is rage, and even that empties out of me.

"Not just NaReau, was it?" I swallow hard as the thoughts rush back. "It was anyone even associated with GEMs. Pert's family. James Morrison... my daughter. All killed. All killed... all gone..."

"I... didn't know that." Soren sinks back a little. Nash's hand hits his shoulder and squeezes it gently. "What... happened on Europa then?"

The word still burns, but not as much as the anger that spills out of my eyes and onto the table in front of me.

We have lost so much more than ourselves.

"It was... our last stand," Snow says to Soren. "Where we hoped to create a colony for just GEMs. A safe space in the JAC that strengthened their place as a solar system power. They wanted to be free of Earth and Mars, and we wanted to help. I guess we failed? At least, I imagine we did. We've been out for a while."

"A long while," Josh's voice is quiet as he speaks. Our eyes meet again: his say so much to me, more than I can even perceive. I miss you, I love you, I know you.

It burns worse than the water from my eyes.

"This station was his idea," I add, choking on the tears in my throat. "I knew about its location, but he's the one that convinced us to go for it. A backup plan that wasn't reliant on planets and politics. He said we could make it ours, an entire city free of rule from anyone who may use us. Plenty of mining deposits and comet chasers around this area, and close enough to the Rift to trade. It was a good plan. It cost a lot to get here, even more to get her up and running but -"

"But we did it." Josh's smile was brief. "And then... Europa."

"The last port before the Rift that was still considered viable at wartime," Nash adds. "All the GEMs who disobeyed were removed from the docks and killed, put out on the streets to ensure loyalty. The cold kept their bodies... fresh."

"The way they teach it on Earth," Soren is hesitant to speak, "is Europa is where you gathered and slaughtered civilians? That's when HUDO took it under military control and bombed the shit out of it. They declared it a dead zone. Radioactive fallout or whatever."

"Civilians?" Josh shook his head. "No. We didn't attack. They did."

"Oh, we did," I growl.

My memory paints the world in shades of gray and red. Europa's sky is navy blue as the foreign constellations watch on. When we arrive, there are bodies in the street. GEMs. Tit for tat. We match them. One for one. Ten for one. A thousand for one. We came to bring our sisters and brothers home, instead we found them slaughtered.

I feel the ice in my veins, the chill of my hands in Europa's artificial air. The rage boils so hot that this sight cools over my compassion like volcanic rock. Memories fly by in alleys, in tunnels. Necks beneath my arms stiffening, breaking, relaxing, collapsing.

"We killed anyone who opposed us that day. They took them all. All of us. Old. Young. Newborns. Loyal dock workers taking drink breaks. Families. Anyone who they deemed in the way. Anyone they randomly picked. We returned the favor. Body for body. Mirroring what they gave, but this time we amplified it."

Josh is silent now.

"The rest of it is a lie. That's not what happened." I hold up my hand, grasping at the Rift in the distant sky above us. "HUDO did not visit Europa. They abandoned the place and all those in it hoping to make a political frenzy. No, they never attacked. We surrendered. They found us outside of it after… after…"

The white noise returns.

The sun takes away the world - until I feel his hand on mine again.

"It was January when we met, April when we started dating, but it was November when we were married." Josh's voice cools the lava flow of wrath in my veins. My heart races in my chest, looking for an answer I just can't find.

I feel breathless.

He continues.

"It was just before you left. We just... did it! I got you a spinner ring. You wore them out so quickly, I bought a horde."

He motions behind Soren, who hands him a small box. Josh opens it and inside are a dozen rings with unique patterns, all silver with dull cores that spin in place when you touch them. He pulls one of the rings out.

Gently, he takes my left hand and removes the rusty bit of metal with care. Then he eases the new one on. I stare at it but somehow it feels unfamiliar.

"Married in November," I say it again, but nothing plays. "Married in November. I don't... it's not there anymore."

"Give it time," Josh's smile is strong and patient, but I can see a sadness under it. "You have been gone for so long. All of you. I'm just happy you're back, okay? That's what matters today. You're back."

I wrap my arms around Josh, even though it feels strange, and his stubble rubs against my neck. I hate it, but it brings tears to my eyes and I choke on them again.

"How long?" Snow's the only one who dares to ask the question.

"Six years," Josh lets out a long breath. "We were beginning to give up hope you were still alive, but I knew my wolf was too hard to kill."

He smiles again.

I feel alive somehow, but even more lost than before.

Married in November - wait. No, something else catches my attention.

"We?"

"Like I said, we did it. Just because our pretty poster boy was gone didn't mean we were." Josh stands; the guards around us move to follow his lead, pushing us up into their middle ranks. "I wouldn't use the word thriving, but this city is only empty right now because a mysterious ship docked without communicating. I assure you, the Sahaqiel and everything we wanted for her is alive and well."

This is the man that takes my breath away.

I feel a return from wherever I had lost it. It is warm, and it hurts, and it turns me upside down.

"Hah. Hah. Ooo-ah."

28

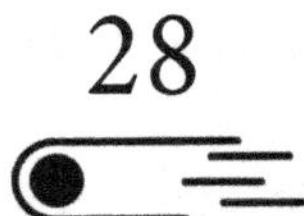

I watch from a perch at a coffee shop. It feels so natural and foreign all at the same time. Hundreds of warm bodies fill the streets, but even then it feels surreal, like a trap - like a dream. I stare at the Rift above us, with its staircase of colonies trapped just in front of it, and all I can imagine is the burning sensation of the sun.

It rips under my eyelids, into my skin, into my mind.

Snow's touch pulls me out of it. I grab her hand with the firmness of warning, but it softens as my heart slows down.

I can feel her nerves on the edge of my mind.

She's as wound up as I am. It feels like everyone is.

"It really worked," she whispers. I expect to see a warm drink in her hand, but not this time. She still wears some connectors for her spacesuit like she is still ready to go at any moment.

I get that.

"GEMs, WIPs, all here. Together. Even some RIPs."

"Partial breeds," I correct. "It feels unreal."

"You don't drink coffee." She sits across from me. "But you used to love coming to these to people-watch, didn't you?"

"Humans think everyone drinks coffee. No one looks twice at someone sitting outside, taking it all in."

We watch the crowd swell and shrink as Soren returns with Parrot and Pert. I worry this will be too much for Parrot and he'll try to climb on the dome outside to nest. It's an amusing thought that's a little sad at the same time.

Is he further gone than most of us, or is he just the most obvious?

It's a hard question to ask.

Harder to answer as I try to roll the name of a moon off my tongue with no success.

"E... Eu..."

Snow clears her throat, and after a moment of thought, she turns back to me.

"I don't remember him," Snow says in quiet frustration. "Josh. I mean, I remember pieces of things he's done, but not him."

I spin the ring on my finger. The metal still bites into bruised flesh, but the pain is comfortable. Clean.

"Me either."

The next time I feel myself taking in my surroundings, Nash is at my shoulder, and Pert sits in the chair across from me, with his back to the entire city. He is peeling an orange, an entire stack of oranges, and I find myself doing the same when I look down. The lapses are becoming shorter, but I can just hear Jimmy's ghost yelling at me from whatever depth of hell he landed in.

"When are we going back?" Pert asks, catching my eye. I look around and see that Soren and Parrot have joined us. I focus for a moment on my orange, trying to formulate the words I need.

They need.

This time, it can't be just a song, but I don't have answers. I don't even have questions anymore. I simply have this. A chair, an orange, and the cracked sky.

Soren finally asks: "Back to what? Back to V'ger? Back to the prison?"

"Europa," I study Pert as I say it, avoiding the fire in my mind. "We can't go back to save the others until we have a real ship. The only way we can get one is if we go to a port. We had ships on Europa. We can access the port."

"And then what?" Nash scoffs. "Steal one? Hope no one's touched anything in 6 goddamn years?"

"Steal one," I nod to Pert and slip some orange between my cheek and gums. It burns. "It's significantly harder to get onto Europa than to get ten ships off of it if we need to."

"I'm not really seeing why we need to go to Europa for that." Soren plays with a device in front of him, writing things down or playing games. "It's been abandoned. Seriously abandoned, quarantined even. Most of the traffic has been diverted to IO and some other colonies along the Neptune Outlay. Siofra, Calganey Bay."

Josh clears his throat at the edge of our group.

"You guys all look pretty... doomful. Can I at least talk you into dinner before you officially decide to leave again?"

"Josh, man," Soren scoffs, but Josh just shrugs. "We're not leaving without LOTS of dinners."

Josh smiles and puts his hand on Soren's shoulder, a thing that makes our young friend blush.

"You learn fast. With them, stopping is not an option. Seriously, though, dinner?"

My stomach churns at the thought. Pert is the only one who raises an eyebrow and holds up his stack of oranges.

"I would at least suggest some rice with that. You don't want to piss orange juice." Josh's smile is knowing, as Pert stares at the oranges with a new intensity.

I'm surprised when Soren takes the lead.

The rest of us follow in a line like his ducklings.

When we get to a building, all of us stop, waiting to be let in. Josh opens the door and waits for us, following behind.

We enter a large building that smells like a thousand flavors our tongues have long forgotten, even if the place looks familiar. It is a cafeteria, not unlike the one in the center of our torment. We all freeze when we enter, watching, waiting.

Soren goes on without us, but Nash, Pert, and I stand still. Children and their parents go in and out of the area freely. Some with food, some without, all with casual smiles. I recognize a few faces, mostly young ones, but only some of them recognize mine.

A few wave, but I cannot wave back. I try my best to smile, but it does not come.

I am frozen, suddenly self-conscious, dirty, shaggy, covered from head to toe in something I can't scrub off.

It seizes my thoughts.

It pulls them out of my head and twists them around. I can feel my hands on my shoulders. The calluses from pushing against stone for ages are rough against my skin. My throat burns from screams that don't come out of me.

My eyes turn away from the light that they never see.

My body is on fire, but not how my mind is. They burn together.

Then hands touch mine. I feel a chest at my back, a gentle swaying follows, and when I finally squeeze my eyes shut, I can see the moon. It is clear, round, cool and welcomes me. Beside me is a man painted only in shadows of lust and power, and I think it is me, but I am unsure what is real and what is not. So, I put my hands on his hands.

"You're safe," a calm voice whispers in my ear.

We stand there, his arms wrapped around my shaking body as people walk by us like river water. We are unmoving stones against their current. I try to focus on breathing, on thinking of something else, but music is the only comfort.

It's a song I don't know.

It's a song I have heard a million times, but cannot repeat.

It is the song that takes away the world.

It feels like my throat is on fire as I hum a single note from it and it escapes into the air.

I wait for everyone to ignite.

I wait for the sun to set fire to the world around me and burn us away in bright light. I watch as each face etches itself in my memory with clear, precise, distinct clarity. Nose hairs, freckles, eyelashes, color, sound of voice, color of clothing, pigment of skin all superimposed over the other as they come over and over and over and over and over.

"Do you want to go somewhere else?" I hear the voice behind me ask. I want to answer, but the only thing I can do is SEE.

See the faces.

See the screaming.

See the light.

See.

"Just… tap my hand if you want to go, or we can stay, right here, okay? You know where we are, right? On the Sahaqiel. Safe. With your friends, Soren, Snow, Pert, Albatrossi."

I find my fingers rapidly tapping his hand. It is so faint that I don't know if he can feel it.

"Okay. I'm going to turn us around, and we're going to go North a little on New 42nd Street and then down three blocks. That's where my apartment is, okay? It's the bottom level, behind the teaching facility."

I nod.

We move. I think. Rivers of people flow by us before we turn to exit. People give me a wide berth. A circle that I live in alone. It takes another river before we move through the door.

Once outside, the river parts, and we make our way forward. It's slow.

Every step feels like a decade in darkness. I try to count, but I can't get past one.

Just move forward.

He keeps saying words, his voice soft, but I can only hear the faintest of things. I can make out phrases. He asks me if I'm okay; he tells me about the station, nothing I don't know, but just... talks to me.

Then we are at a door; we pass through an empty classroom.

He opens another door.

We lay in bed.

He turns something on and we are staring up at the stars that would be over Earth if we were there.

The air is cool, his hand is warm, he is humming, but how tired he is shows in the way the notes sag. I wonder how much time he's spent waiting and now, here I am, missing in place, missing in mind.

"You could do so much better, Josh."

"Shut up, Stargon." He punches my arm, and all I can do is stare into those tired eyes of his. "I love you. It's okay. I know none of you can talk about it yet. About that place you were in, about Europa. It's okay, I didn't expect..."

He lets out a long breath.

"I don't know what I expected, but I knew it wasn't going to be some sitcom ending, Star."

"You've been doing this alone for so long."

"Alone?" He looks at me like I just stepped on his toe. "No. Not alone. I'll introduce you officially later, but trust me when I say most of us are right where you left us. We even have some new ones, bright ones, ones taking charge and turning around the way we think and teach. The only ones missing are the ones that went to Europa. You're the first I've ever seen return."

"Comet prison," I stumble over the words. "They had us in an old mining comet. Emptied deposits so we could sleep in the holes. No light. Barely any water. Deprivation… so long without… anything, but we could hear each other, you know?"

"Hah. Hah…. Ooo?" He tries his best to mimic the song. It brings a smile to my face, then it makes me laugh.

And I laugh.

It's too much of a laugh, the laugh of a stressed mind that wants to let go.

I roll into giggles that make my lungs cramp and my body ache. He tries his damndest to stop laughing with me, but it doesn't matter, we both are laughing, cuddling and breathing under an artificial sky.

When I am done and wipe away the tears, I kiss him.

It's warm and calm. Best of all, it's right.

29

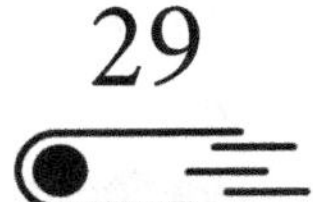

4:00 am.

My eyes open without permission. They know the time better than I do. I find my hand tapping out seconds. I lay next to Josh in the dark for a long time and listen to him breathe. Is this what sleep was like before?

I don't remember.

I force myself out of bed before I begin to chant. The name, the word Daylight, itches at the edge of my lips.

Time for a shower.

The water is cold and keeps me grounded.

Shave - hair, then face. It's smooth, it's clean, and I note the need to tend to the rest of my body hair later, but the razor is too dull. I'll sharpen it after lunch.

Lunch.

My stomach growls as much in anticipation as it does in protest of this new bounty of food we have access to.

There are 20 white undershirts in the top drawer, folded in perfect sets of 3 with a divider between except the one that is missing. I pull out the next one in order, and slip it on. Sweats next from the drawer beneath. Socks pulled high before lacing up one of the three pairs of boots.

Military grade. Black. Fully laced.

This all feels… right.

Stretches.

4:30 - time to run.

I stand at our bedroom door. Josh left it open a crack, but I still wait. I tap at it a few times, waiting for the sound of chains and gears, but it doesn't move. Panic rises in me as I try to open it, but I can't bring myself to. I hear a groan as my zombie husband lifts himself out of bed, opens our bedroom door, and then the front door.

I kiss him.

I run.

Seven blocks north, three blocks east, then back. Not much time to take in the scenery; no one is really up and about, so my view is limited to abandoned buildings and well kept bots managing well kept greenery.

The only thing that's awake with me is the sky. The Terra-centric settings on the dome make it appear blue with fluffy clouds, but even artificial light can't block out the Rift and its brilliant array of lights. In the distance, I also see the faintest outline of Neptune as her rotation brings her close.

She almost looks like the moon from here.

I think I am growing to like the moon. Even as the heat from the sun the ATMO-shield is generating is absent, I still can feel her soft eyes on me. Today, I am just glad there are no stars.

The stars… are always off putting. You grow up with a certain set of constellations and when you get further out, they always seem like ominous strangers. It's hard to get used to.

Just like doors.

I am not surprised when I find Pert jogging next to me.

We speak little; we rarely do. I wonder sometimes if there was a time we did, but I know the answer. There was a time *I* did, but he was never much one for conversation. Pert. Brother in honor and war - the only way it can really count for a GEM.

What I do not see until it's too late is the look on his face. It's new, something I haven't seen since before - well, ever, in my memory. It's something I would almost consider a smirk as he points to my other side.

A red blur jogs on my other side and it takes a moment for me to cool my pace down to get a good look. She's tall, lean, larger than life in every other way. She has hair that streaks up into the sky in shades of red ranging from neon to blood and an outfit that tells you she will live up to every promise of her name. Blunt Force Trauma.

Pert's smile spreads to me.

She smiles back.

She does not have the same wide, unnatural grin as her brother. No, it's far more complete. It's small but wide, graceful, but unfathomably comfortable. I jog in place for a moment and hold out my arms.

She sticks out her tongue and gives me a smug look before bolting off ahead of me. I glance at Pert, who waves me forward.

I run after her, pushing my weak muscles to their limit.

We make it two and a half blocks before she turns down an alleyway. I almost stumble as she comes to a complete stop and shoves a stick of honey, chocolate, and oats into my mouth. My mind doesn't really remember what to call them, but my stomach calls it gold. She doesn't give me much of a chance to react before I am lifted in a hug.

She is almost half-a-head taller than me, so it's easy for her.

"Hey, little girl."

She squeezes a little tighter; it is something between happiness and warning. My back makes a few noises I haven't heard in a long time, and the ache in the center of my spine forgets to exist for a few moments.

"Oh, that's nice." I laugh.

She opens her mouth to say something else, but doesn't. She was never much for talking, either.

"You made it here?" I ask. "I thought we lost you."

She nods a few times and shrugs. Then she flicks me in the forehead. I'm not sure how to interpret, but it doesn't matter. I think it is permission to leave, so I make up for lost time by adding a little extra speed to my jog.

I get home with only a minute and a half to spare.

I knock and wait.

When I get home, I see Josh has removed our bedroom door and I lose that last minute to the beating in my chest.

5:30 am.

100 sit-ups.

100 pull ups.

100 squats.

100 push-ups.

He's staring at me over the edge of the bed when I get to 40. I stop counting out loud as he traces his fingers across my shoulders. He gives me a smile and rolls out of sight. I continue counting out loud.

He counts with me.

I don't know if it annoys me or if I love it, I just know I need to get to 100.

"100."

I hop to my feet, my body appeased. I hold out my arms and pull him into a hug. He holds me there for an unknowable amount of time.

"Breakfast," he smiles and starts towards the kitchen. It's gray, with hints of brown and red. That seems to be his color scheme of choice. Rustic yet modern. I take in the room like I am seeing it for the first time. There are stools, a couch, blankets. The place feels like it's been well lived in, with pictures on the wall. The faces are hard to see and the frames don't match. It feels foreign to be in a place so decorated, and I feel like I should leave.

I don't *belong* in a place like this.

Still, I try to push through it. I make my way into the kitchen and I pull a pan out of a drawer and flip it over in my hands. I offer to make - "No omelets." - I put the pan back.

"I'm honestly not even sure what an omelet is right now."

"It's 6!" The floors creak with the changing of weight as someone bursts through the door. "It's 6 — we're here! He done?"

James Morrison comes through the door and for a moment, I know I have lost my goddamn mind.

There's no mistaking him; he's like Trauma in that way where you *know* her if you see her. Jimmy is wide as the ocean and blacker than anything in space. He wears all white, but the clothes never quite fit right on his gigantic frame.

The only thing he ever has trouble finding is gloves that fit his dainty doctor's hands. His hair is long and in twisted sections, and he approaches me with his arms spread wide.

He hugs me.

I hug back as take him in. His smell, his strength, his softness.

"Jimmy?" I croak, but I don't know if he hears me.

A parade of people follow, including Soren, Snow, Parrot, and Nash. There are others in the group that I don't recognize. Some I do, most I don't, because I feel reality leave me.

Disassociation, my mind calls it.

Ground yourself.

Who are you?

Jason Pechard, but I prefer Stargon. Stargon. Stargon. Hah. Hah. Ooo-ahh. That's me.

Where are you?

Sahaqiel.

Space station and GEM refuge far off the Neptune Outlay. A little piece of heaven far away from the prying eyes of Earth gov. Our piece. Josh and you. You and the rebellion.

You.

Stargon.

Josh touches my shoulder.

"Would it help to make omelets?"

"No." I kiss his forehead. It's so warm I worry he's going to burn away. The bruises on my body tell me otherwise.

I think this feeling is satisfied?

Yeah. Satisfied. It's an uneasy feeling.

James takes a few minutes to approach me, and when he does, it's with caution.

"Jason. Star?"

"Hey, Jimmy."

The embrace, again, is instant. It rivals Trauma's, but it's wider, burlier. It's less like I'm going to be compacted into dust and more like I am being pulled across steely pecs. Jimmy. My brother in blood, loss, and saved lives. The only way a GEM can be a brother to a WIP.

"You are dead," I whisper.

"Oh," Jimmy laughs in that deep belly laugh way that makes me smile out of instinct. "No."

I furrow my brow together, trying to tell him that explanation is not enough for me, but it's too late. He looks me over.

He tries his best not to evaluate, but he touches my wrist, the bruises on it, the shackle that the Cession hangs there. I pull it back instinctively, and his gaze carries a question. I can only roll my eyes and glance at Josh. There isn't disapproval written on his face, but there is the note of a future lecture.

"You are dead," I say again.

"So are you," he says back. "Except maybe one of us went into hiding with the mafia's help while the other established a safe place for us, hm?"

"Hiding," I say the word out loud, and the image of a house fire comes to my mind. So do a few other things. Trading drugs, extracting information the *fun* way, and a clinic full of GEMs. Partial breeds too.

They were so *young*.

He squeezes my shoulders and turns.

"What's for breakfast, Josh? Need any help?" Jimmy's accent is thinner than it was when we were on Earth. One tenth less Jamaican probably makes it easier to understand for all the Russian and Chinese speaking spacers on the station.

Josh responds, but my mind is too full of new things to hear.

I watch breakfast unfold.

I try to remain present for most of it. I succeed to a degree. When I come back, I am counting. It's something I do now when I am no longer present. It lets me know how long I'm gone for. I wonder how long I've had this habit and if it's new or if it's just exploded since...

One.

Two.

Three.

...

Forty-five.

I can barely eat.

They're both disappointed, but Soren more than makes up for what I miss. He really is a ravenous beast. They don't lecture or bring it up, but they pull me aside afterward. They talk about me for a moment like I'm not there.

"How'd this morning go?" Jimmy asks Josh.

"Fine. The routine through and through. Run was a little rushed but I gather Trauma couldn't wait. "

"I saw Big T pick him up on the way. She's a hard one to hold back when she wants something."

They laugh.

"Good." they both turn to me now. "Good."

"I had to remove the doors. I think doors are going to be a problem." Josh sighs and gives me a smile.

"So," James stands up, "I want to examine you. Give you a few supplements, but more than anything, I want to look into your psyche. I want to see what we can do about bringing you into the here and now."

"Take up psychology while I was gone, old man?" I tease the best I can. It's a pale shade of paint over an obvious flaw. "No, you wouldn't be so careful with your words if that were the case."

"I was thinking of something specific." Jimmy hesitates and looks at Josh. I can see the disapproval written all over my husband's face. "I was thinking we would let YOU talk to you."

I stare at them dumbly for a moment. I'm not the only one, as Soren even pauses for a laugh.

"No offense, man, but I think that's the last thing he needs," Soren says with a half-full mouth. "He's almost as gone as Parrot."

My eyebrow quirks, but no other part of me is surprised or interested in what's going on. My body is just happy to be fed.

Is this how it feels to be safe?

It's strange. The absence of anxiety makes me feel anxious.

"Talking to myself would be the least strange thing about this whole week," I find myself speaking thoughts out loud. "I imagine you want to use La Blanc?"

"Good to see it's not all gone," Jimmy nods to Josh. "Yes, but under strict supervision. Monitors, with another person, CERTs, the works."

I nod idly.

James and Josh come to a silent agreement, but don't rush me as I lose myself staring at a wall. Sometimes the words that come out aren't associated with images anymore, just clips of experiences that make little sense together.

La Blanc seems to bring to mind so many.

Sex, music, dancing, the Eiffel Tower and a snowstorm with warm tea and more sex.

"Why?" I suppose it's a more innocent question than either were expecting.

"No offense to you and your friends, but you have literally come straight out of hell from, well, another layer of hell." Jimmy hesitates to name the place. I can feel he means Europa. "We don't know what happened to you all. We don't know what path to take, and the last thing I want is for you to relapse, or worse, break."

"You think I'll have a psychotic episode on the ship? Full of food and surrounded by people I love?" I ask breathlessly. My heart rate skyrockets. I pull out all the ways to exit the room, the building, the ship from schematics I've been drawing in my mind.

It's Soren that grabs my wrist now, putting a boiled egg in it and pointing at it until I crack it.

"No." Jimmy's words are calm, purposeful. "I just don't know what we're going to find in there, Stargon. I'm not sure what will come out, and Jason. We are dangerous men."

I stand up, a hundred emotions swarming through me. It takes a few breaths to engage again.

I sit down.

I stand.

I pace.

I can feel their emotions through my skull, through the walls. A hundred eyes - no. Not possible.

Grounding.

Focus on the now.

Who are you?

Stargon.

Where are you?

Home.

"Why?"

This time it is not an innocent question, it is a direct, angry accusation. James is happy to take the brunt of my anger, but Josh shies away. James moves closer to me, more imposing, his frame twice mine, which is no small feat of nature. If the GEM program were to run again, they would steal his DNA while he slept to make something from such a perfect being.

He hisses out one quick breath before saying: "That song."

"Song?"

"The song you're singing. Right now, do you even know what song that is?"

"Song?" I search my mind, my mouth, my darkness, but nothing comes to it, just emptiness. "No. I don't know. What song?"

"You started singing it last night, too. Then some of the others started panicking. You called it the diameter of you. Now, again, you started singing it and I can feel something terrifying in that song." Josh's voice is timid but not intimidated. "It's the same song we get from Europa when we send scout ships. Like Tidings broadcast, but... worse."

"We're worried about what you might have seen down there, who you might have met, who you might have become." James puts his hands on my shoulders. "If we go into La Blanc with you now, we can find some answers to these questions. We can find out what happened, and then we can start helping you."

I sit back down.

Worn.

My body finally feels worn.

All I want to do is sleep and maybe eat again.

"Water."

Josh is halfway back with a glass before Jimmy gets to me. "It is good to have you back, Jason."

"He doesn't want me to do it." I look at Josh and gratefully swallow most of what he gives me in one go. "Why do you?"

"I know better." Jimmy rubs his hands together. "You're obsessive. I'd rather go with you than have to clean up after you've gone and done it alone. Truth is, Stargon, your sync is mighty high. The kind of crazy you are pushing out right now is making other GEMs… wrong. We want to at least tame that."

Josh puts his hand on my shoulder, leaning his head against the top of mine with a heavy, heavy sigh.

"Not asking the right questions is how I lost you last time. I'm not letting it happen again."

Terms of Light

30

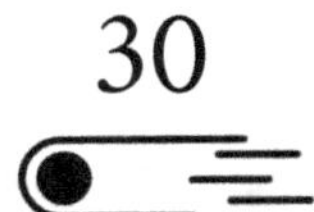

"Therapy."

The word falls out of me naturally as Josh squeezes my hand a little tighter. The room, La Blanc, once sterile white and unmeasurably small, changes. Where there were no shadows or even corners before, now there is a back alleyway and a street that stretches out endlessly beside it.

A single light post, faintly blue, shimmers to life and even though Josh's hand is still in mine, he feels far, far away. I look at him, confused, but he is not there. A pair of invisible fingers turn my face back to the streetlight.

"I know this place."

My voice seems to echo in the dim light. Like I am in a large city, but it's dead. Empty.

It feels too much like I do inside.

"You should."

I turn to see a figure flicker into existence in the lamplight.

I stare into violent eyes.

They are blue, small, sharp, with furrowed brows. His hair is dull, shabby, but familiar, and that is when I realize they are *my* eyes.

The face is different from that in the mirror. It's well shaved with the same sleepless circles, but more full of life. Calloused hands look official, warm, ready to hold on to something worth holding. Again, fingers turn my face, but this time it is up to meet those eyes.

The image flickers again, just for a moment, as if he is a projection and yet, when he stands in front of me, he is *so very real*. I feel like the imposter in front of him.

"You can't be serious."

The violent eyes turn and talk to the space where Josh stands. Josh appears, like he has been brought back from distant shores by waves that threaten to remove him at any moment. This new me's voice is deep, lower than I normally speak, and more formal.

And he hates me.

"We can't do this."

In my mind, I call him the name that Captain Oswald used. Pechard.

I touch my dog tags and rub them between my fingers absently. When did my empty necklace turn to dog tags?

Josh addresses Pechard with a small nod.

"I know, but -"

"No buts. We can't." Pechard turns and looks behind him with annoyance. "Kill the program before it's too late."

"Oh, oh, oh, oh, oh, it's too late. It's FAR too late."

Another person emerges from the darkness. It's rough around the edges. Hair sits uneven across his scalp, cut awkwardly by a straight blade as he twitches it open and closed in his hand. He is draped in leather that's filled with holes and denim that is the same. He tucks away his razor, fiddling with it out of sight. I can feel the blade deep in his pocket, whittling away at fingernails. It's like they're my own hands.

His eyes are like chaos and fire all at once. When he looks at me, the room flashes with a bright light, and the sky - just for a moment - turns green.

I swallow. I try to count, but my brain cannot get past one.

One.

One.

My mind calls this one Dutch. Pechard is quick to address Dutch with firm eye contact, but never a hand - no, he knows he'd never catch us. We're too fast for real authority to take a hold of.

I smirk, I frown, I'm... confused.

"What the hell is this?" I ask. "Is this me?"

Dutch laughs.

"No. It's not. I am, but this asshole -"

"Yes. We are all you," Pechard interrupts.

"You're not in charge here, bitch." Dutch's voice is soft and far more frightening than the deep commanding voice of Pechard. Dutch steps closer to me, almost too close, but I'm not uncomfortable. I can smell his leather, taste his eyes as they roam over every part of me. "Let's look at you, sweetheart. Hm. Too thin, too pale. Shit. It looks like him, but I don't know who this is."

"S——."

The voice is broken, fractured, and the static is not just my mind. It sounds like that to everyone. It comes from the darkness of the infinite street, but no one emerges. Josh sighs in relief.

"Please."

Of the three, this one is steady with the shake of someone who isn't sure what they want to say. It comes from the shadows and repeats once more.

"Please."

"Therapy." I say the word again, and it draws all of their attentions. A command word? Maybe just one that makes all three of these men - of me - uncomfortable. "Is that what this is?"

"What *this* is?" Dutch mocks me and teases the blade against his hair. "We're so fucked."

Pechard turns his gaze to Josh.

"You need to end this. You can't feel it, but we can. We know what's behind the wall he keeps up."

"Okay." Josh takes a step forward. "Well, this wall has... cracks. Things keep getting out, and we're worried about what could happen."

"Shhh." The darkness whispers again. "Josh, it's all gone. You have to rebuild it."

"Rebuild it?" Josh looks at me. "Rebuild... what?"

The quiet one sighs and reluctantly takes shape, but he is hard to see through the density of fog. It looks like the fog from our comet, from the sun, but it can't be. It's almost like the figure has been corrupted, broken.

What does form is half gone. I can see soft hands, a wedding ring, and a bracelet made by a child out of string around a wrist. His hair is long and tied back. His eyes do not glow with *any* emotion. He doesn't seem well, honestly he doesn't *seem* at all, he Just... *is*.

Just's words seem to falter as he moves his hands to talk.

"These are Slates," Just explains after several false starts. "They're programs created by this room that emulate a real person. You.

You used to program them with real-time data from the ship, the station, from what you knew or heard. You would input data from c--era feeds or from events you wit--ssed and build them, but you never built yo--self. You just input data and let the program sort it out, syncing with the room to let it imprint on you. So you never kn-- what you were going to get. These three, *we* three, are y-u and not you. They are y---self, and not so self therapy."

By the time he's finished talking, he seems more real. More 3-dimensional even as he sits heavily in the darkness. Incomplete. I touch his throat, and I can feel the strain in his voice.

It makes me worry.

"So, why are you broken?" I ask.

Dutch chuckles, and Pechard shakes his head.

Just stares at me.

"Re-compile, reset us, and you will find us the way you left."

"Re-compile. Reset?" I look at Josh, who just shrugs. "Then why aren't you that way now?"

Pechard motions to me, Dutch turns away. Just flickers.

"We are filled with the data we have picked up from others, and now, from you," Just whispers.

"Broken mirror, for a broken man, but fuck." Dutch clicks his tongue three times. "You're pretty broken there, sweets."

"Enough." Pechard folds his arms. "Leave."

"He's right. You should leave. Engaging now… we will bury you." Just fades in and out as he does. "We will bury you in stress and pain. We have nothing good to offer. Josh, there is a hollow man here. It won't ever be what it was."

I stare at the broken piece of… myself.

It's so familiar it hurts.

I'm not scared of the fragment I see before me, no in fact, it's better this way. My eyes fill with tears - oh, and I am so sick of tears - and I push them away to make room.

"I used to call you Jason," I say it aloud as Just cracks his neck in response. He turns to look at me, his skin is pale and strange, but now his eyes sparkle with that same bright blue.

I touch the slate's grayed out skin. It's cold, no real sensory return, and yet this feels too real not to be.

"I called you Jason. The therapist, the lover, the masochist, the one steeped in sorrow. You bear all the pains of the outside."

Silence answers.

They three take one full step away from me, Pechard looking away now, not to Josh - just away, in contemplation.

"Pechard, my strength, my will, my unending need to move forward, my will to live, my... love."

Josh smiles. "Yeah."

I squint at Dutch, and he folds his arms in irritation. "Who the fuck are you?"

"Dutch," we say together.

He rolls his eyes. "The chaos. All that shit you have inside that's screaming to get out. The things you love that aren't allowed, the hate, the blood, the passion."

"Everything I keep inside." I say with him.

He spits at my feet and flips me off.

"Fuck off, man. Don't put your burdens on me."

I turn to Josh.

"I have to admit, if the sex weren't as good as it is, I think I would have left me."

Josh coughs to cover his laugh and shakes his head.

"No, that's... this is... the extremes."

"I dunno." I look at all three of them. "I kinda like'm. I get'm."

I fold my arms as Pechard does.

Just - no, Jason, does not turn back to me, but continues to fade in and out.

"So, the part of me that is broken is love?"

"It's a fuckin' METAPHOR!" Dutch throws his hands in the air. "If it were that easy, a kissy kiss from Josh would have healed us all up. Sutured all the wounds."

"You're not ready for what's broken," Pechard growls the words. "And pressing it will make it worse."

"It can't really be worse." Josh's words stick in his throat.

"Europa." Pechard says the word and the world flashes in bright white with a hue of green.

I hold my hands over my ears and crouch. When the world does not fall apart, I stand again and look at Josh. He takes my hand and his lips twitch a few times in a question he never asks.

"Yes," I answer before Josh can. "We want to know what happened on Europa."

"Death," Dutch shrugs casually. "Ask me what happened after."

"After?" Josh asks this time because I can feel it like a swarm of hate in the back of my head. "After Europa… what…?" he takes my hand firmly, pressing his palm into mine as he asks.

"What happened after Europa?"

The room turns dark.

It's so dark.

It's so, so dark.

I can hear weeping.

No, maybe I am weeping?

I feel like I'm floating, but I know I'm standing. Am I? Am I? Where am I?

"Shhh…" my voice whispers from the darkness.

There is light.

It is blinding.

Oh, it is blinding. A wicked smile, no, a pleasant one. They hold above me a glass of water. A question asked that I can't hear, my ears… my ears don't work so well after the explosions. All those ships falling from the sky. I lean closer; I want to ask, but my mouth doesn't work. The electricity has numbed it.

Electricity?

Light?

It's hard to see. It's hard to remember. It's so… far away.

It's *so* dark.

"The answer, Joshua, is that we don't know." Pechard's voice is powerful from beyond the darkness. "We can't see into his head.

We can only see what is given to us, but we can tell you *after* matters more."

"More," the fragment of Jason whispers.

"Hah. Hah. Ooo-ahh." I tap my ring against the cool bars as I wait for the sun.

There is silence. I tap for days.

One.

Two.

…

One-hundred.

…

One-thousand.

…

One-million.

"Hah…hah…ooo," the darkness whispers back. It is breathy, musical. A chant. A heartbeat. Our song.

"The GEMs." I look to my right. Josh is still planted there, and he is a ray of brilliance that my eyes can't handle. He is there until the darkness swallows him. He is there until I turn to stone. Until…

Until…

The darkness becomes… comfortable.

I lean into his grip.

"I was the first. They wanted me to be the only. I was alone in that prison. Alone in here for so long. They thought if they put me in there, that it'd be over, but there were more. So many more that the war could not keep hidden.

They put us in the darkness. They took away our food, our light, our space, but not the gentle sound of breathing. The count of our heartbeats. The songs we would sing to each other to sleep. Words didn't have to make sense. At first, it was anything I could remember. Some of the others would join in. It was Sky Ways Break, Frank Sinatra, Power Carnivore, Mozart - anything our brains could leak through bars, but eventually it just became one… just one… just…"

The darkness is filled with music.

There is a brightness in the distance. The comet is passing the sun in a way that it hits something other than the solar generators. There are a series of vents at the top that filter our air. The flash of light is brief, but it becomes something we look forward to. The sun prickles my skin, fills my lungs with fresh air as the pressure releases and recycles.

We count our terms in light now. Some are mad with the desire to see the sun again. To see anything but this darkness. They wait and they climb. And they fall.

Another bright body plummets into the pit in flames. No one will know who it is. Guard. Friend. Foe. We have all forgotten our names, but we mourn the only way we know how.

Hah. Hah. Ooo-ahh.

They belong to the Whispers now.

"Oh, for the sweet shadow of death. Oh, for the call to arms. To walk among the others. To wake to daylight's call," I whisper the words.

In the surrounding chambers, I hear others call out the word we both long for and fear the most.

"Daylight."

"Daylight," I whisper back.

I glance at Josh. I suddenly feel shame that stabs me like a knife. It burrows deep into my chest, into my heart, and into the back of my brain.

I didn't want him to see this. He knows me, the me that is here in front of us. The soldier, the lover, the storm, but not this. Not the Stone, the dust, the shambles of a man that was.

That was.

That… *was.*

"This is all there is now, isn't it?" I feel tears fall down my face in shame, in fear, in every other feeling I don't have words for now - maybe I never did.

I wasn't meant to have them. I'm just a fucking GEM. Just a construct of perfection for the Humans to play with.

How could I ever be anything other than…?

Jason steps closer now.

In the shadows of my prison, he doesn't look broken. He is one of the stones now. He is thin, outlined by the faintest light from the artificial hope above. His eyes are a promise to bring a fire into the world.

"We have to go back." we say it in unison.

Josh pulls back a little, not letting go of my hand, just letting me experience… me. My mind. Myself. I study Jason, even though he feels incomplete, he isn't. He's familiar. He's… stone.

"I want to talk to the others." My mind grabs hold of something. The room becomes brighter, lighter, more like V'ger and her dull walls and ambient light.

I glance at Josh and with a gracious smile, release him from his protective duty. He is hesitant, but respectful enough to let go.

"James." I call out, knowing he can hear me. "I don't know the answers to what happened, but I know what I want to do now."

Pechard smiles in the background, folding his arms as he glances at Dutch. The chaotic, younger version of myself just tosses up his hands and grunts.

"About fuckin' time."

Josh's eyes are wet with tears. I can feel echoes of fear, happiness, and sadness all at once.

I can only kiss away the first set before James takes me to see the others.

31

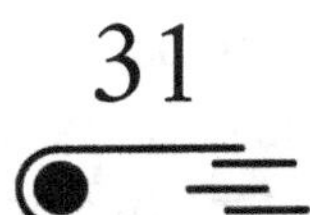

Sleep hits at me like a runaway truck.

I sleep without thoughts, without dreams.

I feel a body beside me on and off, and when I finally wake up, I am hot and weak and ready to move. Still, it's like there is something new inside of me, something that is as much ashamed as it is repaired. A wound reopened and cleaned.

Now the part I am not good at.

Healing.

When I finally get out of bed, I shower.

I spend every moment in the shower drenched in dread. I don't want to see how Josh looks at me. I don't want to know if my brain was out causing others trauma while I slept.

So, I wash slowly.

Eventually, the timer ends and I dry off. I don't bother with the routine. I do not shave; I do nothing. I wear what I find on the floor except that I open Josh's drawers, and take one of his shirts and put it over the rest of what I wear.

There is still no door on our bedroom. It's stuck in 'open' and sealed with metal. I trace it and when I poke my head out of the room, I see all the rest of them are gone too - well, except the bathrooms.

Still, I wait.

I hear Josh moving around, maybe making food, maybe cleaning up. I can't tell. I want to know, and I don't. Eventually, I close my eyes and take a step forward. I do not know why this is harder than running from the sun on the back of a comet.

I do not know why this is harder than staying alive.

There's a small itch at the back of my head that says it would have been better for Josh if we had died.

Then I see his eyes. They are tired and sad, but when they see me, they are bright. He doesn't approach me, or do much of anything. He sets down what he was doing, leans on his elbows and stares with a soft smile.

I think maybe I know that smile, but the haze of sleep and fear pushes true thoughts far away from me.

"Good morning," he says. "Well, evening. Glad to see you up."

"I'm sorry."

"Stargon." He takes a step around the counter and comes to me. I squeeze my eyes shut, dreading the touch I know is inevitable. When it doesn't come, I open my eyes, and he is sitting on the couch, patting a space near him.

I sit, but not directly next to him, near him.

"Stargon, I know that you won't really hear me when I say this, but you have nothing to be sorry for. You have nothing to be ashamed of, and, most importantly, I still love you. All of you." He takes a breath and clears his throat. He makes a kind of gentle, sad laugh before looking at me again. "Whatever that is now, and will be again. I didn't build us a home together to turn away when the world got ugly - when it got hard."

"It doesn't…" I don't have words. It's not fair to him, not right. I love him and I offer him nothing. He takes care of me. He must be so tired. So angry. So done with all of this.

"Why don't you go for a walk?" he says with a smile that I can't help but mirror. "Clean the slate. Get out of your own head for a while. See what you helped us build."

So, I do.

He, of course, insists I get something cleaner to wear first, and I agree.

I lace up my boots. Grab the next pair of socks, the next pair of sweats, but I keep his shirt. He touches it before I leave and smiles.

I make my way towards the center of the space station. The upper half invokes memories of an earth city with its skyscrapers and parks, but I have no memory of the underbelly, except for the docking area.

I find a ramp that takes me down, and I am reminded that space can work in three dimensions. As I get below, the world comes to life in a strange way. The ceilings and walls are filled with working GEMs, gardens, and conversation. I do my best to remain in the background and take it in, and it is easy.

Unlike the coffee shop upstairs, when I watch the world? It's more real to my mind. A strange feeling, since I was never raised on a colony, but something about it is… right.

I hear Sparkle. The sound of it is hard to follow, which doesn't surprise me. It's a GEM language made up of words from across the Solar System smashed together to create the shortest version of words. Efficient communication - and hard to follow. I am very behind as I try to decipher a few words I have no context for.

Goash. Clab. Fritz.

The words tickle parts of my brain that want to problem solve, so I sit, and I absorb. I take it in. The smell of air that is fresh in my lungs, the way the artificial light is dim enough to not burn on my skin.

I hear laughter and a bright spark of red catches my attention. When I look over, I see Soren wrestling with a few younger kids. He has a ball and fakes falling to the ground as they pile on top of him.

He is laughing, and something about it makes my chest ache.

I stand up and move on, making my way through laundry lines and various workstations. People hand out supplies and have polite arguments over services make me smile. Memories of another float back to me, smelling of mildew and sea water.

I walk until I find myself some place less full, but louder. The heartbeat of the ship is close to my ears, and I can feel it under my feet.

One-two-three.

One-two-three.

I am surprised when I am pulled, called, or just unlucky enough to run across Nash as he stares up at something broken and beaten. It is not our Comet Chaser, but it is bigger: meaner looking.

I stand next to him. We say nothing for a long time until he finally opens a small bag of potato chips and offers me one. I gingerly remove one from the bag and he is satisfied with that, starting in on the rest.

"Cargo runner," he eventually says in his gruff tone, as if that says it all. I just nod in response. He takes me inside and tells me what's wrong with it. It's all words that I know, but don't hold any relevance to me.

Calibration for the foosywasy is all glibglorpbed, and it needs some wheewanzas, or whatever. We walk the ship, it's large, tall and wide. Good for carrying a lot of things, but in need of some serious love. Still, he sounds different.

He sounds *hopeful*.

Then he stops as we exit again. After another round of staring up at the large ship, he finally addresses me.

"I missed this. I think I was missing this," he says with a somber awe.

After a moment of ignoring as his eyes burn into my side, I turn. His fists are clenched tightly and his mouth is pursed into an expression I don't recognize.

I think, perhaps, he is lonely?

"I have this dream," he starts. "I have this dream where I am in a chair. There are lots of these smiling people around me. They all have knives and blades that curve and glitter. Sometimes they pull out my teeth. That hurts, but I don't care about that one. Other times, they cut my hair. It's not the same smiles, not the same people. It smells like ice and beer."

He reaches up and touches his proud and round poof of hair, and then his hands fall to his side.

"I hate it. I hate it more than anything."

"Nash does not like bladed edges," I recite.

"I wish I could recall why."

He crouches now, tracing his finger in familiar circle patterns along the floor. I think it is one of his comfort patterns and recall it in the dust and ash of a cell we would sometimes share.

I crouch down next to him.

"The brain breaks in predictable, uncomfortable ways. Trauma hides from us all that we cannot stand and all that we love in the same instant. It is indiscriminate, cruel and the only reason a lot of us survive to the next day." I reach up and tug on his beard. "I'll get you a laser beard trimmer, and maybe Soren will complement your nice hair with this out of the way."

"Excuse you?" he says gruffly, standing. "I don't need a fucking trim."

I smirk and shrug, recalling in some distant way that the best way to deal with Nash is to let him figure it out.

"Okay."

"Unless you have one." He frowns. "Then I will try it."

"Hah. Hah. Ooo," I say, and he pushes at my chest angrily. There is no genuine force behind it, but when he stops, his hands are still on my chest. I see a few things flicker across his face before he ends up with a sneer.

Disgusted, he turns away from me.

"Fuck off, already. I have work to do."

"Always more at home with the machines than the men."

"They don't betray me." He lifts his arms towards the cargo runner. "They tell me what they need and when they're all better, I know what to expect."

"He is pretty cute," I offer without context. "You should talk to him."

"Fuck off!" He pushes me for real this time, and I am more than happy to comply.

32

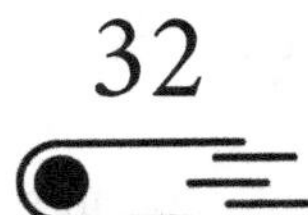

Snow is the most hesitant to put the CERTs on her head as we stand in that impossibly white room, but eventually she does it.

The CERTs (or Cerebral Emission and Rebuffering Technology) are strange little devices that Josh and Jimmy say will help our brains connect with each other. I find it hard to believe we need the help.

They also added it will stop us from spilling our minds into each other any further, preventing sync shock. That sounded much more like what we needed.

"I don't understand why we're doing this." Snow folds her arms as she studies the room. I put my hand on her shoulders and her eyes widen as they meet mine. Some part of me wonders if she sees the stern gaze of Pechard's eyes?

Is that the me they've been missing?

I wonder how much I miss it.

I wonder how much I hate it.

"I want to find out what happened to us." I say it calmly, even as my hands shake. "I want to know what happened on Europa."

The word still tastes like lava on my tongue.

No one says anything. When I look them over, they are all faded echoes of themselves. All except Soren. I nod to him. He is one of us now.

Talking to Jimmy, he said things like this were easier if we had a focus. Something that could bring our broken pieces together. So, I brought the only glue we all shared. Soren.

I didn't tell him that.

It feels wrong, but for the right reasons.

"Well, this place is very clinical," Soren scoffs. "Greeeeat. Very excited for whatever this is."

I put my hand on his shoulder and he jumps, his bravado briefly gone. He rolls his arms up into his armpits like he's cold.

I lean closer.

"Don't worry, it will be less white in a minute."

"This is Josh." The overhead com calls softly, "Remember, Jimmy and I are right here. We're going to try to keep you grounded and hopefully put things to an end if they go too far."

"What is this place?" Nash asks, irritated, as he makes his way closer to Soren. His edginess is worn on his tongue. "It's weird. No shadows. I do not like this."

"The White Room," Jimmy's voice booms from above us.

I am the only one that doesn't look up.

I can't look up; it's like I'm staring into the infinite when I do. The white holds no shadows, and it makes me feel like, in here, we don't exist. However, here also feels like it is one of the few places I *do* exist.

I stroke my own hands, trying to ease the anxiety.

"It's a place where our minds can be connected. Reminded," I state.

The others shift, slightly uncomfortable as the room dims. Soren backs against me as the sky above us changes to the reds and whites of Jupiter's large, lingering storms. The room is gone and in its place is the vast open arena of a far away place.

We all know it well, except Soren.

This is the docks of Europa.

The CERTs on their bodies spark to life. Pert's are on his neck, Nash's in his hair, Snow along her temples and Soren's are on his coat. After a minute of watching him try to eat them, I put Parrot's on his ears, and he frowns in a way that is almost cute.

After a minute, our minds connect. The others don't seem to notice, even though I can't ignore my own CERTs buzzing in the back of my head. I briefly wonder if I should have put them on my nipples to make this more fun.

The air chills.

I know this is all in our minds, but I can see my breath in clouds before me. I suppress the images from other's minds as we linger on Europa. Some are of the darkness, others of the wall of fog on the comet's surface.

The others shiver as the image settles, muttering to themselves. I am surprised when a gentle wave of energy pours over me. I don't think it's from the room as the thing that is me changes. Like a projection of myself onto myself. My waist is thicker, my arms no longer weak, and I wear a leather jacket trimmed to my rib cage and leather pants.

The most devastating thing I wear, though, is my confidence.

Soren takes a step back, holding his stomach subconsciously as he does.

"Whoa. Wait. Where are we?"

Snow steps forward. She is draped in armor that would go well in a painting. It suits her style, her power. It is all deep browns and grays with a subtle hint of orange that begs the eye to look at it.

She wears confidence like a scarf and surveys the crowd that walks by us. They are faceless, faded shadows.

She steps closer to me.

"I remember this."

"This is a place where our memories can come to life. They can feel real, we can touch them, but they are *not* real." I explain. I cannot tell if anyone hears, as they are absorbed into the moment, the memory we stand in.

"Europa," Parrot whispers, standing tall at his full height. His shoulders unfurl from their arthritic stance and goggles are now tightly attached to his face, along with a deep frown. "So many people, so many undocumented GEMs."

"These docks," Nash mutters. "Don't make me come back here. I don't want to see them do this again. I don't need to see more dead brothers!"

Pert changes little. His skin is a brighter white, his stance brisk as he closes the gap between us and stands close enough to me that he is both shadow and protector. Soren shivers in the cold and whatever energy changes us, summons him a winter jacket with a bright red scarf.

I turn away.

"You gotta change that," I order, motioning to his throat.

"Change?" He looks down. Shocked, he focuses on the scarf and it turns a soft green. He yelps, something between joy and surprise, as a smile covers his face.

"How did I? Wait. Did I do that with my powers? Wow! This is amazing."

The com above us crackles to life, the sound coming from the sky as Jimmy speaks.

"The environment you are experiencing is directly projected from your collective minds. It's leveraging the CERTs, and with all of you working together, it can get pretty elaborate."

Soren takes a moment to take in the scene around us. I put my hand on Soren's shoulder and push past him. The rest of them follow my lead. As we walk, we fall into a natural pattern. I am three steps ahead of everyone, even Pert, as we march.

We pass the docks and I can hear ships docking behind us, their ATMO-shield's evaporating into rainbows of color as their stratus-bubbles pop.

We make our way past the bars and the inner boil of the city. This is where all the WIPs stop to drink, relax, take it in, but I can see the hidden scuffs all around it.

Four GEMs sit among the refuse of the alleyways. Two are loading cargo too heavy for any single human to carry. One is sitting, staring forward, counting slowly to no one.

Starving.

Starving.

That hunger echoes in my gut - pieces of the room flash to Sunken Brooklyn. The streets, the rain, a safe, warm place underneath the bridge of the auto-ways even as the smell of mildew and sea water permeate the air - and I push it back.

Back on Europa, one GEM watches us pass. Her eyes are unfocused but Pert nods to her. They communicate with a non-verbal version of Sparkle.

She understands.

We make our way into the shadows of the back lots, past a scrap yard, past a docking disposal zone to a place where there is life so quiet, so fluent in its own Sparkle that it is a low hum of noise instead of speech. We slip under the streets through a well-hidden opening and find ourselves in a grand set of underground caverns.

Soren pants as he stumbles in. "This place… this place is enormous."

"This was our base of operations." I motion around but go no further. The thoughts that hang here are heavy.

It's cramped, damp, like the sun might go out at any moment, but the light from above is artificial and won't leave.

I'm not alone in the feeling. Even Snow, even Pert hesitate to want to go any further into this darkness. Not because of what lies ahead, but the fear of not being able to leave. To have to live this again, from the start.

The shimmer around me crackles.

I remove all the doors.

"What is this place?" Soren asks quietly.

"This is where we worked," I say.

Snow smiles. "Danced."

"Drank," Nash shrugs.

"Spoke." Pert adds.

"Died," Parrot mourns.

"Why?" Snow finally asks.

She finally addresses the itch that's been nagging at the back of her mind for hours. It's her hesitance that scares me more than her question.

"Why are we here, Jason?"

"To remember." I touch the walls of the tunnel. "To try to find ourselves."

"Not lost." Pert confirms boldly.

"Maybe we don't want to find it." Nash whispers. "Maybe we're fine with what we got."

"I need to find it." The scene dissolves away as we are pulled out. "We need this. We need to -"

I turn to Snow, who's now got a hand on her pistol. The world dims as emergency lights flash.

"Why the alarm?"

Now we stand in our base, the part that overlooks the docks from deep within the city. The world shakes. We hear Europa's thick ice crack.

The sky turns a shade of green we have never seen.

The alarm blares.

Warning.

In another place, another life, it would be a hurricane siren, but here it means *pray.*

"Volcanic activity?" Albatrossi asks.

"The alarm isn't seismic activity. We have incoming!" Snow shouts, and a dozen screens pop up with views from all over the colony. The docks. The sky. The ice.

I process them before the screens can fill with what my mind projects.

"This can't be right."

"Sir," Nash barks from behind. "We're getting heavy damage down at the docks. If this is a military raid, they are going to pulverize us unless we get people underground, now!"

"Understood. Pert!" I grab my brother's hand. "Coordinate the civilian effort. We have ships on the outskirts that can hold off a military attack and direct them into our brigade on IO. They need fifty minutes."

He salutes. Soren's figure fades into the wall as the scene plays out.

"Sir." Snow again brings up the screens and this time the room fades into a 360 display. Above, below, and beside, as if we are the eyes of Europa itself. "It's not a fleet, but a mass. Alien."

She points up; the room rotates, so we see it in front of us now. We both fold our arms, unsure what to say, what to do.

A silver orb.

Time stops, and the room dissolves into bright light.

"What's happening?" Josh whispers in my ear.

I touch the com, but my hands shake so violently it takes a moment.

"Daylight. DAYLIGHT! I- I mean... I don't... have the answers."

Pert looks to Snow, Snow to Nash, Nash to - "Parrot?"

We glance around the room, but he isn't there.

"I see him on the cameras. He went back to his room," Josh reassures. "I think it was too much for him."

"Too much." I touch where dog tags should dangle along my neck and wince when they are not there. "He was there, wasn't he? I can't remember."

"I don't know," Snow answers coldly.

Pert shrugs.

Nash takes Soren's hand and tugs him to the side of the room, where they whisper for a moment. I try not to focus on them. I try not to focus at all.

The light dims and as we stand, once again, in a blank white space, it is hard not to feel like we are reflections of it. Thin bodies, worn and tired, shake and blankly question their existence.

Snow pulls off her CERTs.

"I get it, Stargon. You need to know, you *want* to know, but maybe *we* don't." Her words are blue ice in the air.

"We need to-!" I plead.

"We don't!" she yells and I see the first tear I've ever seen roll down her face. "We don't *all* need this. We don't remember what happened for a reason. No one else is going to say it but we need to - to -"

She stops. I'm not sure why.

It's like my gaze chokes her words off and I tear something out of her and she is left breathless. The silence sneers around her lips and eats her words.

"On Europa." I motion around us. "What did we lose there, Snow?"

"Ourselves." She pushes past me. "Maybe we should stay lost."

"If we don't find us, then who will?" I ask.

She pauses as she opens the door. She tosses the CERTs on the ground.

"No one. We're already dead."

"If we fight here, maybe, just maybe, we can LIVE this time."

"Or we stay dead."

"We lived! As only GEMs can, because we fought well past when we were supposed to die. We live or we die, but we always fight," I finish. "Fight with me."

"Some days I hate you." If she could have slammed the automated door, she would have.

33

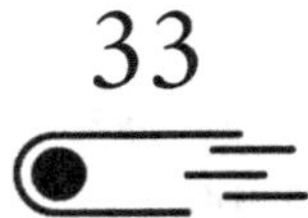

For days after the White Room I am nothing but a lump in Josh's life, and I hate how much it takes out of me to do these things. He asks me questions; we watch films, but I retain nothing. I am a ghost in my own body, pleading, waiting for life to return.

It does.

But slowly.

I learn I can cook. I learn how much I hate that what I cook is not perfect every time. Josh laughs when I tell him. It makes me frown, but I serve him what I think is mediocre vegetarian lasagna, and I eat it with him reluctantly.

"Sorry it sucks," I mutter.

"Some things don't change," he laughs. "You have not perfected lasagna yet, I promise. A man can only eat so much, though, before he's tired of it."

I don't understand his words, but when I look at the counter I see four other night's worth of lasagna pans waiting for a final cleaning. I grumble and eat faster.

Then I clean.

It starts with the pans, then the kitchen.

I open a pantry and find the plates in the wrong place, and I move them to the other side. Then the cups. The silverware, the pots, the pans, and I only stop when I sense Josh's eyes on me..

I set a few of the serving dishes down and worry if I've done something wrong. A small bit of panic slips into my mind and he just smiles that cute goddamn smile and looks at me. I hate that smile. I'd *kill* for that smile.

"I think you're ready." he says and heads to his office. This is one of the few doors he has not removed and, after I finish placing my last dishes, I follow. He leaves the door cracked so I know I can come in.

It still takes effort, care, and consideration, but I make it.

He shuffles through some drawers, his office a mess of papers and unvacuumed floors. I note where everything is and that it's not mine to clean, but overlay it with an older image of a spotless version of this room.

It satiates the desire.

"You're cleaning again." His words sound like they are searching for others. "That's good. It's your comfort activity. Some have math, some have sounds, or patterns, some need silence, but you were always cleaning. Spotless house - how I missed you!"

He laughs and pulls out a remote. He selects a few buttons on it; the music turns on and he grunts. Another button and on the far wall there sits a corkboard. Old school, cute. God, I love him.

I love him more when it pops open to reveal a set of printed papers and screens behind it. He shuffles over and summons me with his hands. I creep over, doing my best not to perch, crouch, or make myself smaller as I do. He opens the secret pin board and I can see a cascade of information.

It is hard to take in all at once, but I see a name over and over again, and it burns my eyes to look.

Europa.

Europa.

Europa.

"When you would go out on missions, you would always go for some unknown period, so, I don't know exactly how long you have been missing. Not to the day." Josh lets out a long breath as he touches a projected piece that says 'Disaster on Europa.'

"I sometimes wish I remembered what day you left, but it rarely mattered. At first, I was a little worried when you weren't home after a few weeks. Then it turned into a month. Then… the reports started coming in."

I look at the way he lays them out. Some are newer, older, they are not in the right order, at least not by the dates on the screens, but they are in chronological order. Some are articles, some blog posts, some are crazy timeline videos from white guys with too much time on their hands.

They are all pictures of me.

No, not me, but us. What happened to us? Some truth and some lie in all of them that lay before me.

I touch one.

"Thousands killed in Europa Slaughter," I read out loud. The words burn as I remember brutalized corpses in the streets. Below it is another one, an article, thoughtfully written, tame and long in its paragraphs. It says, "How They Lied to Everyone About Europa."

"The answer is, no one knows." Josh talks as I study pictures and screens. "I don't have answers for you, but what I can say is there are those that care enough to ask the question. To remember it another way than they have fed it to us."

"Another way…" I shiver. "They locked us away to die."

"And they will again if they find us, but the worlds are changing." Josh touches my hand. "Not in a big way. Not yet, but the cracks are showing. The planets can't survive without one another, and the belt has resources they need."

"I don't care about the planets," I say.

"Me either, but what I care about is this one." He points at a page that talks about Mars.

I read it aloud.

"Martians deport Ritz-hybrid children to Rift."

My blood runs cold.

"Look, I know you're not ready to fight again. You may never be, but there are others here that are. Others that want to know what we can do. We don't need an army, right now we need a way to… to…"

"Stop it from happening to them," I breathe. "To stop Soren from becoming like us."

"But I think that starts with this."

He taps a picture of a blocked out zone around Europa. It says quarantine zone. There are articles that seem to agree and disagree with each other referenced. One says radioactive disaster, another says superweapon, the last one says catastrophic airborne disease.

'Evolving situation' is what Josh has underlined.

I smile at a term I used to use in the military all the time.

"We fucked up."

"Yep."

"Then what's on Europa?" I ask. "What's really on Europa?"

"Does it matter?" Josh asks.

My brain spins a thousand tales as I study the board in front of me. I see small articles about scavenger ships that have been destroyed. About military blockades with dwindling numbers. A thousand different ways that they are screaming to me that HUDO doesn't know what happened either.

There is something there.

Something big.

And I wonder…

And I wonder…

And wonder…

And wonder…

Until -

…

28,850.

"Hey."

It's Soren. He's looking at the board too now with me. I don't know when he got there.

"Did you do this?"

"No. Josh." I motion to where he was - where he *isn't*.

I look at the time. I have been here for almost 8 hours. As I look at Soren, I rub my face and groan, and a thought occurs to me. I tilt my head towards him.

"Do you like lasagna?"

34

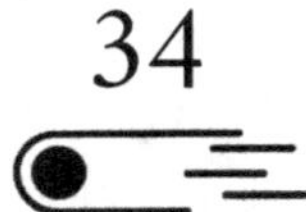

Soren and I lay on the hood of a car. The cool air wraps circles of ice on the edges of the windshield. He looks at me with a quirked eyebrow, and I point up to the stars. "The constellations aren't the same here, you know?"

"Well, it's more than halfway across the solar system. Technically they are, we're just at a different angle." Soren pulls his knees closer to his chest.

I smirk.

"You sure you want to do this again?" he asks. "I worry it's going to set you back."

I shrug.

"I need to know. I *want* to know, and it's easier."

"Easier?"

"Easier." I tap my head in the place where memory is best kept. I know that in there are the Shadows, Stones and Whispers of a comet that still spins so very far away from us. I know that right now, I struggle to remember I'm not still there. Sometimes in the darkness, I still wait for daylight. For doors.

To wake up.

"I need this."

Soren summons up a pair of rabbit fur gloves for his hands and rubs them together as he stares out at the landscape.

"You guys went through a lot of shit here, didn't you?"

"This is your memory, too." I motion around us, the old-growth trees, the road. Things that colonies don't have yet. Then I motion to the city below us. "What city is that?"

"Grand Rapids. It's a town in Michigan." he shrugs. "I guess a few buildings are from Chicago. I wasn't there long, but the city was so big, no matter where you were in it."

"Earth was lonely." I glance at him, the cold pressing at me from behind his thoughts. "Europa was cold, but not lonely."

The twinkling lights are too brilliant and too numerous to exist in the lightscape below, but it doesn't matter. This is what our minds have in common: a love for space and a love for secret places above the chaos of a city. It invokes in us the same pathway to happiness, the same... love.

It lets our minds connect over the CERTs' electronic transfer.

I pull my hand away from having unconsciously grabbed his, but he doesn't say anything.

The chill around us is a figment of our minds, but one he clings to. He tugs at a jacket that wasn't there moments ago. I smile, and with a thought, we are standing on a dock on the dark side of Europa.

"Have you ever been to Europa?"

"Nope." He slides off the car roof. "Not that I remember. Maybe? I don't know. If I did, it was in the hungry years. Your memory goes to hell when all you can think about is food - well. You know that."

Our stomachs ache in a familiar pattern.

"So much of my life is blank." He hates using the word as much as I hate admitting I understand it. Forgetting something is entirely different from knowing it's missing. Losing control, missing pieces of someone you may have been. I change the scene before us to the edge of the main docks.

We are stepping out of a small shuttle, one attached to a larger ship that floats in space. Above us are distant outlines of ships too large to dock up in the artificial atmosphere. They fall into orbital patterns that match Europa's rotation like a threatening storm.

My mind echoes, and buildings flicker to life and disappear as Europa in its many lifetimes dances around us. Pieces of my memory play out around me, inside me. I project the things I love - Pert is at my side, Snow at my other, Soren between them - and we walk with rebellion on our minds.

There are so many versions that overlap as we walk.

This place, this dock, represents a thousand terms of light we never thought to save anywhere. At my side, Snow talks to someone, guards a GEM who has been beaten, shoves someone, fights someone, and then yells over a mostly empty bottle in celebration.

Pert does the same, but his actions are muted, and instead of fighting, he kills. Images of me are almost always the same. Standing, watching, waiting.

Smiling. Enjoying.

It's almost unnerving.

Soren doesn't move and takes in what he can. His eyes meet the ground and stay there for a while. Then, when it slows down, we move together in silence through a town with no people.

He clears his throat several times before he speaks.

"I bet it was never this quiet."

"GEMs." I motion to the alleyways, the streets, "We made up 80% of the population, but almost all the noise you hear was from

WIPs." I put my hand on his shoulder. "Sorry, I shouldn't call them that."

"No." He shrugs. "I don't care."

"Stand down, soldier."

A man appears beside us, faceless and in HUDO whites with blue stripes on his arm. "I said stand down."

"You killed them." The words escape my mouth as swords form in my hand. I am ready to gut him, to spill his blood on the pavement next to that of the silent bodies.

"They rebelled. They paid the price. Now, get back to work, soldier."

"No."

"A mutiny here will only cause shipments to other colonies to cease. You will be responsible for the deaths of millions more. Starting with your own kind."

I stare at this face that I can't see, and an echo of me steps forward, out of me. Words cross my lips at the same time he speaks. "I can live with that, can you?"

"GEMs. You have no idea what you're doing, do you? No concept of family, of pride?"

I turn Soren's head to the side and pull us past this memory.

"You don't need to see this."

The argument continues behind us.

"How could you put so many people in danger?"

"It's easy. We learned from you. We learned it all, General. How to kill, how to give up, how to leave behind the unwanted. You don't care about the colonies, you want to make your bosses happy. To line your pockets and look away. To have us fight and die while you write news stories about it."

There's a gunshot.

We're done talking, I hear clearly in my mind.

We keep moving forward.

I can see the questions in Soren's eyes, but I don't want to answer them. So, I ignore them.

We move fast. There are more echoes that I can't push away, I can't control.

Josh drags me into a shop, scolding me for eating something I shouldn't have and bitterly I follow. We kiss outside the same shop; he rolls his eyes and I stick my hand up his shirt.

Pert guides my hands as we stretch in some fantastic ways on the street. He is more flexible than I'll ever be, but I try. People watch on with embarrassed expressions; and my body feels so good.

Jimmy kneels down and does a magic trick for some kids. His giant frame makes the kids scared, but no one can resist his charm. I keep telling him to leave, my expression grim.

There is a rumbling under us. A kind of quiet as even the echoes sound muted.

I know something is coming.

Snow dances with a woman in red; I know her name, but it still hurts to think about. Trauma. Her name is Trauma. They dance, but as soon as they get to the edge of the bar, Trauma gets shy.

She could take down 1000 soldiers with her gravity hammer, but when it comes to meeting new people, she's always shy. Snow takes her hand, drags her in. Moments later, they stumble out half drunk and all smiles.

Practically sisters.

A man with only one arm approaches me. My gut churns with this echo. It should play out beside us, but he watches us pass. I keep my arm in front of Soren as he approaches.

He says his name is Gracin; he used to draw art on men like me. His smile is sick and sweet and he tastes like beer. He puts his hand up another me's shirt, and my smile twists in all the wrong ways.

He is painted in the windows of a run down tattoo shop we pass four or five times.

He threatens violence more than once, while admiring the art on my body.

In several windows I see us dancing, fucking, kissing, plus one where I'm on the floor. My arm is broken, my eyes are black.

His fist is raised and he yells. He had two arms back then. I recall removing the one that broke mine and the windows all turn red.

I look to the side and I see us walk down another set of streets, ones I don't know. It occurs to me that Soren's ghosts might follow him here, and for a moment I worry. He does not look at them, or tries his best not to.

He sits on the roof of a car with a young girl. They are drinking, even though they are too young, and talk about the future.

There's a girl with a gun. She points it at his head as he tries to talk to her. He's got a guitar on his back, and it glows a bright red even though he's terrified.

All he can think about is his music and how he shouldn't have bought her that ring.

Then I see Fresh standing beside him. They are on a ship and he is in chains.

His face is an expressionless void as he stares out the window.

I hear a few keywords.

"Pirates. We need to land somewhere else."

"There isn't anywhere else. He's a prisoner. This isn't a goddamn day spa."

The captain drops them off.

The last thing I see before I look away is a pair of familiar doors that lead to an airlock. A faded logo on a distant comet. The only way into a prison full of forgotten names and faces.

"Hah. Hah. Ooo-hah," I whisper as I touch his hair.

He looks at me and does his best to school the expressions that slip on and off his face.

We move to the back. An icy shiver runs through my body. I don't want to see anymore.

I have to.

We have to.

If I can face this here, the others can face it.

I can find that piece of me that wasn't left behind on a comet to rot.

The further in we get, the quieter it gets, but it's not quiet: it's digital conversation. Every GEM is illuminated by light and text that means nothing to most. I can see all the colors of code, the excitement of conversation. The warning.

Two flashes in white, one in blue.

"We're being followed." I tell Soren.

One green. Unknown affiliation.

"Do you see anyone behind us?" I ask Soren quietly.

"Behind?" He turns instinctively. I grab his face and pull him into a kiss, pressing us gently against a wall. His eyes go wide, his mouth is limp, and his fingers turn cold as they press into my hand.

I glance to the side. Three men pass.

Three unfamiliar faces. The signal across the road says it's clear.

Hide.

I pull him beside me into the shop. It is eerily empty, but I pay no mind, as we are quickly out the back and into another alley.

We skip through a few more shops as the adrenaline rushes through my body before coming to a junkyard of parts stacked higher than the city is wide. I take a moment to laugh, invigorated but exhausted.

"What?" he stammers, wiping at his face anxiously. "What the hell was that?"

"Saving our asses, Sunshine." I tap his shoulder with my fist and shake my head. "Those guys have been on to us for a while. Watch for the colors. The GEMs are always watching."

"Stargon?" His voice is full of concern. "This… that didn't happen. Not to me, well, *not to me*."

He takes a moment to find his words. "Are you sure this is a good idea?"

I realize what he's trying to say. He's worried I'm in too deep, that I'm losing myself. The memories are too real.

I stare at my hands as I see them age, grow thin.

The feeling is so strong.

I think the storm is coming.

"Yes."

The shadow passes over us. The storm is here.

I don't want to look up. My whole body freezes in place. Soren has fewer hesitations, he looks up, but what he sees is not written on his face. He looks confused, curious, but not afraid.

The shadow makes the world darker.

"Is that it?" He asks.

"Sir," Parrot, no Albatrossi, speaks with a hurried voice. "Sir, that signal I was talking about."

"Shit." As I whisper it, the Cession in my wrist writhes with attention, but I dare not say it too loud. "You mean the Tidings?"

"Tidings?" The professor scoffs. "Don't be stupid. That's a rumor, practically a myth! Superstition!"

"Then what is it?!" I can see the fire in my eyes even from here.

"Sir, we've lost all communications," Snow's voice chirps. "We aren't receiving any communications. There is no signal."

Now, I look up.

The shadow is a ship, no. Not a ship, but something much, much bigger. It's so close to Europa's orbit there's no way it isn't being pulled in by her gravity. Is it crashing?

No.

She's stable. She's just… there.

It's almost as if Jupiter herself has come to punish its little moon, but something strikes me as odd about this thing above us, this moon? Ship?

It has green eyes.

They twist into a face; a beard, red hair that weeps above us even as it smiles.

"What is that?"

The Europa we walk on fades away. Now instead we sit on a gray street with gray walls, but the heavy shadow remains over us.

So does the silence.

"I don't remember this."

"Oh, no… oh no…" Soren is curled up, clutching his knees as he crouches on the ground. "No, please, no please, no please, not again."

We're now on a ship.

The red lights blare in warning of a breach. The heavy sound of a saw weaving in and around metal as pursuers break through.

Soren is frozen in place.

"They'll find me. They'll find me. Find me… please, no."

I kneel by him; I wait as the words pass by us. We begin to overlap.

Don't find me.

One-two.

Don't find me!

One-two.

Don't find me!!

One-two

I tap it out, my ring against the pavement as he repeats the words in an overflow I'm not sure the CERTs are handling anymore. A river of words passes between us. He grabs my hand and stares into them with ferocity and pain.

"Go. They're coming."

"Not yet," I whisper into his ear. "You have to see it."

"No, no, please, please don't make me." It's hard to pull his voice away from the one that's screaming in my head. I pull him up and straighten out his legs, bracing us against the pavement as the shadow is now almost completely upon us.

"They'll find us!" he screams.

"They've found us," Snow's voice echoes.

Soren's voice is barely a screech under whispered pain.

"No, I don't - I can't - I don't -!"

"Sir. That's not HUDO or Ritz." Albatrossi stares up through a ceiling that parts ways as the sun appears above us. It burns so brightly that I can't look away.

I feel...

I feel...

Soren screams. His screaming echoes tenfold around me, but it's not only him. I can hear so many... so many...

"What is it?" I ask again.

My mind is on fire.

Every inch of my being is on fire. For a moment, I think I am one of the GEMs falling down the pit, into the darkness, to the sweet release of death surrounding me.

I crave it. I want it. All of us. Let us die.

No.

"Hah. Hah. Ooo-ahh," I whisper. "Oh, for the sweet shadow of death."

The fire stops.

Screams silenced, sound gone, sight empty.

I am alone, standing in a room but also far away.

The artificial sun beats down on my dry skin, on my parched lips, and for the first time I know I am broken.

They can have of me whatever they want.

My fingers hurt. They ache with callouses from clawing at the stone. My tongue no longer tastes anything but ash and dirt, and my stomach churns in agony at ages and ages of empty longing. The sound of water pouring overhead is torture. I hear it every night as the machines turn us towards the sun and gather water from the surface.

If I am not stone yet, I will be soon.

"Daylight." I whisper into the darkness.

The first time the machines break, they give me orders. They tell me what I am going to do. Who I am going to take.

"Fix the machines and we will bring you one cup of water."

"Why me?"

"We want you to die first."

"Two cups."

"One cup for you, or half for the entire prison."

My mouth is so dry, stomach so empty that there are a thousand pinpricks in every part of my body and I nod. There would be tears down my face if I had enough water to spare them, but I don't.

All I can spare is a smile.

How did I get here?

Is this what the sun promised when it said it would take away the world?

I'm pulled back to a ship.

Red lights beat overhead, and it shakes violently. Soren stays completely still as he stands. Two men, draped in shadow with eyes that burn like the sun, glance over the room. I pull him closer as we hide deeper in the pile of bodies around us.

Echo trauma, I recognize. The CERT buffers on my head saved me from pieces of his, but did it save him from pieces of mine?

I watch the shadows pass us.

They never say words I understand. Not because I do not know the language, but because Soren's memory refuses to understand. The screams begin as a man questions a woman for information. Soren's infinitely younger in my arms. All I can do is sing to him.

"You are my sunshine,

My only sunshine,

You make me happy,

When skies are gray."

The song plays in my head, but I do not know the words.

I understand it, bathed in daylight, I understand it all.

I am all. I am none. The alien light turns the sky green and takes everything I am.

It sings to me as it takes away the world.

"-----?!" Snow's eyes are wide as she stands in front of me. She is out of breath, her hair is singed, but she is fine. Every word she says is like she's speaking underwater. "Jason, what the hell happened? Did you see that light? The sky turned green and… they're… they're gone."

I look at my hands. Albatrossi is beside me, balled up as he mutters to himself quietly.

"All alone. All alone."

"They?" It's the only question that made sense. Words are… hard to understand. It's like breathing smoke. "They?"

"Everyone." She motions around. My eyes pass over houses, pass over shops, streets, but all that remains are blinking lights from fallen coms and emptiness. It takes a moment to sink in, the sheer emptiness of it.

It was never this quiet.

Still, I don't understand.

I take a few steps forward. The shaking starts when I open a door. I am almost tossed from my feet, the force so intense it's as though the moon itself is rejecting me. I look at Snow, her body is shaking as she stares up at the sky.

The shadow is still there, cold, unmoving. The sky still screams in shades of green.

An emerald sky.

Streaks of smoke plume from the junkyard as overhead shuttles lose their orbits.

It is then I understand. The storm has come.

The dark sun above us has done what we could never dream. It has destroyed everything.

Shaking and cold in my arms, Soren wanders the ship. His stomach craves anything, but he's afraid to leave the REC room where he was left. He's too afraid to know what happened, he's too afraid to see Jan's face as he rounds the corner, so he stays.

He stays.

The scavengers come: they are superstitious and drop him off at a colony. He passes between as many ships as he can to get food. One ship is eager to have him, a strong, young male with a friendly smile.

"You ever want kids?" The man asks.

Soren glances at me and shrugs.

"Yeah, a dozen or so."

"Ever since those GEMs wiped out all those good folk of Europa..." the man spits "We could always use more good people around. C'mon, I think I might have a job for you."

There are fifty of us when the shuttles stop falling.

The AMTO-shield's life span empties within a week. No matter what we do, the communications don't leave the station.

We are alone.

As the air becomes unbreathable, we all don space suits. We make our way to a shuttle, already knowing what we'll find up in orbit.

A dozen empty ships greet us as we leave. We hop on board to scavenge what we can, but it is like the stories of the Tidings. There is nothing left. No corpses, no signs of a struggle, just nothing.

The same as the homes that surrounded us on the surface.

We wonder if we've been transported to hell, or if we are even alive at all.

We wonder if perhaps we are the Tidings that scare sailors when they cross paths with an abandoned ship.

We make do with what we can.

But we do not speak.

The answer comes a month later in the form of a sparkling white ship with blue words on its side.

It aims its guns at us as a Racial Purity Alliance crew dock and pours into our little shuttle.

We don't have it in us to fight.

I've lost so many... we're so afraid of what happened, we don't dare to spread it to anyone. When they ask us what happened here, I tell them it was us.

"We killed them. All of them. Even our own. Please... I don't want to see the sun anymore."

They take me away in cuffs. I do not know what happens to the others.

No one fights.

Soren pulls off the CERTs, shaking as he does. The room fades to the blazing white with no shadows. I stumble as I am summoned back to reality.

"That's... that's not what..."

"I needed to see." It's all I can offer in words.

If the CERTs were still on, I could show him that we shared the pain between us. I could show him that I know what he fears in the dark. I could show him that we — he throws up.

I kneel beside him and all I can do is chuckle.

He pushes me away.

"Not... my cutest moment."

"Thank you." I pull him into a hug. He smells like ass but reluctantly touches my arms as I hug him.

"I don't really think you should be thanking me for that," he shudders, body still quaking.

I hold him until he's ready to stand.

All that comes to mind, all I can even utter, is all I know to say.

"Hah-hah. Ooo."

35

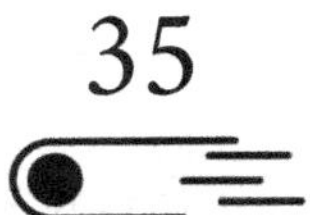

It takes Soren a while to look me in the eye again. When he finally does, there is an understanding between us. It serves us well in the next few weeks. Josh says that I stop screaming in my sleep and with it comes a kind of quiet.

We're not sure what changed, but the effect I have on the others and some of the missing time fades. Where once people gave me a wide berth because they were afraid of what I would do to their heads, now there is little space.

I am ignored.

Soren keeps telling me he'll monitor things. He thinks he understands what's happening and will work on it when he can. Sync shock. Ravyn. Tidings. He said a bunch of words that made my mind bleed white noise.

I try to take every day one at a time as memories fill themselves in, and my body allows itself to heal.

My mind?

It depends on the day.

I find out pretty quickly; I am obsessive. Josh teases me about lasagna as I try not to make it for lunch and dinner, so I switch my focus to something else.

I loathe the change.

"You were always good at self-punishment," Pert whispers to me when I bring him into La Blanc. "I am not surprised you have still been going. Your fire has always been a beacon to us. You know we would have fallen if you had."

"Not really the reassurance I was hoping for."

He smiles.

What we see in his white room echoes mine, but darker. Colder.

He does not think about the sun, Europa, or our fallen brethren. Instead, the echoes he brings are of a family. The play we see is of the darkness that drove him deeper into that madness. Of flesh that falls from the ceiling as the people above call "Daylight".

Of food.

I don't press him too hard, because I know Pert is healing too. I think it's easier on him because he has someone.

His sister, Trauma, has been nothing but a rock for him to stand on when he needed. Not that he ever would admit he needed it, but I know how the quiet can creep, how it can seep into you when you think you are safe and tear away what you think is real.

He takes to the less acidic fruits on the station, and sometimes even pudding. He grows. Glowing. Before long, he's almost as vibrant as the first time we brought Trauma to the station with us. He lets his hair grow in shallow patterns on his scalp. They help accentuate the paint that Josh helps him make. They forage them from some of the organic materials we have on the ship.

He and Trauma have paint fights on the concrete pathways outside. Sometimes others join in, and their smiles are contagious.

Snow busies herself with books.

Fiction, nonfiction, filling the space in her mind with something not as quiet. Seeing her read, I find a hundred books I can call up at a moment's notice in my memory. It's easier when I stare at a page, even if that page is full of other text. Soren always teases me about how I'm never reading what I'm holding.

Still, Snow dives into the now and tries not to focus on the then. She takes to the nets and with Josh's help, learns more about what happened to the worlds outside of our lives.

She tells us about our deaths.

Us.

We go down in history unnamed but powerful.

The Europa Massacre that began and ended with HUDO's victory. It was a shame we got that virus/ bomb/ unknown alien weapon took out all those people. All agree, humanity is better for not investigating further.

That's what the propaganda says.

The users of the nets whisper other things. The most vocal outliers, of course, are the IO colonists. They are the true hearts of the Jupiter Alliance Colonies. Earth native people who are familiar with fighting against unearned power, and claimed the rich soils of IO as their own.

She buries herself in a world that exists after her own death, but I visit often. She won't return to La Blanc with me to fill in the blanks.

"I don't want to know. I dream about it. That's enough."

"Are you sure? Even Parrot talks about it?" I shrug.

"I guess? If you call that talking." She shoves a pillow at me and shakes her head. "I'm not eager to learn, Star. I want to move on. I just want to… be new."

It's a sentiment I envy.

I let my hair grow out, but shave further up the sides. As it gets longer, the edges curl and Josh ties it up for me.

Buns.

Pig tails.

I try it all. I even let my beard grow in.

I find myself quiet, though, as I sit among a growing group of people I recognize. The young woman in the mask who tried to fight me becomes a sparring friend. Others join us. They are rowdy, spirited. I love them. Unfortunately, that doesn't mean it comes easy. If I spend too long with them, their faces fade out, and the sound of crashing ships and the smell of smoke fade in.

Garth - Nash - Garth approaches me one day with a certain amount of fear. He still busies himself with ship projects. He tells me about them. Ten ships, all ready to haul anything we can imagine across the systems. He even talks about acquiring a Ritz engine or two.

Working with his hands makes him feel again, makes him want to do more with himself.

This visit wasn't about ships or dreams, however.

"Soren." It was a question and a statement. Classic Garth.

"Stargon." I motion to myself.

"No. No!" he grunts, a screwdriver twisting in his hands. "I want to ask you about him."

"Sure, what's up?"

"Are you…?" He hangs his head low and bites angrily at his lip. I move closer to him, probably too close, and tilt my head so our faces are on the same level.

"Are we fucking? Lovers? Dating? Enemies?"

"Yeah! Are you?"

"No."

"No." He repeats the word with relief. "No."

"Not interested. I'm married. I can barely tell what day it is or where we are half the time. The last thing I need is a moody lover. Not that I would mind." I wave my hand at him and keep reading, but pause for a second. "Does he… talk about the green eyes in the dark?"

"Yes." Nash stiffens up. "Well, not talk about them, but he sees them. Tells them off sometimes when he thinks he's alone."

"He needs to talk about it."

"He's…" Nash has never been good with words. "Working on it."

I smile.

Parrot avoids me. 'Me' is perhaps too specific; he avoids the world.

He vanished for a few days after the incident in La Blanc, but when he came back, he was worse than before.

Fragmented.

He stops creating maps and regresses into something with fewer words. Less song. All scribbles and mumbles.

He nests one evening on the top of a fire hydrant and hasn't moved. At least he brought a datapad with him. Something settles in him once he finds it. Access to the nets, to reading, and math, I think helps him find a part of himself.

Still, I watch him suffer, but try to give him space. Everyone else tells me all the time they're sick of me.

Sometimes, for fun, I will sit by him and talk at him in several languages.

The look of disdain I get reminds me of the old Albatrossi.

I wonder *how much* the sun changed him.

The old him is as far gone in my memory as he is.

The itch settles into me, and one day, without thinking too hard, I bring him to La Blanc and let the place fill with the images of his mind. Cascades of equations and annotations and stars spread across the room like vast, infinite galaxies. At the very edge of it all, there is a bright white light. It seemed to consume his ideas as soon as he looked away.

I knew it was the sun. That thing that took part of us all away.

Even as it consumes all he makes, he's never afraid of it. Instead, he continues to create and create and create. His room fills with numbers, music, constellations, and a thousand other thoughts.

After an hour, I am an empty shadow among a universe of music and math and light. Somewhere, while composing, he places a hand on my arm and whispers, "Don't. Leave."

I move his nest inside after that.

He spends most of his time on the kitchen table. One morning, I wake to find him helping Josh with breakfast. We find out quickly, he'll go to war if we try to cook omelets, and potatoes he hoards and eats raw.

We started boiling them for safety before we bring them home.

Then there's Josh.

When I first told him I was hungry, I think he cried. He fed me everything he had in the fridge until I told him I really had to stop. He still waits for me to tell him to stop, but he's happy with the results.

He tells me every night as we lay in bed, staring at artificial stars.

He talks to Soren a lot. I think they're friends?

It's hard to tell with Soren, he's very moody.

"At least he *is* moody," Josh teases.

I must have said it out loud.

"What's that mean?"

"You're all a lot more like the other GEMs now. Blank slates you used to call them. GEMs born into a duty without too much thought about their life outside the orders they were given. Almost as if they really were artificial people." His voice lingers for a moment. "You always coaxed them out of their shells. I wish I knew how to do it with you guys."

"Time," I say. "We've forgotten how to be anything but stone, anything but notes of music on a blank page… it's… "

It's hard to put into words.

His expression tells me he knows.

"I can wait."

"Don't you ever get tired of waiting?"

Josh traces his fingers along my jaw, up to my hair, until he rests palms on my scalp.

"No. I know you. It never takes too long."

"How do you know this time it won't?" I lace my fingers around his arm.

His face shifts into something unexpected: amusement.

"Because you're already planning."

"Planning?"

"You don't think I know what you're doing with Parrot, Nash, Soren, and Trauma?"

I contemplate that thought without any real direction.

"Know... what I'm doing?"

"Planning a rescue. Going back to the comet. Parrot's been talking to you about directionality and orbits for weeks now. Trauma's almost got a good flight crew, and Nash and Soren have been repairing our old fighter-cargo rigs. I imagine it's going to be... another few weeks? If that. You're always impatient." His arms slide around my neck and he kisses my ear. "You sure you don't want more potatoes before Parrot gets them?'

"I'm good."

I stare down at my datapad and wonder for a moment if it's true.

A list of names.

Possible ports. Medical supplies.

Docking keys.

One note keeps repeating itself over and over: Daylight. Daylight. Daylight.

I look over at Josh, managing a half-hearted smile. I imagine the surprise is written all over my face. He winks and finishes packing up dinner.

How the hell did I get so lucky?

36

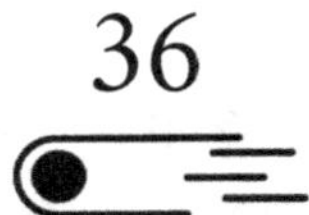

I swipe the record button to run and project the screen onto a
surface. Josh tells me, this was me before. Always recording, always
trying to prove I existed.
The screen floats in front of me and waits, seconds ticking
away on it. Flashing.
It feels right, but I hate it. It puts all my flaws on display, my
pores, my rough beard, the way my shoulders sag.
I stare at it, that blinking light, for a cold moment. Unsure
I want to know what will come out of me; unsure I want to feel
anything come anymore.
I shake it off.
This isn't *for* me. It's *to* me.

"Love is hard.
Let me start again.
Love is the stone that sits beneath your feet all day and
night. It never leaves, but that doesn't mean you're always sure it will

hold you, that it will stay. Love has been something both unexpected and beautiful, but impossible to maintain.

Today…

. . . .

. . . .

Let me start again.

Love is hard.

There's a million poems spread across a hundred languages that will tell you that, but they never tell you why. Love is simple - that's why. It's like air, it's like water. You forget they're there until they're gone, until you need them.

Keeping love is hard.

There's this place in you that empties slowly. Sometimes you don't notice it until you're completely empty. Then, something comes along to remind you that you're *you* again. Refills you so you have more to give. That's love.

Small or large, that's what it is.

That brush of nerves against the back of your neck reminding you someone cares. Reminding you - that you exist, and that is good."

I touch my face as I say the words. Something feels right about this.

I think… I smile. The reflection of me on the screen smiles, too.

Damn, he's got nice teeth.

The smile turns into a smirk.

"I know of one love I have neglected for too long." I turn the camera so it faces a window. Soren stares out of it, one of his favorite pastimes. He is a silhouette against the darkness outlined in white light from the window's edges. The stars peer through as the lens adjusts itself to the contrast. They twinkle around the void that is my spark.

"Space."

Garth grabs the camera and moves it to his grumpy ass nose and knitted brow. I shift the view it so I'm back in frame, and glare at Garth.

"Space." I repeat, to clear up any misunderstanding. "Spaceships too. She's no V'ger, but Garth tells me it's going along well. Garth and Soren have been working on this for the last few weeks - weeks, is it weeks? I'm not really sure. We have an ATMO-shield around some ships, but they don't turn on the cycles because it's distracting to colony GEMs.

Apparently, they like the way it creates rainbows when the precipitation gathers around a hull. Apparently, they also like to throw fish in it too.

Ah well, Soren approached me a few days ago with the idea. 'When we go back -'"

"Oh, no." Soren looks at me and looks over at the camera, then back to me. "What the hell was that?"

"I'm going over what's happened over the last few days." I motion to the camera. "Giving context to why I'm standing in a ship? The last log I have was on Europa and -"

"No, no, I mean that voice. What the hell was that?" Soren puts his hand on his hip in that way that makes me laugh. His eyebrows, his face, even his hips scream, every emotion passing through his mind. "Was that supposed to be me?"

It makes me smile more. I should have refrained, but I don't. I tilt my head a little, and in my best Soren voice say, "Is that supposed to be me?"

It's pretty damn good.

"Okay." He throws up his hands. "Off the ship."

"Nah." I turn back to the camera. "When we go back, he said, I want to make sure we have enough food and water to get all of them. I haven't figured out how we're going to fend off the guards yet but, I've got a few ideas."

"No." Soren shoves me gently. "Stop that, it's weird. Just… talk. Just talk, because you know how to talk, right? Like yourself? Don't do impressions of me."

I ruffle the tuft of silver on his head and lean close.

"I know how to do a lot of things, but I think Garth has most of them covered."

"No sex!" Garth barks from behind some console in the back. "Stop making him uncomfortable, asshole!"

"Uncomfortable?" I scoff. "Nah, if I was going to make him uncomfortable, I'd talk about last week how he was swooning over that blue sweater that Josh had and you went and bought him a green one but he won't say he doesn't like green."

The slap of a hand against steel reverberates in the air and I look at Soren, who in fact, looks uncomfortable.

Win for me.

I nod, satisfied, and turn back to the recording screen.

"This is all gold. I don't see how I have any other choice than to record it."

"That is STILL not what I sound like," Soren insists.

Garth grabs the com away from me, turning the record button off and looking at Soren apologetically.

"It kind of is. Go do this somewhere else, asshole!"

"You wanna put a sir in there, soldier?" I ask with a devilish smirk.

"No." He shoves the com in my hands and then, with a deep frown, mutters, "Sir. They'll be ready in another week if we can get the right supplies, like I said."

"Supplies." I glance out the window at the emptiness that seems to span infinitely before me. "How do we even get supplies here?"

"Normally," Soren explains, "as I understand it, they go out for some supplies. IO's a friendly trader, but there are also ships. They're kind of like anti-pirates? Similar to Open-air colonies, but specifically traders that float around the depths with goods."

"Why not ask Bound to make the Renegayed stop by?" I ponder the words as they come out of my mouth.

"Renegayed... Renegayed... I'm seeing a giant Blue Phoenix with a laser crescent and a Royal engine on the outside. Half-Ritz stored in her belly along with a few dozen artifacts, including the thing that tore a hole in the sky."

I look to the other two for confirmation. Garth raises an eyebrow and tosses his wrench in the air at Soren, who catches it deftly.

Soren clears his throat and says, "Right, well, I need the last few parts and we can go... do whatever we need done."

"None of this rings a bell?"

"It does." Soren is hesitant to speak. "But more like myths than actual things. The Blue Phoenix... I used to lust after that ship. It's supposed to be -"

"A safe haven for the half, or the none of Ritz," we finish together.

"That's the way Satou wanted it." I shrug. "But Bound never had the right marketing team."

I revel in some new found cache of knowledge. Garth disappears and Soren lingers for a minute. He moves closer, puts his hand on my shoulder and when I think we're going to have a moment, he moves close to me and says, "The beard."

"Yeah? You like it? It's taken a while to grow in, but has a bit to go."

"No." Soren shakes his head. "Look, I don't have to stare at your perfect but grim face all day anymore, but I am begging you to shave it off."

"You really don't like it?" I rub my hands along it, the rough hair bothering my fingers, but the change is as relieving as it is annoying.

"Star. Jase." He wears a serious expression on his face, "I'm pretty sure, if you keep wearing that beard, Josh will never want to fuck you."

"He hasn't complained so far."

"He - wait, you guys are already sleeping together then?"

I shrug.

"Yeah, pretty much every night since I've been back."

"You-!" His hair fluffs up and he blushes, annoyed.

"You're telling me he slept with you when you had that ratty ass awful hair and were nothing but skin and bones when we first boarded?"

I look him over as if trying to note the projection that seems to be happening.

"I'll shave."

"Please." Soren shakes his head. "Not even Josh can stand that forever. Also, get off the ship so we can finish."

"I'm feeling like maybe the Captain of this ship ain't very respected by his crew." Pulling myself off the console, I start for the door. "I can take a hint."

"Since when?" Garth mutters in the distance.

"Good bye, Stargon. Don't let the door hit you on the way out."

"As it is literally not attached, that seems quite impossible," I chime, thinking myself far more clever than I felt.

Love is hard.

37

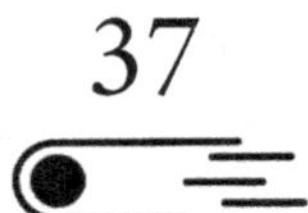

"I moved Parrot to the living room." Josh washes a counter for the fourth time. It's an action that keeps his hands busy. We had a fight earlier today, but I know it was because he is tired.

Some part of my memory recalls grading papers used to occupy his mind, but I don't even know if he teaches anymore, or if I stole him from that job, too.

"I saw that, thank you." The data in front of me was making less and less sense. Maybe I need a counter to clean too.

"You're distracted."

"That counter is way too clean for me to think *I'm* the one distracted. But… yes. I can't focus." I rub my eyes to try to get them to stop my head from spinning. "Maybe this isn't doable. Maybe I should let it go. Let the others handle this."

"You won't."

"I won't?"

"You'll think about it." He sits on the table in front of me, placing feet on either side of my thighs. "You'll consider letting someone else do it but it will keep you up at night and eventually you'll go less prepared and probably end up losing an arm or another eye."

I run my finger over the scar on my left eye. I can tell there used to be a tattoo there, my mind tells me when I look in the mirror, it was a star, but it's faded, skin torn away from beatings and age.

It's a pang that comes with a dozen memories.

Josh yelling at me about something that doesn't matter. A fight every time I go off to save another colony, or run another rally without him.

Josh's arms when I come home.

"I'll come back," I whisper.

"Because you'll go prepared. Talk to me. What's wrong?"

"Why?"

He leans closer and puts his forehead on mine, and like the patient teacher he is he asks, "Why what?"

"Why did they take us there? Why did they keep us so far away, so in the dark, it would have been easy to crucify the GEMs without putting us through that?" I close my eyes and try to quiet the memories that try to edge out of my control. "Why didn't they let us die?"

"Silence is powerful." Josh lets out a long sigh. "If they had given you a name, someone would have come for you. You would have said something that would have cascaded down the line like dominos.

If they had put your face on anything, put you in prison that someone could find or discover, let you exist, it would already be over for them. People were ready to give GEMs a voice, but the people in charge weren't. Instead of fighting you, or calling you enemy, they did something far worse: they did nothing. They let you be nothing. They hid you in silence."

I touch my chest as pain shoots through it, across my shoulder and elbow.

"Silence…"

That's when I make the choice.

I didn't want it, but knew it. In my heart. In my soul. It had to be done.

It was time to get the rest of my brothers out of silence.

Terms of Light

38

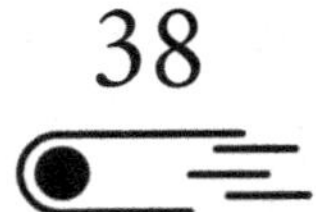

When I step onto the ship, something feels different. It's like ice over a freshly opened wound. Refreshing, numb, but with a bit of pain.

She's not V'ger, no, this ship is pieces of other ships strung together with Cession and love. Part long hauler, part cruiser. For the last hour, I think, I've touched every hem, every centimeter of her, memorizing her lines and numbers.

Soren keeps poking his head in to ask the same question over and over.

"Are you alright?"

"Yep."

I don't bother with a longer answer since I think it's his way of determining where I am. There's a question he doesn't ask, though.

The question no one asks out loud.

When do we leave?

Instead, they ask it in their actions, in the way they avoid me. It's the question I keep asking myself, too. The answer isn't easy, and the stakes change day by day as I feel out my crew, my family. Josh would leave at the drop of a hat. I think I would have to literally tear him into pieces to stop him from joining us, but the others…

"You alright?"

"Yep."

"Maybe," Garth interjects, "you should let us do our work."

I study him.

I know he has little work to do; the ship tells me with the way she vibrates. She is ready, but now she's waiting for us. It's then I can see it has nothing to do with the work, but with the company. Garth has become… attached.

He'll deny it until the day is over, but the way he holds Soren's hand in the absence of conversation, the way he hovers around when Soren lingers in a conversation too long, all the way down to the way he keeps his hair trimmed and his beard shaved all tell me Garth has it bad.

I wonder if Soren knows?

So, Garth will go where Soren leads. Soren will go when we're ready.

Two down.

There isn't a crack of doubt on the horizon that Pert would follow me anywhere I asked him to, but some days I watch him meditating outside under the artificial sky and wonder if it's fair to even ask.

I wonder if just this once I should let him grow roots? Let him and Trauma find girlfriends and wives and die happy and old. He is, after all, five years my senior, and at our age, that puts him much closer to death than I am.

Then again, my Pert needs little more than a well-shaved head and some berries ground into paint to be happy. He spends hours in meditation; I wonder on what. Part of me thinks maybe his mind is as broken as mine and he does this to make sense of it all.

When I close my eyes, all I can see is space.

Does he see the sun?

Does he dread the idea of going back out into the unknown? The idea of that dark prison? The idea of going back inside as the doors close behind us?

"Daylight!" I find myself saying.

"Hah. Hah. Ooo-ahh." Pert whispers at my side. I look over; I guess more time passed than I thought. We share an understanding without words.

"You found the sun."

"I found the sun."

"Why is it then, you worry about it?" He motions around him to the ship. "There are other things to face that we cannot beat."

"Yeah… but I feel like the sun is the most important." I struggle to find the words again. I touch my chest, I point to him and I point to myself. He seems to understand better than I can phrase it.

"You do not fight alone," he reiterates.

It doesn't comfort me.

"What if I want to? What if the only thing I want to disappear is me?"

"Then you should go back to bed. You are sick." Pert puts a carrot in my hand and slaps my shoulder gracelessly. "You lead or you die. That is the Stargon you are."

"What if that's the Stargon I was?" I run hands through short hair, aimlessly checking with my fingers to ensure each is equal length. "What if that Stargon was left behind in pieces? What if there is not enough left of him to fix?"

This time the carrot goes in my mouth.

"We leave soon."

"Yes." I hesitate. "If Snow has made a choice."

"She will come," Pert grunts. His voice must be sore from so much talking. It makes me nudge him. He settles at one of the navigation seats in front of me.

I busy myself with more inspections.

Soren is the one to stop me.

"You know I've already run all the tests, right?"

"When's the last time you flew a cargo cruiser? What about the other pilots?" I apply a few sealants to the outermost frame of the storage unit. He glowers at the ground with sudden interest. I toss him the sealant tool and point to a spot.

"It never hurts to have another pair of eyes, that's all."

"You're obsessing."

"I am." I flick him in the forehead. I can see his bangs flare up in response but little else. When he doesn't engage in some greater, more spirited way, I frown. I suppose part of me is ready to fight. "It's who I am."

"Do you think there will be enough space?" Soren asks. Finally, the real concern surfaces.

"Space?"

"There were so many levels to that place." The shiver visibly rocks his body. "There were so many voices. I dream about them. I dream about not having enough room for them and having them stacked up like bricks in a wall - and they can't breathe."

I grab his shoulders. "There will be enough space. We have three ships going, but even then, we'll find a way. Even if we have to have some stand. Even if we have to turn sheets into hammocks and hang them in layers, there will be enough space. Focus on what we can control, Sunshine. Did you get all the food and water I asked for?"

"Double."

"The medical supplies?"

"Triple."

"Sounds like we might be ready to go." Josh swings his jacket over his shoulders as he comes in. He looks Soren over with a smile, squeezing his arm before draping the other around my hips. "Unless we're having second thoughts now?"

"Nope," Soren confirms.

The shift of his body is hard to read, but I think it is between confidence and envy. I'm not sure why either.

"I think we're ready."

"Then let's go." Snow pours in, followed by the tall red obelisk we know as Trauma. "Before I change my mind again."

It's sudden, it's strange, worse of all it feels right. Josh's scent surrounds me, and I can see the determination on the faces in front of me. I nod.

"Get Parrot, Nash and our second pilot and we can go."

"Should we say goodbye to anyone?" Soren asks softly.

"No." Josh's reply is confident and smooth. "You'll be saying hi to them again too soon for it to matter."

Slick, beautiful bastard.

The ship detaches with barely a sound, just the gentle shuddering of metal expanding beyond the limits of its compressed design. The engines roar to life beneath my feet and within minutes my heart syncs up with their rhythm.

One-Two.

One-Two.

"Our Projected target is six days' travel with the Drift the way it is now towards the Neptune Outlay. The other ships will be hours behind us." I say to everyone. We all stand in the same room, somehow a million miles from where we started.

"There is always a chance we won't find the comet, or worse, what we find is not stable enough to land on. We could end up dying there, that very place we fought so hard to leave.

There is always the chance we could come into contact with HUDO or pirates, or something worse, and even in the best-case scenario here, we succeed and have to fight our way in. Our brothers and sisters will not know us. They barely know themselves. We cannot expect them to, but we promised when we left to return. So we will keep that promise and whatever consequences come of it."

Soren takes Nash's hand, Nash takes Pert's, Pert eats an apple, Trauma takes his hand anyway and Snow takes my hand, and Josh takes the other.

"We will come back from this." Josh echoes the sentiment. "We will come back and they will come with us. There is no other choice."

"Then what?" Nash's bitterness pours through. "I mean, saving them, yes, but to what end? Back to the station? Back to a life hidden in the shadows of Neptune?"

"One step at a time," I whisper. "We will answer the sweet call of arms, but first… we have to get there. Six days stuck together, six days between here and an eternity ago. Try to keep yourselves as close as you can, that's all. This is going to be hard on us. Not just seeing the others, but I fully expect the effects on our minds to be bad."

Snow hesitantly adds, "We'll be here for each other."

"I lived through it once," Soren snarks. "It won't be too bad if you all devolve. You still kicked a lot of ass."

Pert raises his knife high.

"I promise to kill you quickly if you are too far gone to return."

Josh chokes on his own air, and I smile at him.

"Right. Thanks Pert."

"Trauma. Josh." I motion to them both. "To hear about it is one thing, but seeing it is another. It's too dark in there to see without light, but the light is the one thing we grew to fear more than anything."

I'm parched as I speak.

"Blessing and a curse. End and beginning," Parrot chimes. "Purge your mind in FIRE. PURGE YOUR FLESH IN DAYLIGHT!"

The silence hangs heavily between us all. The engines sing a song for us, a steady beat that brings our hearts together.

"Hah. Hah. Ooo-ahh," I whisper. "We ride into the dark to be victorious."

"The enemy will come." Snow recites a song I don't know the title of in her words. "We will fight, we must if we want to be us."

"Take it all. Let us fall," Parrot chirps. "Let hell sing our praise!"

"After this night. After this fight," Soren's voice is a gentle stream in the echoes of a forest. "The world will never be the same."

"Hah-hah, Ooo," Pert chimes.

We join him.

"Hah-Hah, Ooo,

Hah-Hah, Ooo,

Hah-Hah, Ooo-ahh."

Josh squeezes my hand with a sad smile painted on his face. He wants to say something, but there are no words that fit the moment.

I kiss his hands and let the silence answer in the best way it can. Hand in hand. Together.

39

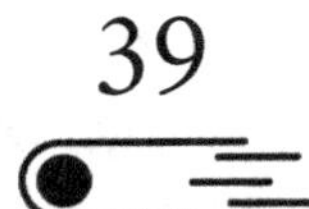

The first hours are always the worst, or the best.

I see both in the eyes of my crew. Soren stares into space and as it goes by like it's his first time seeing a star. He can't take his eyes away, and I envy him. Every star burns a thousand times brighter to me as the image of the Sahaqiel fades away.

For Pert and Trauma, it is different.

They spend the first hour in meditation or stretching, then the next they are reading, then a few moments later they attempt to find peace in the other's company. It results in a fight.

A rare thing, a silent thing, but a thing.

When they almost come to blows, Pert draws a circle on her forehead in paint, and she full-on tackles him. Their war rages for a while before the concept of time releases them to space into a pile of limbs and laughter.

Nash finds his space gut in a matter of moments. The engines sing to him; the hull busies him with its false promises of being secure, and he hums while he works. He is more alive in space than he is on the station.

Every now and again he glances back to Soren, envious of whatever star he is staring at, but not eager to remove him. The soft smile on his face lets me know there is some hope for him, after all.

For Josh and Parrot, there is an uneasy ease into the rhythm of things. Parrot changes very little, finding a nest among the supplies we brought along for the prisoners. He makes an adopted son out of the fridge and demands that people call it Toddrick.

Josh falls into the role of trying to maintain some sort of order to the chaos that is our merry men. I think he's anxious, but he takes it out in fixing whatever Parrot deems worthy to tear up for his nest.

As annoyed as he is, he smiles and he worries.

"What is it like?" he finally asks. It's the first time I've heard him sound like Soren.

"Cold. Dark. Dark. Dark," I answer. It felt better in my head, but my head still can't find words for it. For there.

For then.

"It's a mining facility," Soren almost whispers to Josh and looks at me as he speaks. "It's hard to breathe. There's little to no light and there's ash and soot everywhere."

"Ash?" Josh frowns and rubs his chin. It's something I've come to learn means 'that's concerning' but in a way he doesn't want to voice. Probably left over from his teaching days.

"From those who fall." It's Pert's voice that catches me by surprise. "They climb. They dream. They burn. They fall."

Josh doesn't ask anymore questions after that.

Snow, as she does best, reflects me. Her hair is now short again, well kept; her uniform, as pressed as it can be for something that is not a uniform. She sits back and watches with that damned smirk on her face.

I put my arm around her. She seems surprised but leans into it after a moment. I rub her shoulders as she relaxes into it.

"Yeah… this is what I was missing…" She moans it softly into a massaged muscle. "This is nice. It's almost like we were born for this."

"We were born to be lost?" I chuckle. "Star gone, if you will."

"How come it's so easy to forget that?" She leans her head back so she can see my face.

All I can do is shrug and motion around me.

She accepts it as an answer. Then again, she was born in space. I don't know how you could forget being born under a thousand suns.

"I was told all my life I wanted to leave, so I did. I climbed to the stars and into the heart of rebellion. I had gone so far out they never wanted me back," I whisper.

"Oh, that's nice. Who's that by?"

"Jason Pechard, something I wrote before… before Europa." I graze over the words in my mind, a picture perfect image with a star necklace dangling by it. A necklace long taken from me as my metal forms it around my neck. "I wonder what we could have done if things had gone differently."

"Does it really matter? Look around us. It almost feels like… like…"

"Like we're home."

Terms of Light

40

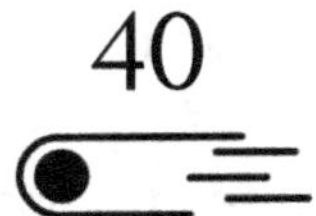

"There is no good way to prepare for this." I start the camera again. "The room is small, but it's mine - *ours*, technically, but it has a desk tucked away out of sight of the bed.

I like it.

I think he knew I'd need it."

I adjust the camera so it focuses on my face and my hands as well. People tell me I speak almost as much with them as I do with my mouth. I rub my face and remind myself to stop internalizing.

"Okay, I'm going to start again…" I hesitate. "I'm not really sure what the date is… what the time is, but I know it's night over the Sahaqiel. The artificial night and day would be opening up to the stars now. Just chilly enough to wear a jacket, but still bright enough you could finish a dance in the park.

I miss it already.

But we'll be back. We have to be. We have no choice. It's home now.

Home."

I take a long breath and let my hands lay flat on the desk.

I motion to the small window behind me and let the recording focus in on it.

"We're on day four of a six-day journey. It's already taken some time to adjust. I've discovered how little I sleep and -" my eyebrow quirks as the camera focuses back on me and I do a little hand motion," how much Soren does. I think he's asleep three fourths of the time I want to talk to him. Man, I don't know if that kid's depressed or he really likes to sleep that much.

That or play music. He keeps trying to take my lyrics and make them into some fighting song or something - I don't like it. Then he wrote another song about a tortilla?

Now, that was fun."

I tap at the desk for a second and think about Soren.

"I wonder what he dreams about? I mean," I shudder, "besides the bugs. Big ol' giant bugs. Which I guess I should talk about. The first time we found out about the bugs was on the Comet Chaser - uh, V'ger - but I woke up to Nash attached to the bottom of my bed screaming bloody murder.

It didn't bother me too much at the time, of course, but when I saw the bugs on the outside of the ship, I woke up a little more. After a while, we figured out they weren't really there, all illusions, but at the time, we thought we'd *really* lost our minds.

Waking Soren up was not an easy feat, but when we did, they went away. That's the first time he told us his powers were illusions. Real looking ones too. Makes me wonder if we have giant bugs crawling on the outside of this thing? Heh."

I roll my neck and sit back, focusing on the images in my mind, the thoughts I've tried to collect.

I close my eyes and it gets easier.

The camera records as my silent witness.

"There's no good way to prepare for this.

Going back to a place where we didn't want to be, going back to a place that we know still holds on tightly to every inch of our souls.

I think the war was less traumatic for us because of that place. None of us know what to call it. Not purgatory, not hell, just silence.

She's got a designation. What was it? Comet HH00-A. Her path pulled her into the solar system a few hundred years ago, but little else was known about it until deep space mining operations expanded to roaming comets. They had some grand delusion about higher quality ores and rarer materials from outside the system being on these rocks.

Idiots.

The only thing rare in that desolate hole was - *is* - the GEMs in it. It was one of the first 'free' GEM mining positions that were offered out in the world, shortly after we were no longer considered property of the NaReau Corp.

That was a long time ago, though, before they took all that back. Before they purchased the GEMs for military use. Before..." I let out a long breath, and I can see myself shaking on the camera. "Who even are you anymore, Jason Pechard? What did they do to you?"

I don't have an answer.

I don't know what to say, what to ask. It all falls apart into that dull silence that grips me again. I squeeze my eyes tightly, still shut, and a few tears roll down my cheeks involuntarily.

At least I don't black out.

I hold on to every second.

Who am I?

Stargon. Sometimes, Jason Pechard.

Where am I?

Aboard the ship that's going to bring my brothers and sisters home.

I let it flow; I try - I try to. I can smell the damp chill of the cells, and I wonder if I am made of stone.

Then there are hands on my hands. Hands on my face, a chin against my forehead. The scent of baked goods, leather and a bit of oil and hands more calloused than they look.

Josh. My Josh's hands.

I shake, I freeze, I try to regain myself, but in that time, he waits.

"Hey," he whispers to me when my breathing becomes normal.

"... Hey." The words finally eek their way out of my mouth. It's more of a breath than a set of words.

"You going to be okay?"

"Always."

"You want to talk about it?"

"Not sure… what to say." The words are a little easier. Chest a little less tight. "I thought I was over this."

"You - Hm." He re-thinks his words, hand held in mine. I trace the lines of his fingerprints in my mind. Like little calming waves of the ocean, my eyes roll over them. "There's not really an *over this*, Jason, it's part of you now. You know that better than probably anyone here. Especially you, Mister Photographic-but-not-always-audio memory."

I trace the lines of his face; they feel so different from the same lines I saw yesterday or the day before. He points to the recording screen behind me.

"I would watch the logs while you were gone. All the things you said out loud, all the things you didn't. Actually, I always thought it was funny what you did and didn't leave out." His smile melts my heart.

"Oh?"

"Like how much you eat. You never talk about food though, that you like food or want food, sure, but I rarely see you acknowledging that you eat it. Less so now, but there wasn't much to begin with." He kisses my cheek, wipes away a tear I didn't even feel. "Sometimes you get the audio wrong, but the visuals? I do not envy that mind of yours."

"It has its ups." My eyes do more than words can as they run over his body.

"Sensual by nature, photographic by design." He laughs. My words coming from his lips always sound so odd. "So, what were you trying to tell us in this log?"

"I was, I don't know, I guess I wanted to go over the last few days, but it's impossible to focus. I have no idea how I used to do this." I stare at our hands, laced together.

"Then change it." He touches my face, but I can't look at him again. I pull away and sit on my hands, trying not to find the floor as interesting as it is.

"I..."

"Or don't?"

"I want to. I want to. I want to be that person. For them. For me. For-for... for..." It's hard to focus on anything but the number of tiles on the ceiling, the uneven cracks along the window's sealant, the hair that falls along Josh's eyebrows, the fact I'm missing three pairs of socks in the drawer, the -

He traces my hands with his fingertips and taps the table, one-two-three. One. Two. Three.

I put my finger on the table, tapping my ring on the edge of the desk in the same pattern.

One-Two-Three.

One-Two-Three.

One-Two-Three.

"Tell me." His voice is so soft I barely hear it. I watch his mouth for a few moments, disbelieving that he is there - that I am here - that I am real.

"Tell... you?"

"Tell me." He smiles. "Start again, but don't tell the camera. Tell me. Tell me what you want to say."

The world vibrates back into place and for a moment, it's me, it's him and this room. This small piece of space that is me and mine and his and ours.

The rest of the world falls away.

It's La Blanc all over again, even if this time the shadows stay.

"There's no good way to prepare for this." I clear my throat and let it sink into his eyes. "Everyone of us is going through our own personal fire right now, not least of all, Soren. Ever since he stepped foot on this ship, I think he's been struggling with something, but all I see in cameras, in footage, the twitches, the uncomfortable look around unknown corners. Even if he's been down a hall a hundred times, every now and again he stops and looks again.

He won't tell me about it though, I don't expect him to.

I approach him at lunch and he settles in a funny way around me now, especially with Josh there - with you there. I don't think he knows how to handle me anymore.

I think part of him misses taking care of us. He sinks a little when I offer to make dinner or when you do. I wonder if it helped him forget whatever ghost is on his wings.

Today isn't any different. There's an awkwardness to his greeting.

"Good morning, Sunshine."

"I asked you not to call me that," he says it, but he doesn't mean it. He pours his soup back into his bowl repeatedly.

"Somethin' on your mind?" I tease him, and it earns me a small smirk before a chiding glower. "Or did the soup offend?"

"It wasn't soup - isn't soup, it was, is, sort of a..." He frowns when he realizes even I can see soup is the only word his mind will come up with. "It's not fucking soup."

"A'ight, a'ight, so did the not-soup offend?"

"No, I just, I'm not really sure I have any confidence in what the fuck we're doing." His words shake out of him like a junkie in need of a hit. "I mean…"

"What if we die?" The words make him flinch, but I don't. "Or is it, what if we get hurt?"

"No, I mean, what if they don't want to come?" He stands up, his eyes are bright with fire. "That kind of pain, manipulation, you know it can warp you. The others, you had them in your little group. You guys were different, but to them, you might be dead. Your deaths could have signaled the end. They could all be… what if they don't want… us?"

I look him over for a long time, trying to find out what other emotion is in there, but he sinks back to his stew and stares deeply into it for answers. There's something else there, but it makes me think. That thought that keeps pouring into my mind over and over again: there's no good way to prepare for this.

"It won't be hard." I'm surprised when the words come out of my mouth. I don't really remember thinking them, but something deep in my head comes to life. Something ruthless, something cruel, but honest.

"We'll promise them water."

Soren's eyes show disappointment, but even my tongue gets dry every time I even think the word."

"It does?"

"Yeah… I try to say anything but the w word."

"Good to know. You're doing great. Sorry to interrupt."

"Nah, you… this is good. I guess I needed a little more Josh in my Stargon."

"Mooore on that later. Keep going."

"We're just going to march in, kill the guards, and promise them water?" Soren says it so dully.

It's actually a far better plan than I had.

"Why kill the guards? Most want off as bad as we did. Forgotten and alone, we could use some on the Sahaqiel - but, yeah. Kill who gets in our way, lead our people to freedom. Did you think this would be more glorious? Like our escape?"

"No, I just thought it wouldn't be about water." He clenches his fist. "It makes me… angry."

"Save that anger for the battle. You have been in a fight, right?"

"A few." He instinctively glances towards the knife he keeps at his boot. The Cession one on his wrist wiggles a little, dying to become a knife, too. My Cession sings back to it. "I don't know if I can take on anyone skilled."

"Don't worry, the goons they had guarding us weren't. They were almost the same shadows we were - BUT." That smile creeps back up to the edges of my face. I have a razor in my hand now, flipping it open and tracing my calloused finger along the edges. "If you want, I think training really will take the edge off. Waiting is my least favorite part."

"Training?" Soren's face says more than his words ever will. "You want me to fight a bunch of GEMs?"

"With." I smile. "We can sync. You'll be a pro in no time."

"Yeah, *knowing* how to do it in my brain and in my body are two different things." He says, irritated. "No, I don't want to get beaten up today."

"You're really putting a damper on my style here, Sunshine." I flip the blade back in my pocket. "First, I'm going to teach you to dance, then we gonna learn how to fight."

Then there's silence.

"Is that what you wanted to say?" Josh touches my face, my eyes long closed, and I kiss his fingertips.

"No, not all of it. I really wanted to point out we can't prepare for this, but we are prepared. We're going to fight, we're going to win and we're going to bring them home, Josh. I owe the world a debt. Payment starts tomorrow."

"Two days," Josh corrects my dramatic tone. "Two days from now."

"Yeah, yeah, you and your math, Mr. Marrick."

"History. I'm a history teacher," he corrects again. I reach for the Com to stop the recording. "That's part of why I love you, you know… always making history."

I turn off the recording and go in for a kiss.

41

When we see it again, it's as small as the top of my thumb. It is incredible, painful, and terrifying to look at. Every inch of me seizes up with tension.

The place with no name, the nothing they left us in to die - it makes my blood run cold.

The ship falls silent.

I can't even hear the engines churning. I'm so tense I hold on to my time with my teeth.

"Hah... hah..."

"Ooo-ahh." Pert's hand touches my shoulder as he whispers the response.

We say nothing more as we stare out into the portrait of space, a dark ring etched on a darker sphere. There's a dark stain on her skin where the Calgary Haut once was. The comet tilts at a strange angle; its sealed doors and windowless features are so benign and innocent from here.

I touch my chest. My breathing is heavy, but Pert squeezes tighter.

He takes a deep breath in, then lets it out for just as long.

I stare at him lost, but he does it again, this time with a hand motion for in.

I follow along even if I don't understand.

In - two, three, four, five, six, seven, eight -

Out - two, three, four.

The tension stays, but as we repeat it, my blood steals.

The Cession around my body writhes and twitches, eager to fight. I can feel it under my skin, in my scars, along all my hairs and trailing through my vision. I touch my wrist and for a moment, missing the numbing injection of my EGG.

I stroke a few icons before the shuttle begins its docking preparations. I'm excited when old military codes from the Sahaqiel grant us entry.

When the docking rings engage with our ship,a time appears in front of us.

Thirty minutes until docking complete.

"Soren. Pert. Snow," I call as I walk. They fall in line behind me; Soren is the only one out of step, but he quickly matches our pace. We can all feel his mind with ours, and we use him as a hub. Though it was not planned, it has become second nature. Fortunately, he will only benefit from it.

Ritz blood grants a few gifts to go along with the flaws.This one we have been practicing. Sharpening him up so he is ready to fight. So the panic with green eyes doesn't set it.

We make our way to the docking bay. It's a small cargo room full of equipment prepped for the incoming survivors. We silently prepare for what comes next.

Pert laces his body with knives the same way one might wrap oneself in war paint.

Snow replaces belts and scarves with bullets and gravity belts. She adorns each inch of herself with a weapon that can either fire, be thrown or cause a concussion when used with appropriate force. The glint in her eyes spins me to darker places and relaxes the tension I carry in my back.

Soren, on the other hand, Soren dons only a few items. He pulls out a sonic gun and slides it into a side holster, a knife in his hand and one in his boot. He contemplates for a while some of the gravity mines, but in the end sticks with thick military style boots and some body armor. Swift, fast, and deadly is what I've seen out of him in training. Let's hope the Shadows get their chance to see.

They won't know what hit them.

He hasn't learned it yet, but his mind is his deadliest weapon. It will be two steps ahead of theirs as the sync processes through his Ritz mind faster than the Human nerves can send their signals. It will be a quick death if it is one for our enemies. The metal seems to react to this idea, I think, it even craves the touch of a Ritz again.

As for me…

I mirror Soren, favoring speed. I wear the metal on me and it forms light body armor and attaches to my gravity belt. Otherwise, I form those two swords from it and then melt them back into my gloves as if they were never there.

Pert approves of my choices, where Snow gives me the look of a woman about to outdo me on a fashion runway. Her pride shines through, and I spare Josh a glance as he holsters his own sonic pistol.

"I'm with her. Screw you guys and your minimalism. I don't move that fast," he jests and puts a hand on Snow's shoulder. "I tried to keep up with him once in a fight! Won't do that again."

"You got the wrong guy!" We hear in the distance from Parrot's perch guarding Toddrick.

"Ha." She shakes her head. "I don't even bother. That's what Pert's for."

"I think you're all missing out." Soren grins and moves ahead of all of us. I try not to smile, but I fail. Every inch of me, even the metal on my back is eager to move forward. The ship shakes gently as the docking rings seal.

The oxygen seal takes the longest. We all wait in silence as the counter ticks in front of us. The doors shudder as the pressure between the two places normalizes.

Panic washes through the hub, through Soren's mind, and back into us. We all hesitate, impatience showing in the flick of a knife or the twitch of a finger. He tries to run through the scenario in his head. Pert's calming presence makes it clear we'll be okay, and Snow is a monolith of concern.

"I'll lead." I step ahead of Soren, who shrinks back only enough to be a step behind me. His fear reduces. "I wish I had a damn HUDO uniform."

The doors open. My stomach clenches.

The bridge extends before us and it is the longest ten meters we will ever walk. Docking rings above give off a dim glow that blocks out the stars and makes the tube around us seem endless.

The door on the other side opens.

A small show of force greets us. Four guards without real discerning rank. They wear black, maybe gray, but it's hard to tell against the harsh light above us. I take a few steps forward, slow and purposeful, to see how they react.

They wait. After a moment, they shoulder their weapons and salute.

I'm surprised when one of them greets me.

"Admiral." He swallows hard as he says the words.

I glance down at my shoulder. I am now draped in a white HUDO uniform with quite a few stripes. A pit in my stomach churns.

Soren? Is that you? My mind asks without words.

Reassurance responds.

I scoff and look at the two Shadows standing guard. My eyes look them up and down with extreme scrutiny.

"What are your names?"

"Davenport, sir."

"C… Conway, sir." the other one stammers, his voice parched from a lack of water? Nerves? It's hard to tell, and I have no desire to feel him through the sync. Soren at my side stays quiet, the other two stay back and wait for us to move on before following.

"Take us in then."

"Sir! Of course. I mean, yes, sir!" Conway leads the way, eager to be away from the eyes of authority. Davenport is calmer, almost eager? It's hard to tell what the bounce in his step means.

They lead me down a hallway I don't remember - no wait - it becomes clearer. I was less conscious, and it's a blur of images.

> *My feet drag on the floor.*
> *My hands are cuffed behind me, my wrists raw and bleeding,*
> *my lip cut, jaw dislocated.*
> *Every time they ask me a question, I laugh.*
> *I spit blood for days.*

I hold back as much as I can from the group. I'm aware of Pert and Snow pulling the doors shut behind us. The darkness is… thick. It weighs on me with a physical presence. It gets hard to breathe.

In - two, three, four, five, six, seven, eight.

Out - two, three, four.

Thanks, Pert.

My eyes focus on the doorway at the end of the tunnel. It's a reinforced door and we know, it's the last chance we have to turn around. This will be the final test of our *plan*. On the other end of this is the Queen of Shadows, Captain Oswald.

She knows me well. I know her well.

I anticipate our games to continue. I'm not sure if she knows, but we go in assuming she does. She's set this. She's been waiting for us.

She is the real test of how well this will go.

Our footsteps are the only sound between the walls.

It's so quiet; the guards are either too afraid to ask what happens now or who we are, or they already know. It's amusing to watch as they prove themselves to be what I've always known: Shadows against the wall as they hide from the sun.

I wonder what our odds are?

I wonder what people have bet on the most?

The Captain is smart; she knows more than most. If she knows, she'll either bargain or she'll mow us down as soon as that door opens - but then why send the four guards?

The two guards beside me stop as we reach the end of another endless hallway. They take their spots on either side as the door slides open. Inside, looking unarmed, Captain Oswald stands in the center of a beam of light. The orb on my body roils and writhes with anticipation.

I know this room. This room is where the orb used to live.

I do my best not to smile as it remembers too, and it pleads to fight, to eat, to not be returned.

"Good evening, Admiral." Oswald's voice is dark and cold.

I look around the room, assessing what I can. I am not sure how far Soren's illusion has wrapped around me. All I can do is anticipate what ever it is she has planned.

Still, I play along.

"It's Deckar. Kain Deckar. I understand you *lost* something very important to us. Are you who they put in charge of this… place?"

The woman with the confident stance seems unshaken. I walk around the guards, who all fidget as I put my hand in the light source above us and make it dance off of their weapons.

"We have called for assists for the last. *Three. Years.*" Her voice quakes as it leaves her mouth, anger pooling at her chest. "We have called, pleaded and begged, but with every new shipment all we receive is word that any decisions regarding our posts are *pending.*"

There's something hard against the back of my head and I hear a few shaky sonic weapons charge and move towards Soren's position. They make the air smell foul around them as they threaten. I hear the words and as they roll around in my brain; I realize she doesn't know me.

She has no idea.

This woman who stared at me from her tower, the woman who watched as everyday someone burned as they tried to 'touch the sun' and did so with a bitter smile, this woman who I played a sick game for access to a single cup of water doesn't see me at all.

Instead, she wears rage on her shoulder like it's a medal.

Like she has been sinned against.

I glance over to her, cooler than any glacier, a tepid smile gracing my lips.

"And you think that's changed?"

"You DARE come here with your white uniform, with your damn entourage, and want to ask us questions?" The shadow is now cast away from her face. "You want to accuse us of losing some psychopath the world forgot and leave us out here to DIE!?"

I turn slowly, not letting an inch of fear trickle out of me.

I have none.

I'm in total control, and that is what she wants.

I know this pain, the pain she feels, the need to fight for your life, to beg, to steal, to do anything it takes to get away from where you have been left.

It was my entire childhood.

It was the service I was sold into because of my genes.

It was the forge that made the weapon I became.

Her eyes are clouded with emotions that cover the rage and hate she associates with the white uniform that Soren maintains around me. I watch her: I see every twitch, every micro expression, every anticipated reach for a weapon.

My mind is no Ritz mind, but it is still that of a GEM.

It is faster than hers will ever be.

My mind expands, even as I filter in the details through the hub.

I hear the reports, even if they are just pings inside of Soren's head.

16 total Shadows in the area.

Likely 20 more outside.

I could never get a full count, but that feels like the right number for them. There are always more down in the tunnels. Two at the door, one with a rifle behind me, four more with rifles raised around me, one left, three right.

The Captain's weapon isn't a threat; it's on, but the safety light is blinking. She's covering her ass, but her emotions shake her fingers close to the trigger. The orb whispers to me translations from Soren's mind.

She has a side arm, and a wounded knee wrapped in a brace.

The silence drags out too long.

The Shadows are nervous, looking to the Captain for orders. Tension is high, but everyone without a weapon is a liability we can take quickly. I don't worry about the two by the door. I'll let the others handle them.

I formulate a new plan, and a way to get us into the ideal positions.

Soren can see it too, we exchange a glance. He quirks an eyebrow to tell me he's - he's having fun? He doesn't reach for his knife.

"Oswald, Terra, right?" I hold up my arms and the room instantly relaxes. I move myself between her and one of her guards. "You've been at this station since damn near the beginning, haven't you?"

"I took over for the build captain, DiGorsi. I don't care for PLEASANTRIES, Admiral. I want off. We want off." Her shaking ceases. The doors that lead into the hall close as she motions taking a step closer to me. "We've been waiting for an answer, Admiral, I suggest you start telling us what we want to hear."

The smile that slides its way up my face where it stops just short of a laugh.

"That's not an answer, Admiral," the Captain warns like a toothless mutt.

"What do you think happens now, Terra?" I know the familiarity of her name burns under her skin in ways no other word could.

It's cruel of me.

I love it.

That dark sadistic thing in me crawls out and paints my tongue in midnight.

"You think you can walk away from this?"

"I think you don't have to." Her finger twitches again, gracing the trigger. I can feel it in her, the urges spilling over into our sync, the desire to fight, to weep, to die - to *feel*. "I think we have all the power here. You better tell me exactly what you're here to do, and you get to walk out of here as a whole man."

"How many staff do you think I brought with me?" I fold my arms. "How many people on my ship do you think you could hope to replace? That is the plan, right? To take our ship, our identities and run? But I only have six with me. Hm. Do they know? Have you… chosen?"

"Shut up." She moves around me and again shoves the weapon against the base of my skull. This time she swings enough that I roll my head to the side. I bow, slightly, in a sort of concession that everyone sees.

"Has she told you who she's taking? Which six?" I ask the greater room. "Do you really think anyone is leaving here? Or do you think, for one second, that we're here to make sure that never happens?"

"A Kill Order?" One of the Shadows in the background gasps. "Oh God, it's a kill order."

"Shut up," the darkness begs. "The Captain isn't leaving anyone behind. They wouldn't put a Kill Order out on us."

"Commander," I motion to Soren, who steps forward, shielded by me and able to aim if I need him to. "How do you see this ending?"

"We came to talk about what happened." Soren's icy gaze takes in every guard's face. It's hard to tell if he is planning or truly trying to take in the faces of the soon to be dead. "To talk about what you lost."

"Then let's talk about it." Oswald pulls a chair from behind her, shoving it at my knees. I stumble and put one foot up on the seat. "What the hell this place really is, and why? What right do you have to ------------"

I tilt my head as she speaks. A momentary break in my reality? No, it's something else, something I can't quite hear, but others can. It's on the edge of my perception.

What… *is* that?

"- inhuman." Her last word is spat at me. "We will not be prisoners of those mistakes anymore. No one deserves this."

"And the GEMs?" My question catches her off guard, but not in an unpleasant way.

"Is that really all you care about? You came here for more weapons in a war we're not even fighting anymore?" Her safety light switches off as she aims at me. A silly weapon for close combat, but too fast for anybody to move away from.

So, I don't try.

I can hear the low hum; a deep noise from far beyond the doors, far below the tower where the Shadows gather. The voices of my brothers and sisters far beneath the surface. I can smell the smoke, the dust, the ash of a thousand lives beneath my feet.

It's a moment before I realize she has been speaking to me.

"Admiral!" Her anger is a fresh edge along my neck. My spaciness taken for disinterest, I imagine, and Pert's edge becomes present in my mind. "I can't believe you would put the lives of GEMs above those of real Humans."

It slips off my tongue involuntarily, darkly, sickly, and without thought.

"Always. Hoo-ah!"

Something hot hits my shoulder.

I turn my head to look at it, separated, as if I am not me. I see the scorch of weapon fire there as my Cession rushes to repair it. The ache is dull, senseless, lost to a hundred other sensations. Others raise their weapons, some fumble, some fall.

We are faster.

Soren reacts first, before anyone, before light meets flesh. His Cession forming a set of short swords in his hands, moving Oswald's weapon away from my head with one motion and cleaving at the guards closest to the door's calves with another. The blood surprises him, but some savage part of him savors it. He kicks the security door behind us open again, and we are no longer trapped.

Pert and Snow are milliseconds behind him. They read the room from a far better angle than I could and take it all in. Pert takes out two before he dashes through Soren's open doors. He wears little armor and by the time they aim at him; he has vanished.

Snow wastes no time dominating what remains of the room. I see a few rounds head her way, and she takes them against her armor with a sturdy grunt. I see someone's finger fly off as a tried-and-true metal bullet pulls it off of a hand. The cold fire in her eyes tells me they will only get those few shots and nothing else.

A few smart Shadows see the action and flee.

Then I hear a song that sings me back to a time long before here. A song that doesn't belong. The heavy, thick sound of metal against stone. Trauma's trademark.

I do not envy the fates of those that run. She will make puddles of them in moments with her gravity hammer.

They will learn fast why we call her Trauma.

The room goes from a small army to a scattered crowd in a matter of moments.

They were not prepared to fight.

They didn't see us coming.

It reminds me that training means nothing in isolation. Soldiers with only fake targets become brittle or fade away. I watch as both happen at the same time. The few brittle ones burn up as they are met by killers. Killers they trained, guarded, and thought they ground into dust.

Anger fills me up, turns me into something I haven't been in a very, very long time.

The chaos in me crescendos into a joyous sound.

I take in every mind around me, those below, those scattered to the winds. I'm aware of the few guards hiding out near the food storage, and two near the outermost exit cringing in fear as the thunder that is Trauma rolls through the halls.

Through my sync, calm overwhelms the other feelings, the silent mind of someone so far gone - some*ones*, so far gone - they no longer have a song to hold on to.

That's when it happens.

Our eyes meet mine and Captain Oswald's. I don't know when Soren's illusion fades away or if it has at all, but I know, in that moment she sees me. Her eyes are smoky glass with fear. Everything she thought she knew about this situation was incorrect.

She is not prepared to face death today.

She was prepared to win.

My hand forms the sword as second nature. I close the gap between us in a time that would make even the Ritz envious. That is what they trained us for, to take what was biologically better and kill it. I always preferred to strangle, I recall; it was far more satisfying than the quickness of a cut.

Today is not about me.

"Ooo-ahh." My lips almost touch hers as the gap is closed.

The heat between us is not romantic or bitter as I grab her head and tilt it up to the right angle. My sword extends through the base of her neck up through the soft palate and into the brain. It makes for a gruesome, and survivable, injury. She hangs from the edge of my blade, eyes wide, unable to breathe. "You wanted answers. I have some for you."

"Stargon!" Soren's shouts catch my ears, barely. "Oh geez. Okay, they're fleeing towards the ship!"

"They won't get far." It's barely said aloud, my eyes still fixed on Oswald's. "Trauma's my gate guard."

"Is that what that sound is?" Soren's mind wraps around the source of heavy, thunderous noise. I can feel him wince in my own body.

I remove the blade.

I let Oswald slide to the ground, sputtering, oozing blood on my boots. From behind us Trauma and Josh enter the room. Soren lowers his weapon and relaxes at the sight of allies. I'm aware of Pert, eager, roaming free in the great halls below and itching to join him.

Snow grabs my shoulder.

"We need to help."

"You should have let me talk to them." Josh's voice is faint as he looks around. "How many are left?"

"Dozens. We can round them up. They are afraid and want to leave." I report, "Snow. Josh. Soren. With me."

"And where are you going?" Snow asks, annoyed at my ease of giving orders.

"What we came here to do!"

We part ways as I enter the darkness beyond embracing the only thing I have to do now: free them.

42

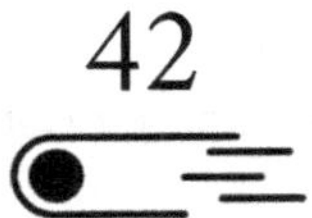

The darkness settles around me like a cloak. I feel it about my shoulders, pulling tight to me, comforting me, giving me power and prestige that don't belong. As I step past the door that I spent years looking at in longing, the world is quiet and I... I am clear. For the first time since I could feel my breath in these walls, I am clear, ready, and prepared for what comes next.

As prepared as I can be.

For a moment, as the artificial hope above shines, I see myself rising from the center of the hole, blades bare, singing a song of the sun. I am overrun by he warmth, elated by the bloodbath behind me, and it is all... *exciting.*

I run down the spiral. As I pass, I see empty doors, open gates, and I gain speed as I pass empty cage after empty cage. My mind races as I focus through the memories that edge into me, overwhelm me. I recall the first few weeks here, how they kept us, how they tortured me. Abandoned me. Then the others came.

We took what liberties we could, choosing our doors, choosing who we could die with every night. Pert was among those that went deeper.

Down further into the darkness to those who had become something else. Not stone, not man, not shadow - something else. The Whispers.

We were all afraid of what they were, while admiring all the same. After all, they had kept a piece of themselves, or found a new one. That was hard to turn away from.

Every step forward is a step deeper into the darkness. Every cell I pass is empty.

Empty.

Empty.

Empty.

Then closed.

I stop at this door, my feet barely able to as my momentum begs to be reclaimed. I stare at it for a moment, waiting.

Waiting.

Waiting.

I tap lightly on it three times. Tap-tap-tap.

Then I press my good ear against it. For too long there is nothing, but I hold myself there.

Hopeless.

Hopeful.

Then, a slow, steady return: Tap. Tap. tap.

My heart sings.

I study the door. It brings back memories of another time, a time when I was something more than stone here, a time when the contemplations of body and mind were beyond the ideology of seeing the light again. I ponder the door, the edges, the curves, and the dust in front of it.

Undisturbed.

That meant they hadn't been let out in at least a term, not with the way the dust has settled here, but was it only this one?

Had our escape led to something much worse for those down here?

Had they been feeding them? Punishing them? Worse? Was there worse?

Too many questions - not enough answers.

I touch the door and stare back up the ramp. It would be easy enough to fight our way into the control room, but something tells me that will take too long. The Cession on my body begs for me to use it.

I know what it wants. It wants me to let it free to eat, not the raw materials of the door but the surrounding minerals. I worry I can't control it if it gets too much stronger. I wonder what it will do, so I hesitate.

I remove my hand and change tactics.

I pull myself up to the small opening that sits outside the chamber. There is a gap that is barely enough to call a window, but in my memory, it was huge. How did something so small keep so many of us alive? It let us share song, let us be prickled by the sun… and yet it is barely a sliver.

I hoist myself up, grateful that my body is now strong enough to do that from food and care. It only takes a second, a glance, before I hop down.

Photographs are easy to analyze anytime you want when they are captured with the mind's eye, but it doesn't ease how ill the results make me.

Bodies.

Stacked, staggered, unmoving, blinking eyes, breathing, waiting, crammed in together like they were made of sausage. I wonder *how long*? I wonder *when*? I wonder…

The Cession, again, pleads with me to let it eat. I still worry I won't be able to handle it on my own, but we are now long past the idea of worrying about dragons.

I place my hand on the door.

The metal spills over it like a rush of liquid as it leaves my back, my legs, my body, leaving behind enough to keep me safe. I have my sword, my blade, my tags, my necklace and my com.

I touch my ear. A faint signal chimes through.

"Josh?" The words are desperate, cold, and clingy. I want to hear his voice. I hate it. I hate this new part of me and how wretched it feels. "Josh, I found them. *Some*. I found some of them."

"Where? They're still securing the area, but I can bring down some water."

"They're crammed in together." I'm talking before he finishes. The metal pours over the door like water. "They're stacked. Compacted. They can't… they can't breathe, Josh. I can't wait."

"Okay." It's a calm, comforting acceptance.

I wonder if he was always this way?

The metal eats, chewing away at the door edges like acid. I hiss at it, a silent urging with my mind to go faster.

Stop spreading and focus!

It seems to enjoy the readiness of my command as it solidifies into a straight line along the door. I direct it towards the seams. Not the one between door and wall, but the one between door and door. Solid metal is expensive and hard to make in single sheets.

Welds are easier to eat.

It accepts this knowledge with a hunger that I mimic in my stomach.

Forever passes.

Black liquid, I assume to be welding waste, streams down the seams of the door. The metal wobbles as I try to focus my thoughts. Next will be the bars, those will be harder.

The door slides away in sheets, and I'm faced by a few of the bars that keep me from the inside. The first thing I recognize as flesh is a knee, or maybe an elbow? It's hard to tell in this darkness, but I kneel by it. I wish I had brought my EGG.

I whisper into the darkness, "Hah… hah… Ooo-ahh.."

Silence.

The metal consumes more of the door and drops another piece, but perks as it hears there may be flesh. I push its desires away and try to coax the Stone in front of me back to being. They are so dirty it's hard to tell what's floor and what is flesh.

What I do touch is clammy, cold, lifeless, and something about that makes me swallow hard. The body is thin and boney. What I touch is barely enough of a thing to be called a leg. The skin is gray from lack of light, sickness or… something else. I tap my ring against the stone beneath me.

One-two.

One-two.

"Hah… hah…" I take a deep breath in. The ghosts and nightmares of this place crawling inside me. "Oh, for the sweet embrace of death."

"Oooahhh…." it's a long, shaky breath out.

Did I imagine it?

I did hear it, didn't I?

I call out to the darkness in front of me, "Hello?"

"Hah. Hah," it answers.

"Ooo. Ahhh," another part calls back.

"Josh." I stand and swear I can feel his hand in mine. A pair of toes wiggles in front of me as I hear others move behind. My heart beats faster. It is the most amazing thing I have ever seen. "Josh! Bring my EGG!"

My joy has no words as the last slab of metal goes down and the Cession moves to feast on the heavier, solid iron of the bars.

"Somewhere," I sing to myself softly, "Beyond the sea~."

I tap out the tune on my thigh as the Cession pulls apart the bars. They twist, tilt, but never break or fall. My impatience grows *painful*. It cuts out every other sense; it pulls away at all of my mind.

It's Josh that pulls me back. His hand on my chest as he motions to a case behind him. It's cold and round and mostly white with a few interface buttons on the side, but I know it well. I open it up. The cool dry mist rolls out of it and, for a moment, I am filled with dread.

I squeeze my eyes shut, knowing seconds now matter, and stick my hand into the container. It is cold; it is biting and then it is sharp. The proboscis of my EGG probes the holes it knows so well as it emerges from its storage. I am alight in shades of pale.

It is easier to see now, the pieces and edges of those inside as they move. I study what is in front of me, and look at the edge behind me, and worry. The gravity flux of the core and the EGGs are something that can exist at odds.

This means as we get further down, my EGG will be less and less effective.

Pert grunts.

It takes a moment for my mind to understand that he is there now. He is paler than clouds in the faint white light emitted by my EGG. My lips edge upward. The Cession seems to understand and pulls itself away from the bars. Pert and Josh follow suit as the EGG extends alien tentacles and suctions to each side of the door. One small tentacle slides behind me, into the gravity well, and surprises me. It tests at the pull of the core, its fluctuations, and tests for stability before removing the bars as if they were toys.

Bodies flow from the cavern in a wave of flesh that crashes against my legs, but does little else to move me. Eyes stare up at me, some blinking, most dusty and glossed, but each set of eyes is *on* me.

There are a few waves of movement starting from the back of the cavern, but all seem focused on one thing: me.

Daylight.

The one who can turn them mad if they stay too close.

The one that gets the full glass when we get half.

The one that trades food and plays games with Oswald.

The unlucky one.

No.

No, it's not me they stare at.

I turn to Josh and the cool, heavy item that he carries. I see now that it is a jug. A large container of water, bubbling softly, cleanly at my side. I pull it from his arms and he stumbles as I offer the jug.

Weak hands paw at it, a few touch my leg, my hands, my arms, my eyes, but all ask silently for the same. Josh struggles to hand out paper triangles and presses something near the front that dispenses water. For a moment, that is the only sound in the world. The water as it ever so slowly pours from the jug.

The stronger ones are quick to take their fill and grab another glass, but they do not take it for themselves. Those on the ground are offered sips. They take it gladly before pushing it on another.

Then another.

I offer the jug up to arms that look like they can hold it. They waiver, barely able to stand with the burden, but as I go to steady them, another approaches. Her arms are built to carry, even weak, and she takes into the dark.

They disappear from my view, and the cups follow.

What felt like years now turns into seconds as water pours in small sections upon the hundreds of bodies that seem to gain life with each drop used. Trauma comes down with another jug as the one we have runs out. Stronger ones from the center take it from her without a word. Two follow her back up and the few who seem eager to walk make their way up the path.

No one says a word.

My joy has no words as I try to help others stand up, right themselves.

Get them moving.

Get them up.

Free - it's the word my mind barely touches on, but it sends a tingle down my entire body.

With each one I help, they pass me as though I am a ghost, a nothing that exists, and for once, I am grateful. Slowly, they begin their climb up the steep ramp. Josh, after a moment of stunned silence, sets down a familiar metal case before stumbling after the first ones. He wraps his arm around one that is having trouble walking and takes her weight on his shoulders.

I watch them leave, my heart light with excitement. It is hard to focus through the buzz that fills my brain.

Pert grabs my shoulder.

The Cession climbs its way up my leg and wraps itself around my body. My joy fades as I stare down the long, winding ramp that melts into the darkest parts of the comet's core.

So many doors.

There is so much left to do.

I look at Pert, my parched mind and tongue finding some way to pull themselves away from the sight of the others. How thin they are. How weak. The image stays with me. It's a sight forever etched in my memory.

"How many are closed?" I ask him darkly. He has seen the open ones too and has the same questions I do.

"At least ten more, but I did not make it all the way down." Pert's words are mumbled and there is something else beneath his meaning. I stare into the darkness and run into it with renewed urgency.

43

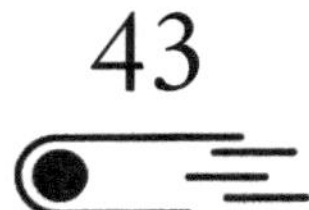

We learn with each cell we break open.

And slowly…

Slowly…

We work gladly, because the work is hard, but the work has meaning. It is the first time in this place the work has meaning. The river of GEMs moving towards the entrance fills with more people as even Parrot joins in helping. Those who can't walk or no longer have limbs able to support them are carried by others.

Tit for tat. GEMs give what we get.

The medical space fills quickly, and we get word the second ship is an hour out.

We get to the third cell. The air fills with a hum; it is softer now, but familiar. Those at the top participate, and my heart murmurs a new chant to my lips.

"Sisters, brothers,

We waited so long, but now,

Just a little while,

Just a little longer,
We'll return.
Water will roll to your lips
Food to your stomachs,
Air to your souls and we again will breathe.
Sisters, brothers,
Your wait is over.
This time we do not beg for freedom,
We walk out on our own two legs,
This time I promise
We walk free."

As I speak the words, I tap the rhythm against the stone. The darkness hums along. A bassy rhythm rises up, sisters... brothers... I am so sorry I left you behind. I wish I could have seen you so much sooner.

What did they do? What did they do to us?

As another door falls away, my heart struggles with staying present, staying far away from regret. I remember the words of my other selves in La Blanc, and I think I understand.

Europa may have been the place where I cracked open, but this place shattered every part of me.

The bars come out. Our new ritual resumes.

Nash has taken to removing the welds on the doors further down and my Cession gladly eats at each stop. It grows powerful. Satiated.

The door fall.

My EGG removes the bars out.

Josh and Nash bring them water, Pert helps those to stand.

Parrot and Soren start them moving, navigate the crowd. They answer questions, but there are so few.

So few.

It reminds me; we learned to stop asking questions. How long have we been broken?

I keep a count in my mind.

Two hundred. So few questions. So few bodies.

When we get to the fourth stable of GEMs, we experience our first loss. When we open the doors, the smell tells us before our eyes do. In this room are at least one hundred. It is Pert that dares to sort through them, climbing on the bodies as he searches for any still left alive.

The way Josh keeps looking away, and then to me, says what I can't voice. What none of us can.

I search for faces I recognize, stones that I may have doomed. That I — Josh touches my shoulder.

"You can't think about you right now. You need to move forward." He whispers in my ear.

I listen.

I move to the next one

I hold back all my thoughts; I banish them to another time, another place.

We have to *move forward*.

Other ships are still coming, Josh tells me. They will be here soon, but we need to keep moving in case there are alarms, or worse. I know he worries the Sahaqiel could not stand a true fight against HUDO if they found us.

So, I keep moving forward.

The next two are half and half. Half living, half dead. I let the others sort out the details and I move to the next cage.

And the next.

And the next.

The deeper we go, the darker it gets.

This darkness breathes, it has its own heartbeat, and I know we have found the Whispers. Even the light of my EGG is a forgotten glint of diamond against the dark stone. I am reminded of the places even the undesired Daylight does not dare to go.

I am reminded of Naya.

The pathway begins to feel like a never-ending loop. It's hard not to see eyes in the walls. It's hard not to see the pleading eyes in my mind of those dead or begging for water.

The walls start to speak to me as sight fades and touch becomes my guide. My feet glide along the smooth surface of the pathway, not knowing how far down it goes or wanting to know. Pert's warmth is right behind me and every step I take, I can hear his breath beside me. It's strange, terrifying, and comforting.

The gravity changes.

I am pulled in different directions. It twists and distorts my sense of where I am and what forward is. For a moment, I walk along the wall and am dropped a few steps later.

I hiss in pain, but keep moving as Pert's hands guide me. This was, after all, his home.

His and *theirs*. I am entering it without permission and I know she will know soon if she doesn't already. If she cares at all.

Naya.

The image in my mind is clearer than it should be, a woman draped in the soft pinks, whites, and grays of her culture. Her stone is etched in dark skin and hair that matches. She was born of the whispers of darkness of other comets and put here with us when she led colony born GEMs to Europa.

It was a bittersweet victory.

I think, perhaps, if she had been more willing to join those above, they would have treated her the same as me. I always believed they put us both in here to kill one another, and we were anything but friends or enemies.

We let the other be; happy to support things that furthered our goals, but rarely interfering otherwise. It was an uncomfortable but necessary peace.

"Naya?" My words bounce and dance in strange ways around my ears, almost like I can smell them. Gravity and sound are enemies, but here, they seem more intertwined. Another uneasy peace.

"Naya, we're here to take you home."

The dark swallows my words. There's a breeze by my head as something brushes past me, pulling strong against the wall that may be more like a floor for them. It's her words that I taste bouncing off of the walls and ricocheting in my head.

"We are home… we are already home…"

"Naya?" I don't stop, but continue my descent and Pert's steps get closer to my own. "Naya. Please, let's talk."

There is a trickle of something wet along my arm and the sting of air before I know the cut has come and gone. It's from a blade, most likely, and the Cession coils around it, drinking my blood like wine.

I hear Pert discard his clothing.

I move forward.

"Naya. We're taking people from the comet, " I say. "It's time to go home."

"Home. Home… we are already home."

The sound comes from a hundred directions, from a thousand different parts of the cavern around me. I know if I am not at the core; I am close. Up above, the faintest light is visible from the artificial sun. The chambers above hang like distant streetlights. It's easy to feel envious of the dead. It's easy to want to leave and let her be.

Still, I move forward.

"Daylight!" The word is hissed, bitter and half feral.

Pert's arm passes in front of me and holds me back, but it's too late. There's a heavy weight pressing against me. It's hard to tell if it's a door, a body, or something else.

Acting on instinct, I use my EGG to move it, to push it far away from me, but as I do, I am thrown from my perch. I am pulled in a dozen different directions as gravity has her way with me, twisting my insides, making me ill until I am slammed into a wall.

Now I know I am at the core as I struggle to breathe until the unstable gravity shifts.

Pert disconnects from me, his mind, his warmth leaving my side as I focus on my lungs. Unable to move, I regret coming down here in such haste. So unprepared.

Trapped, unable to move, I imagine being one of the bodies crammed into the cages so tightly. I imagine days, weeks, unable to move, waiting to die. No longer questioning if I was real, if there was hope, wondering *when* it would be over.

I imagine not hearing the song that kept me alive, not having water touch my lips. I imagine escape, death, life, all squeezed into infinite waiting.

I imagine hell.

Just like this darkness. Eternity feels so heavy and covered in ash.

It tastes bitter in my mouth as the gravity shifts and I pull myself up. Or is it down?

I breathe. I wait. I prepare.

I try to reach out with the metal's help, with my EGG, but this is *her* place. Her world. Even Pert was cautious when coming to live among the Whispers.

"Daylight!" she screams the name *she* gave me.

I feel more than see her body come towards mine. I brace myself for the impact, but let my EGG know it has some heavy lifting to do. The tendrils wrap around me in a circle, ready to bend and twist for gravity the best it can.

If we could be seen, I bet it would have looked elegant and alien.

Impact.

Naya and I twist together, twice, the EGG's tendrils wrapping around her cloth wrapped body before she spins and removes the tendril. The spin pulls me away; she glides one way; I fall another.

The metal on my body writhes and wiggles with eagerness, but I calm it. It is eager to turn to knives, to blades, to cut her open, but I owe her more than that. They never tell you that the metal knows as you teach it, but it learns, too. It knows when I am on edge; it anticipates commands; it is far more the enemy here than I am.

"Naya."

"Daylight."

It's hissed again. From above me? Below? It's hard to tell, but I think the tumble has shifted where I am. I think I am standing on what was once a wall.

"Leave us alone."

"There's nothing for you or them here, Naya. We're leaving. Come with us." I state it desperately.

Pert grabs me as another attack comes my way. This time it is from behind, and it is not Naya. As my metal reaches out, it tells me there are many, many bodies down here.

All whispering breaths.

All waiting to attack.

Another takes their turn at me. And another.

"Traitor. Traitor." I hear behind me as Pert tugs me to safety.

I realize with each attack we are being corralled, moved and then we are both trapped, a gravity spike so heavy it brings us to our knees. I can sense the edge of other's minds, not their presence but their state of being around us. Each one is hungry. Each is eager.

They want to turn us into meat.

Pert hums low in his chest and grips my hand tightly.

I can hear his words without words: This will hurt.

The fists come with the blades, never at the same time, but fast and consistently. It hurts as the gravity releases, then it begins again.

We are corralled, beaten, and released.

My EGG struggles and I retract it so it cannot be hurt anymore.

I get a sense for the timing. They have done this practice a million times before - perhaps on corpses, perhaps on the living. Well wrapped hands tell me this may be the fate of those who burn when they try to touch the sun. I grit my teeth and take what I can.

It hurts.

I grunt.

I scream.

The Cession, frustrated, lashes out, not as blades, but as sheets. It forms in front of me and Pert, like a shield, blocking every blow, cutting off every slice before it can make contact. My EGG, now sensing it is safe, sparkles my hair to life, and it burns as it flashes through my veins with adrenaline.

I glow with a radiance that lights the ash that sparkles as it twists in the gravity bends of the cavern. It smells of death and heat, and I howl in a rage I have no control over.

"Naya! STOP, or I will stop you!"

"Never."

"Together."

I say out loud to Pert, and he understands, even as I think he will hate me for what I am going to do.

I leave Pert behind, and he proudly grabs his knives and begins his deadly dance. As I move away from him, he fades into darkness; I hear another round of attack from the Whispers. This time, the pattern changes into a mud of grunts and the smell of blood.

I try not to worry. Pert can take care of himself.

I push forward towards Naya's last sound and she easily grabs my hair. I swing wildly. The thing in my hand is a straight razor as it cuts into her leg, then her arm. She is fast, but I am fed.

I am stronger, and I am ready to fight.

She lets go, but I don't let her leave. I grab her arm and hear an unearthly howl as a few stray fists head my way from another direction. I see fists. They hit me, knives cut at my skin, but I pull Naya's throat into my arms as we twist in the unstable gravity.

We are slammed into a surface.

My metal surges to life with a light it borrows from my EGG, and now I can see her wrapped in my arms. We struggle.

Fists on my ribs, fists in my armpits. Wherever she can grab she does. My EGG tries to fling her, my metal tries to cut, but each time we are stable, the gravity shifts again, and she is more familiar than I am with it. The gravity fights against me at every tumble.

We are pulled together as often as pulled apart.

My mouth is sliced along with my eye, and the blood pours down my skin.

"Stargon!" I hear Josh's voice from above.

Distracted, she jumps away from me. My body shakes in anticipation of more attacks, and even the adrenaline struggles to keep me upright.

What comes next?

The Cession tries to take care of the bleeding, but I can't feel it moving around me. I'm so numb. It's hard to breathe as the gravity presses on me again and the air is now mostly ash around us.

The Cession shows me its frustration in a new way.

It envelops me.

It fits around me like a perfect orb, floating in the nothingness of the comet's core. It's like it has put me in time out as light veins into my skin and into the orb's outer edges. I feel like the EGG and Cession have been conspiring while I've been beaten, as those veins are mirrored in the orb's surface.

The pressure of fists and blades test the strength of the orb.

After I catch my breath, the Cession around my body relaxes.

The Cession does not break open, but swallows me when it thinks I'm ready. What erupts from that floating, alien, shell out must have looked like the sun itself had come to smite the darkness. I don't see it; I only know what my mind tells me.

Head to toe, I am metal etched in the bright hot white of an alien sun. Wings adorn my back, and the heavy darkness of the core is replaced with my brightness. The Whispers, 22 in all, are born into the light. I can feel the terror of it all ripple through the gravity wells as they scurry back into tunnels.

The only ones that remain are Naya and Pert.

The EGG tells the Angel Suit how to land, and I stand in front of Pert, blades raised. I can see her in only shades of pale as my eyes are so bright I can only see shapes. The figure that is Naya raises her blade towards me. I see the slashes she makes in the air, but I make no move to attack her.

Perhaps she cannot see either.

She motions to the deep inner mining shafts that even the Shadows upstairs wouldn't use because they were certain death, then she drops her weapon, a rusted blade, and walks away.

It is a slow, purposeful walk. It is not a surrender, or a defeat, it is a statement.

We are staying.

I watch her leave; the gravity twisting around me as my EGG does its best to steady me and Pert. My brother grunts at my side. I finally see him and he is pale and red and tired. Blood pours down his white skin and I imagine I look similar under the suit of silver and light.

We make our way up as the others take bodies from the cages. Josh comes to us first. His eyes have questions even as his mouth is parched of words.

He is unsure what to say or ask.

So am I.

"They are… staying." I tell him. I swallow hard and add softly, "This is their home."

I look at Pert, worried that he will make the same choice after he moves the others out. He studies his flesh, his blood, his skin and sighs.

"I want to go home," Pert grunts. I'm surprised by it, but not very.

"The second ship is here." Josh's voice is soft, almost angelic against the echo of battle and gravity still ringing in my mind. "I really think you might want to turn down the savior look, though, before you help anymore."

"Savior?" I say, looking at my arms as they glow with the kind of light that can only be summoned by fiction. I relax my body and the Cession recedes. The EGG retracts its alien tentacles and the light in my eyes and hair return to normal.

My legs give way and I grip the wall and Josh's eyes flash wide for a moment. "Stargon! Your eye? Are you bleeding?"

"They can stay. Let them stay," I repeat. I'm not sure why it's important, but it's the last thing I say before I collapse.

44

I feel pain in my lungs, my chest, and my vision is a blur of light and spots of darkness. The air smells like sheets. I can feel tubes inside my veins, inside my arm, but I don't feel the strength, the motivation to remove them.

I feel empty but *satisfied.*

I wonder if everything that happened was real?

A face bobs gently in front of me.

It's not Josh, but it is familiar. Her face does not match the face in my memory. It has aged, streaks of white, and bits of purple and blue framed eyes that contrast with bits of orange. She leans forward and touches my forehead gently, a sign that she's real, a sign we developed on the battlefield when silence was our only language.

Her hands speak for her, because her voice cannot.

You probably have no memory of me.

"Of course I do." My head aches at the hoarse sound of my voice. "Miranda. I thought we left you on Corsica."

She shakes her head and describes in shorthand the epic adventure my eyes can only catch parts of. I sign back to her that my sight is poor. She laughs. It is an irony that we can barely communicate with each other at all. Me with one hand, her with no voice.

I sit up.

One arm hurts like hell, but I tug the tubes so they give enough for me to pull them out. I'll get yelled at later, but I don't care.

She tries her best to finish her story even as my one good eye struggles to keep up. Then she asks something that gives me pause.

What happens now?

The question surprises me. Not so much the question itself, but the way she asks it. Her expression lacks urgency. It speaks of patience and anticipation for silence.

I shrug and give her the only answer I have.

"We go home."

Home? She signs, but it's a question, not an answer. *Where is home?*

"That's..." I take a deep breath. "Wherever the future takes us."

Shouldn't home be where we take us? She asks with a smile. *I used to be a therapist, you know.*

"I remember." Pulling my com up from the nearby side table, I pull up the display so I can type and she can read. "I recall you telling me many things, and also trying to deter me from leading the rebellion."

She nods.

Look how that turned out.

"Look at *you* now." I motion to my ear. She nods.

She lost her ears at Corsica, that much I knew. She could hear like me, and faked it mostly - like me.

Corsica was just a little asteroid, barely worth defending, but I could still recall in clear detail being stuck there for four days longer than anticipated. We barely had supplies for the two weeks we were stationed there, but it wasn't because they couldn't give us supplies, it was because we didn't matter.

I lost half my unit on that mission. It was the last one I fought for them. Miranda was one of those that lived, but barely. We left that colony in a HUDO ship and ditched it when pirates attacked it. They couldn't have known a GEM crew had already taken the ship.

They never saw it coming.

I remember feeling so alive.

The words pull me into a dark place, one where all I can think about is how lonely a death it is to be forgotten in the depths of space.

It crushes me.

I pull myself away from those thoughts, from any last bits of Naya I have in my head. I respect her choice, just like I have to respect my own.

Taking in the rest of the room, I see remnants of my life. Josh's worn coat sits on the chair across the way, and the book Soren's reading sits in the chair next to it. Hopefully, they were resting or getting food. It was hard to tell where we were, but I was hoping we were on our way home.

Home.

The word sits with me.

"How many?" I ask with text. I don't want to know, but I have to. I remember a number. It burns into my mind. 3227.

She tilts her head and looks behind us. There are so many other beds. I can hear the machines breathing for some, beeping for others. She seems hesitant to tell me.

1298.

My heart sinks. Less than half. The machine to my side beeps louder, faster. A woman comes around and checks on my machine. She looks at Miranda, then at me and she understands. Her hair is a bounce of purple curls that tells me she is a GEM.

She has seen too much today to not understand.

I let my mind slow. My breath calm.

I move past it. I move my mind to the future and I make a motion, trying my best to describe Soren with it.

"You know the red spark with the silver bangs?"

Yes.

She raises an eyebrow but doesn't push for more information. I explain the best I can.

"He is a half-alien. Not Human enough to be Human. They're where we were. They will need help. They are like us."

Like us.

It sits in my stomach like a stone. It makes my mind itch.

So. She smiles and signs: *Then what comes next is more fighting?*

"If I have to," I say into the screen as I look up at the ceiling. "I don't know if I know how to do anything else."

Miranda smacks my arm gently. *You can be anything you -*

"Put your mind to," I repeat out loud. "I know, I know. I just don't know if I can change what I am."

The computer types slower than I speak.

I came to sit with you to see how your head was, she signs, *but I think it can wait for a better place.*

"Look at you." I try not to talk while I type, but it's almost impossible for me. "You look pretty good for someone who's been locked up for so long."

Her body says it all as she turns away from me a bit. Her hands are still, but the way they shake speaks of things she isn't ready to talk about yet. No doubt even the shadows had a need for a patient ear and advice every now and again. The exchange of services for food or water rations was not uncommon after we had lost a sense of time.

Unconsciously, I tap my ring against the metal bar to my side.

It beats in time with the engine.

One-two. THREE. My mind adds.

One-two-three.

There's a long way to go.

Miranda squeezes my hand. She says nothing else before she leaves, but leaves a reminder on my com to speak to her. I wonder if we have other therapists on the ship, but I haven't ever sought one out.

Why would I?

I'm unkind enough to myself, I'm enough therapy for me, I say. Confidently unconfident in that statement.

I close my eyes and I let myself rest.

Sleep comes easy.

45

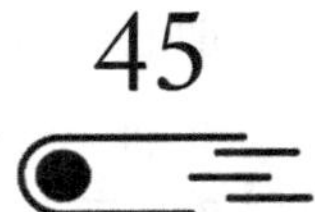

Recording Start

He sits at his desk, one arm bandaged, new scars on his face, but there is something new in his face. Something somber. Something complete.
He smiles, sucking on one of his eye teeth before closing his eyes and leaning back into his chair to begin the log.

Where was I?

Right. After... *that place.*

The trip back to the Sahaqiel is covered in familiar faces washed with a thousand feelings. Confusion, regret, anger, and relief are among them. It's hard to tell which ones are going to make it and which ones aren't.

It's the longest six goddamn days of my life.

The first few nights are quiet, as all the rescued ones are full of fear but hesitant gladness at the abundance of food and space.

People don't speak, so we play them some music. Soren entertains the best he can, pulling from his random bits of broken love songs and tortilla ballads.

More than a few die on the way there.

I try to remember that we do the best we can, but my heart takes every loss personally.

I make them dog tags to put in a memorial on the station. We hold simple, silent services for them. There are few, if any, tears, as most who remember them are still too far gone to feel it yet. I worry about what will happen when they have to re-enter the world.

I try to take one step at a time.

The first steps onto the Sahaqiel are full of many things. Six days is enough to bring many of them back to life, and to identify who may never return.

We guide them into open areas and let them take space wherever they can.

Life goes on.

Somehow it goes on.

I watch as Blank Slates fill themselves up with color and life, and I watch as others are like Parrot. Changed. Different, but trying.

There are 1298 among another 22,000. 23,598, total.

My heart sings at the number, as beautiful as it is bittersweet.

He taps his fingers on the desk in patterns of three.
He shakes his head before smiling at something that rolls
across his mind.

The others make themselves at home as our war ends and another is brewing.

Snow is the most restless, but starts working on the Sahaqiel's docks. The work is quiet, but somehow after she starts, it's less so. We start taking in traders and ships with regularity.

Josh comes to me with Soren and whispers too often of the kids being shipped off of Mars. The half-ones, the abandoned. Those that aren't old enough to defend themselves. Soren wonders at how many more like him survived birth only to be handed to death.

The war is 25 years old, but the peace is so much younger.

Parrot makes a few friends. He also brings the fridge from the rescue ship with him. Since he's a 'dad' now, he also insists on getting his own place. Josh often gives Toddrick 'gifts' of food until he's confident that Parrot can go hunting for food without poisoning himself.

Nash and Soren get a place just above ours. I'm glad not to have him too far away. We drag them down for game days. It starts with board games, but as more of the recovering prisoners come to want socialization, it becomes various sport-like activities.

We avoid teams since too many people want to take bets on who wins.

And no one bets on *me*.

The white noise in my head becomes a background murmur. It still hurts, it still haunts me, but I care less. I can find more pieces of me, even in the static.

I laugh more.

He rolls his neck and then looks at the calendar on his com.
He shakes his head.

It's Soren that asks me first. Six months into the recovery of the comet prisoners, or, well, yesterday, he comes to me with a hand on my shoulder and motions to the stars outside.

"What's next?"

It's a question more and more people ask me as restlessness sets in. So many of us, against our every wish, can't stay in a place like this: solitary and alone.

We need more.

We need to explore, to reach, to be… star gone, as it were.

"People keep asking me that." I let the rest hang in the air.

"And?" He nudges me forward, and I lose my balance a little. Catching myself on the window, I let out a long, dramatic sigh.

"I don't know enough about the world out there anymore to move it, Soren."

"Said Atlas," he adds.

"I mean it."

"Let's be pirates." He flips his daggers neatly in the air. Now, for him, having them in his hands is second nature. The Cession takes to him like they were made for each other, and maybe they were. "Let's abduct GEMs and partial breeds, free colonies, and raid Breeder ships. Let's free some half-Ritz kids."

"Easier said than done. We barely have a steady supply line, and our ships are makeshift cargo runners."

Soren waves away my statement.

"Let's start with Europa."

I snort, but his expression doesn't shift. It's serious. Emeralds stare at me from under that bright spark and my mind itches.

I wonder how much time and thought he's put into whatever plan he's hatched?

"Europa," I say it as a prompt.

"We start with Europa, and we move the supply line to the friendly JAC colonies that Josh already trades with. They're already our contacts, we might as well try? We'll become more valuable. Europa's cut off, no visitors, few military from what we've seen. It would be an easy target."

"And when they find out what we're doing?" I ask. "When they finally find the Sahaqiel?"

"They?" Soren snorts. "Who the hell is 'they'?"

"Earth. Mars. Anyone else who wants us dead?"

"We stand with Jupiter." He stabs the knife into the table dramatically. "We become part of the Jupiter Alliance and we welcome everyone else the worlds have rejected with open arms."

"A misfit alliance," I mutter, folding my arms and staring out into space.

"It wouldn't be!" Soren pleads, ready to fight with me.

"No, I'm not mocking you, just recalling what someone once said to me. A man named NaReau, he once called the GEM rebellion a misfit alliance, fit to topple unstable kings."

I can see the man clearly in my mind. It was never clear to me if he was an unsung angel or a twisted devil.

Politicians, am-I-right?
He slaps the table at his own joke and snickers.

"Exactly." Soren's voice fills with hope and excitement.

"And you wanna just hop on a ship and become pirates?" I smirk as I ask, knowing full well there's more.

He doesn't disappoint.

He pulls the screen up on the window in front of me and zooms in on a small prison base far on the edges of the Belt. Tapping it with his finger, he says, "Okay, so instead of starting with Europa, let's start here."

I raise an eyebrow, putting my thumbs in my pocket to play with my straight razor.

"You want us to raid another prison?"

"No. I want us to raid a spaceport that people think is a prison. We've watched the launches from there, there's no way it's human cargo. This is where they're launching junk, too. It's a trash depot."

"I'm really failing to see how we take over the world by invading a trash depot." I tease.

"It's HUDO shipyard trash." His smile is now almost as bright as the sun.

"I like the way you think, Sunshine." I trace the scar along the right half of my face unconsciously. A reminder of my last encounter with Naya. It sits heavy with me, but so does the anxiety that comes with waiting on this ship for something worse to happen. "Does Josh know?"

"Do I know what?" I feel a hand at my elbow. Josh waits a solid second to look over the plans. "Oh, good. You told him?"

"I told him."

"Finally." Josh slides up next to me, arm draped around my waist. "What do you think? Up for going back out? Trying again? Making some mayhem? Saving some kids?"

I look him over and feel my lips tighten against my skin.

Everything in my gut says no. Every inch of me screams for something else to take the place of this. This is hard.

This will be impossible.

We will die and fight and lose and die again, and I know it.

… And they know it.

And I want to become part of the stone again. I want to fade away into the darkness and drift away until there is nothing left of me in this world except a piece of stardust that sparkles in Josh's eyes.

I want to stop.

But…

I know I can't.

I never could. I never will.

I shrug, and a smile itches its way onto my face as Josh and Soren's eyes dance before mine like stars.

In them I see a future, and the light is blinding.

- End Recording -